Do You Really Know Camille?

Also by the author

POETRY

COOKBOOK

Do You Really Know Camille?

A NOVEL

BY

SHARON JETER

cooper broadwater publishing
RALEIGH, NORTH CAROLINA

Do You Really Know Camille?
Copyright ©2020 by Sharon Jeter

Cooper Broadwater Publishing, LLC
Raleigh, North Carolina
www.coobro.bigcartel.com

All Rights Reserved.
Printed in the United States of America
Second Edition
January 2020

If you would like to use material from this book,
prior permission must be obtained by contacting the publisher.
Thank you.

Write to Permissions:
Cooper Broadwater Publishing, Inc.
604-1011 East Front Street
Clayton, NC 27528
coobropub@gmail.com

ISBN-978-1734501803 (paperback)

Throwing Stones

A pebble cast in the ocean
Creates ripples that spawn into eternity
That's what a pebble will do
Carelessly he threw stones
Birthing infinite waves
And repercussions

Do You Really Know Camille?

A NOVEL

BY

SHARON JETER

CONTENT

....

ONE

....

daddy-daughter dance

INNOCENCE had forsaken Camille before she was even born, although she didn't know it yet. And even had she known, there was little that could have been done about it. The circumstances were beyond her control, as they often are. Unfortunate in this regard, Camille was forced to see and know things that no child should.

By all accounts she was a good kid.

Her bed was made every morning, not a requirement, just something she saw her father do. Camille always put her toys up after playing with them, except for when she was staging a silent protest out of anger or sadness. She would even change out of her school clothes as soon as she got home, unless she was excited about something that happened during the day, and only then would she have to be reminded.

When Camille was five or six, her mother taught her how to fold and hang clothes, something she's been doing ever since, even though dissuaded by her mother. Lynn was meticulous about the linens, she liked them a certain way, something passed down from a military upbringing. And even with Camille's best efforts, the child simply couldn't flatten the fitted sheets evenly enough when she folded them, if she tried a million times.

Camille's chores included dusting her bedroom and the living room, requirements for Saturday mornings. Often, she would start these tasks on Tuesday or Thursday, without any prompting. From experience, she had learned that it would take too long if she tried to do it all on Saturday, cartoon day.

Sometimes her mother would praise her extra efforts, but it didn't matter to Camille, her mother's praise wasn't her motivation.

It was a quiet morning. No school, no crying baby sister, no TVs on in the house. All this was about to change.

It was going to rain.

Camille had already made the bed. Her favorite lavender comforter was spread untucked across the twin-sized mattress. Two plush Gund teddy bears rested against the wall where a headboard would normally be. Her lone pillow was situated between the stuffed animals, almost as if they were reclining against it.

Her sister's crib had been transformed into a petite bed, just big enough for a two year old. Camille placed the outfit she prepared for the next day on the bed most nights, her sister rarely slept there.

A small bookshelf was stationed against the wall between the windows. Camille loved to read. Her mother was a teacher and always bought the girls books as presents.

Jubilee was her mother's favorite. It was neatly stacked on the shelf with all the girls' other books. Camille tried to read it on occasion, though finding it difficult to comprehend without her mother's interpretation.

Camille loved the Junie B. Jones series, especially *Junie B. Jones and The Stupid Smelly Bus*. She read that book ten times, at least.

On the occasion that her sister slept in the bedroom, they would sometimes sit together on the beanbag chair, near the nightlight, and Camille could be heard reading to her baby sister. *Goodnight Moon* was Tania's favorite, it would put her right to sleep. They would always fall asleep on the floor, their mother quietly placing a blanket on the girls when she came to check on them throughout the night.

Although it was gloomy and gray out, the sun exposed a tiny section, speckled with salt and pepper clouds. Strong winds accompanied the darkness, rare for residents in this part of the southeast.

As the rain made its appearance, the trees swayed back and forth with the wind. Droplets of rain plopped out of the sky at an accelerating pace, splatting against the homes on Bartlett Court.

Camille played quietly on the rug as the darkness flooded her bedroom. She was compelled to rush to the window. She loved the rain and loved to go outside and play in it but was never allowed to. Her mother feared the child would get sick, or struck by lightning, or even worse, get her naturally coarse hair wet and matted.

"But what about when you wash my hair, Mom? It gets wet then," the child would reason.

"That's a bit different, baby," her mother would say, disguising laughter. Then her father would chime in uninvited, telling the child to stop sassing.

The back porch was a rectangular concrete platform, the size of a small coffee table or large ottoman. An overhang protected the porch from the elements. Sometimes, Camille would sneak out on the porch when it rained. In her bare feet, she would dangle her legs out as far as they could stretch, just to be able to feel the rain against her skin. Something about touching the rain made her happy on the inside, almost as if a tiny piece of heaven were trickling down just to be with her.

Camille stood at the window and peered at the clouds with fascinated eyes. The section captured by the sun was still white in some spots and looked like cotton balls. Not the kind you buy from the store already shaped into big tater tot looking blobs, but the misshapen puffs growing wild in cotton fields. She squinted her eyes and imagined unicorns, dragons, and cotton candy, familiar shapes she saw floating across the sky.

A sudden BANG startled the child. Lightning would have been the obvious cause, but the storm could not be blamed. Besides, Camille loved the rain so much that she wasn't afraid of lightning. Rain was like a calming melody that soothed her little girl's soul. And lightning was rain's annoying friend, simple rationale for a child.

Right now, however, the calming rain was being drowned out by the commotion emanating from the adjacent room. Distracted by the steadying cadence pounding against her bedroom wall, Camille stepped away from the window, sat back on the floor and began to play with her doll again.

BAM! BAM!

The thuds repeated.

BAM! BAM! BAM!

Over and over again.

This wasn't the first time she heard the thuds, but it startled her all the same. She was unable to enjoy herself anymore, neither the rain, nor her baby doll comforted her.

All she wanted was to float away on those cotton ball clouds, or a strawberry sundae with bananas from her favorite ice cream parlor. Better yet, her mother's gentle embrace. Camille was still of an age where her mother's hugs and kisses made her warm and fuzzy, and she wished that she could run to her mother right now. Funny thing though, the thuds only occurred in her mother's absence.

Camille tried to imagine her mother's voice in her ear, singing one of those 'you'll be all right when the sun comes out' songs. With closed eyes, she could feel her mother's soft kisses on her cheeks and the rocking back and forth in her mom's arms, and just for the briefest of moments Camille was transported to a place where the bad feelings were washed away, where she imagined herself playing with her baby sister, where her world was as it should have been, safe and ordinary.

The sounds of moaning and grunting stunned her back to reality with her doll, the one that her grandmother Bet bought for her from Franklin's Toy Store last year.

BAM!!!

Again and again.

Then the ritual would begin.

She'd hear the banging.

She'd start making noises.

He'd yell for her to stop.

She'd keep making noises.

He'd get mad.

He'd yell some more.

She'd continue singing and playing.

The banging would stop.

He'd burst through her bedroom door.

She'd smile at him.

He'd yell some more.

He'd put her over his lap and spank her.

He'd stop when his anger subsided, or she cried.

Camille held her baby doll in her arms and rocked her back and forth like her mother would do. She rubbed the baby's hair and kissed her on the cheek just as her mother would. Then the little girl started singing to Betty, her favorite grandmother's namesake, a song that she made up.

Pretty, pretty Betty pie.
I see you looking with those eyes.
Brown, brown they are so cute.
Betty, my Betty I love you.

Her repeated chants helped drown out the bothersome noises. Singing softly at first, hoping to somehow escape the clatter. With the gradual yet deliberate crescendo of an esteemed songstress, the child sang louder and louder until a voice from the other room yelled for her to hush.

"GIRL CUT THAT RACKET!" he shouted. The thuds eased only slightly as he tried to control the wish-filled melody of the child.

Under her breath the little girl looked at the wall and repeated the command, 'you cut that racket', and then she started singing all over again until he had no choice but to stop what he was doing and deal with her.

When the banging ceased, she knew he was headed her way. She could hear outrage in his every step. He burst through her bedroom door like a bull taunted by a matador's cape.

"GIRL, DIDN'T I TELL YOU TO CUT THAT RACKET?" he yelled.

Camille sat on the floor playing with her doll, singing almost at a whisper just to infuriate him all the more. "Yes Sir," she said in the sweetest of voices.

The smirk that he hated was written all over her face. He leered at her and she knew from experience what was next, but she didn't care. All she wanted was for the banging to stop. However temporary, once again she had won.

Camille had mastered the routine. After the first few times, the fear of punishment no longer held her hostage. She fake-cried to get him to stop spanking her and was ordered to go to bed. He returned to his bedroom and in no time at all the banging resumed where it had left off.

TWO

....

mother of invention

THOUGH seeming to be at odds the pair shared a common interest, keeping Mrs. Young in the dark about what the patriarch was doing. Camille's father wanted to keep his affairs secret, for obvious reasons. He genuinely loved his wife, even though his ruinous behaviors betrayed this fact. And of course, the child wanted nothing more than to protect her mother. Even in Camille's naivety, she knew that it would kill Lynn if she ever found out that her husband had been unfaithful. Not to mention that many times he carried on his exploits under the roof of their home while Camille played in the next room.

Instead of telling her mother, Camille concocted ways to make her father just as miserable as she imagined her mother would be if Mrs. Young found out what Mr. Young was up to.

So that day after her beating, after her father returned to his bedroom, after the banging started again, Camille got up and quietly slunk her way to her parent's bedroom with her doll in her hand for support. She knew the door would be unlocked; it always was. There was a 'no locking doors' policy in the Young household, one of Mr. Young's rules that he would soon regret.

Camille cautiously twisted the doorknob oh so slowly, so as to not alert the room's occupants. She slithered into the room, like a lioness stalking its prey. The thunder and rain had moved on though still gloomy. The only sounds being made were those of her father and his mistress. And although the blinds were closed, there was just enough sunlight peeking through for the child to navigate her surroundings.

Camille got close enough that she could distinguish the features on the woman's face and stared awkwardly at her as the woman moaned. To a child, the mistress appeared to be in pain. As Camille attempted to understand what was going on, her father said something to the woman, scaring the child and causing her to drop the doll that she was holding.

"Dadddddyyyyy," the whining little girl called out as she stood eye to eye with the woman who occupied her mother's bed.

The woman who at that moment was pinned beneath the child's father, gasped in horror and hurled the man off of her with the strength of a bucking bull, knocking him on the floor, ass out and all, right next to his daughter. The child picked the doll up off the floor and stretched it toward her father, as if showing him the doll's tears.

"My baby doll is sad," the child whimpered.

The woman grabbed the covers that they had messily tossed to one side of the bed, covered herself, got up on the opposite side of the bed from the child and her father, quickly gathered the clothing that was on the floor, dressing as she scuttled out the house.

The man was incensed with his daughter but couldn't do anything until he found his clothes that were now scattered about, chaotically tossed to and fro by the fleeing woman. Camille walked hastily straight to the telephone and called her mother. She knew her father was coming to get her and didn't want another spanking today.

"CAMILLE YOUNG!" he yelled from the bedroom.

She remained quiet and nervously waited for her mother to answer. 'You have reached the voicemail of…,' her mother's voicemail said through the receiver. Camille was hiding behind the kitchen counter, feverishly pushing redial in the hopes that her mother would answer. But she did not.

Suddenly her father walked in the kitchen. She was discovered. With the belt in his strong hand he charged toward the girl. She steadied her breath, not daring to make eye contact. Close enough to feel his fuming breath on her back she began to speak into the phone.

"Hi Mom. When are you coming home?" Her words stopped him cold. "Okay, you're not far away," she said and paused. "Okay, so you'll be here soon." She paused. "You want me to do what?" she asked and paused again. "Okay, Mom," she said. "Mom, my baby is saadddd," she spoke into the phone. She paused. "Mom, Dad's right here," she said, peeping over her shoulder. "He's angry with me," she said and paused. "Well..."

Her father stood still at the sink listening to his eldest child. "IS THAT YOUR MOTHER, GIRL?" the father interrupted.

"Yes Daddy," she responded, in the cutest of voices. "Here Dad. Mom wants to know why you're yelling at me," the child said as she stretched her arm out to hand her father the phone.

He grunted and said something under his breath. "I'll see you when you get here," he said out loud without taking the phone from the little girl's hand.

"Dad said he'll see you when you get home," the child repeated into the receiver. "I'll go get the mail from Ms. Sally's, like you asked," she continued and then paused again, "Okay, I'll tell Daddy goodbye for you." Turning to her father, she told him, "Mom said she'll be home soon."

He said nothing. Instead, retreated to clean their disheveled bedroom. After which he sat down in the recliner, turned on the TV and dozed off.

Luckily her father had been too infuriated to take the phone when Camille offered it to him. Had he known that he was pranked by a grade-schooler, her hind parts would have been sore for weeks.

Camille pretended to run the errand she had fabricated. She hid out at the park for a while, giving her mother time to get there. But when she got back to the house, Lynn still hadn't arrived. So, Camille waited quietly on the porch, hiding behind the large planter until she heard the car pull into the driveway.

The embarrassment of the situation would cause any normal person to change, but Mr. Young was not that person. His pride wouldn't tolerate a child dictating his actions. So, he continued having women over, opting instead to lock the bedroom door, underestimating the child's creativity and resolve.

A locked door was a slight deterrent, but nothing that would stop an ambitious child. And since Camille's singing no longer had any effect on her father, she opted to concentrate her attentions on the things at her disposal.

Camille contrived schemes, skills developed out of necessity, for self-preservation. She hid garments and car keys, and cut itchy jute cording into tiny pieces, placing it in the paramours' clothing or car seats. And sometimes when there was nothing else left to do, she'd sit outside her parent's bedroom until her father and his company came out, acting as though she were cleaning, intentionally spraying air freshener in the departing woman's direction.

On one occasion, seeing a woman's clothing scattered about the living room, Camille went into action. *How dare she leave her clothes all over my mother's floor*, the child thought. "My daddy always makes me pick up after myself, why should you be different?" she said under her breath. "Let me just help you out, so you don't get in trouble," she said, chuckling.

Camille took all the clothes she could gather in her arms and used them to wipe the mess the dog left on the porch. And since the clothes now smelled so badly, the only thing she could think to do next was throw them in the garbage. So that's what she did, placing the feces-stained garments in the driver's seat of the woman's car, afterward she returned to playing quietly in her room.

When the adults emerged from the room ecstatic from what they had just done, they searched for the woman's clothing.

"I know I left them out here," the woman said.

"Are you sure?" Mr. Young asked, returning to the bedroom to look for the clothes.

"I'm positive," she said, standing in the middle of the living room in her pink and red lace and satin negligée.

Richard went back into the bedroom in a desperate search for the woman's clothing, upon his return he found the woman bent down on her knees against the couch, frantically sweeping her hands underneath it in search of her clothing. No luck.

He immediately looked at his child's door knowing all too well that Camille had a hand in these shenanigans. He didn't have time for discipline, only to help his guest in her departure. Against better judgment, he gave his guest a t-shirt and sweats from his wife's wardrobe. She rushed out without even a goodbye, never to return again.

"CAMILLE YOUNG!" he yelled. He made his way to her room intending to spank his daughter yet again. But when he tried to open her door, he found that it was locked, angering him all the more. "CAMILLE MARIE YOUNG! UNLOCK THIS DOOR IMMEDIATELY!" he yelled louder.

She got up slowly from the edge of her bed where she waited to see what all would unfold.

"CAMILLE!" he yelled again. "OPEN THIS DOOR!"

"Yes Daddy," she whimpered, still moving as slowly as she possibly could. "Ok Daddy, here I come." She walked the three-foot trek as though it were the green mile. She was poised to unlock her bedroom door when she heard her mother come in the house with Tania following closely behind.

"Hey Richard, why are your shorts on the porch?" Lynn asked, holding the shorts in the air with her thumb and pointer finger, the smell was repugnant.

"What?" Richard questioned.

"I found these on the porch," Lynn said.

"I don't know. They must have fallen out of my gym bag," he offered.

"They are funky! What's that smell?" she asked.

"What does it smell like?"

"Shit!" she said, pausing briefly, then reiterating, "They smell like shit!"

"I don't know," was all he could muster.

He shook his head at the stench radiating from his shorts as they passed from his wife's pinched thumb and pointer finger to his. Camille came running out of her room into her mother's loving arms. The glare from her father could have burned a whole in her back but she pretended to be oblivious to his presence.

"What's that smell, Mommy?" Camille asked, prodding her father with this sly inquisition.

Mrs. Young didn't respond, just grimaced at her husband in disgust. Richard retreated to the back porch where he took the soiled shorts and threw them in the garbage outside.

This game between Camille and her father had grown old for the both of them. Although this way of being had become her normal, the child longed to be a kid again and do little girl things. Innately she knew this. That is why months earlier, she befriended Mel.

Learning from past experience, Camille knew her father would never approve of play dates had Mel's father lived in the home. Mel had what she needed, not the innocence of friendship, not the childish banter that little girls partake in, but a stable home with a single successful churchgoing mother. And what made things even better was that Mel was an only child.

While Camille's dad was outside taking out his garbage, Camille made her move. "Mom, can I play at Mel's house after school some days?" she asked.

By the time she posed this question, Mel was practically family. Camille cunningly dropping stories about Mel and her mom regularly at the dinner table, while driving in the car, when they would visit family in neighboring towns. Everyone knew the mostly true stories of Mel and her mother. Of course, Camille embellished some details for flavor.

Lynn didn't see why it would be a problem but had to square things up with her husband and Mel's mother first.

Within a matter of weeks, Camille was a child again, doing little girl things, like playing with baby dolls, book reading picnics, talking about the boys who had cooties, and splashing around in the mud after the rain.

THREE

....

gone girl

TWO decades had come and gone since Camille was a child, yet the dysfunctional remnants from her youth clung to her as noticeable as lint on black clothing. Her toughest battle was squashing that part of herself that was like him. Flaws that were buried deeper than the roots of a wild fig tree, that in her unconsciousness, often rendered her actions beyond her control.

And that's why she was leaving. Not because she wanted to, not because she hated her life or the man she was with, but because she didn't know how to stop herself, she was just like her father in this way.

The last shirt she was taking with her was the light pink polo that John always liked to see her wear. She placed it on top of the other clothes before closing the suitcase. The neglected phone vibrated intensely on the nightstand next to their bed. Her surprise wasn't the only one looming that day.

She walked from the bedroom through the living room, out onto the patio, and back, making her way to the kitchen. She was surveying the surroundings one final time. Each step felt as though she were ascending the peaks of Everest.

People move through life gathering souvenirs, tiny reminders of where they've been, who they've met, things they've done, that at the time of their acquisition they evoked joyous reverence. But as time moves on, life forces forgetfulness about the feelings these treasures once conjured, until a situation or event triggers nostalgia.

Camille found herself lost in reverie. The couch that they meant to replace, now spoke to her in hinted whispers. Their friends from Ghana gave them the richly colored throw-blanket that hung over the right arm of the overpriced cloth couch and reminded her of the first time she ever told anyone she loved them.

They had traveled to Africa with their Ghanaian friends. As they ate banku and tilapia, prepared by the friend's grandmother, something about the gathering caused Camille to profess her love for John. Maybe it was the five generations flocked together as one, laughing and dancing. Maybe it was the children playing outside on the stoop. Maybe it was their humble accommodations. Whatever it was, it was raw, and it was real. Not an overly emotional gesture on her part, just a simple kiss on the cheek and a silent motioning with her lips. And although they were surrounded by people, Camille was, in that instance, all alone with John.

And for the briefest of moments she was back in Ghana, remembering bliss, until she saw John's raggedy old lamp that sat on the side table. She smiled, counting the times she tried to get rid of it, only forfeiting her objection to the eye soar when learning its history. A handmade keepsake of his great-grandfather Ted, the lamp was one of the only pieces of furniture that John brought from his condo when he moved in with Camille, as well as the medley of indigenous artwork he collected that was on display throughout their abode.

Sorority pictures that hung on the entry wall reminded Camille of the trip that she, Tamara, Ann and the girls took to the beach last summer. The trip where the world's number one bridesmaid, Ann, met her fiancé, Ben.

In her office, on the mahogany desk that she bought from an antique shop in High Point, with the money she made from her first 'real' job, was the computer he purchased for her as a surprise. When she asked what it was for, he simply told her, 'just because.'

A snippet cut from her grandmother's plant that cousin Nixon sent all the way from Highland Park, blossomed in the mosaic tile planter next to the patio door. This was the only memento she had of her great-grandmother's, aside from the picture in her phone that she took the last Christmas the family spent in Detroit.

In the corner of the living area, just behind the couch, their diplomas and awards were hung with pride, symbols of their achievements interspersed alongside photos of family and friends.

Every piece of furniture, the rugs, the glasses in the cupboard, the fixtures and the photos, all had memories attached to them. When only yesterday they were just things around the house, today they told their very own stories, taking her back to places and times that had been filed away long ago, contemplation that only prolonged the inevitable.

Love was palpable throughout their home. And looking at her life from the outside, one would think that she was living the American dream, white picket fence and all. She even thought this herself. The only thing that didn't fit was the suitcase full of inconsequential belongings that sat by the front door, awaiting John's arrival.

As she finalized her exit, the faint sounds of 102.1 The Shark played in the background. Camille made her way through their home soaking up all the keepsakes, like a person thinking that time was running out.

The DJ announced in his smooth baritone voice, "…next is one of my all-time favorite Steve Perry classics. After leaving Journey he went on to pursue a thriving solo career. This song is from his 1984 debut solo album, *Street Talk*. The release never made it to number one on the charts, but it was one of his greatest hits…. *Foolish Heart*." Then the song began to play.

Foolish heart hear me calling. Stop before you start falling…you've been wrong before. Don't be wrong anymore.

The lyrics, piercing her soul like bullets – *foolish, foolish heart, don't be wrong anymore.* Camille's first dismissed thought was that the song was a sign, telling her to stop, telling her not to be wrong again, telling her to get control of herself, to fight for the life she had built with John, to fight for their love. But she was far too committed to running to be certain now. Her mind, a one-trick pony, every action, every thought lead to goodbye.

The tiny spare bedroom beckoned her uneasy treks, she had been avoiding it, but had to see it one last time. When they found out she was pregnant, they decorated every detail of that room with love, Camille recalled.

The dresser was painted with pastel shades of pink and purple and sat against the wall with a backdrop of a mural painted with different tones of the same colors. Opening the top drawer, she pulled out the favorite sleeper. Wailing in anguish, Camille forced the cloth to her nose. It smelled of preciousness, a mixture of cocoa butter lotion and bubblegum baby oil. Reels of memories poured out like waterfalls.

Evoked by love she was forced to add the tiny garment to the limited wears she previously packed. To preserve the fragrance, she folded it tightly and stored it in a Ziploc bag that she got out of the kitchen drawer. Then she placed the garment in her purse for safekeeping.

Wiping the tears that streamed down her face, she sat quietly on the couch of her uptown condo contemplating her decision to leave. Her mind was made, convinced that she was doing the right thing.

Unfortunately, Camille's dilemma was that her ability to make the right decision was clouded by events and circumstances from her past, causing her to believe that leaving was the best solution, maybe something she wished her father had done. Because of her twisted perspective, Camille was about to make a terrible decision based on the flawed history of the little girl that still lived inside her. And although her affection for the both of them made the decision nearly unbearable, fear was a much more powerful emotion.

John would soon be home. Camille grew stoic in preparation.

Standing as his keys unlocked the barrier that stood between them, she slowly walked toward the entrance. An inherent coldness descended over her as he opened the door. Her belongings betrayed her before she ever uttered a single word.

"What's going on Camille? Where are you going?" John questioned, befuddled.

There were no words that could explain her behavior. It was gutless, so she had none. With luggage in hands, she pressed on. "I have to go," she said, unable to look him in the eyes.

"Why are you doing this?" he asked in anguish, standing between her and the door.

She fought back her sadness, offering nothing for his pleading. "I left some papers on the table for you," her final words.

She sat her baggage aside just long enough to kiss him on the cheek and give him a hug laced with sorrow. Then she secured her belongings and marched out the door. John grabbed her arm, but she would not be stopped.

"WHAT ABOUT SAMMY?" he yelled, and then mouthed again, "What about…Sammy?"

He stood at the door, speechless, and watched her walk away. John knew that the woman who had just left was not the woman he loved. Stunned, he pulled a small box out of his right pant pocket, her surprise, staring at it for what seemed like hours before throwing it against the foyer wall. He surveyed their home and forced composure, he had obligations to fulfill, their daughter still had to be picked up.

Camille appeared calm, considering. She popped the trunk of the car and threw her belongings in. Frazzled, she neglected to close it. She got into the driver's seat, started the car, and looked in the rearview mirror before turning around to back out of the parking space.

She had forgotten all about it, sitting there glaring at her, a consummate reminder. Her baby girl didn't yet weigh enough to ride in the car without a car seat.

Camille jumped out the car to close the trunk and thought about placing the car seat at their front door, but decided against it, thinking it would just add fuel to an already out of control inferno. Not thinking clearly, she drove to the dumpster, unlatched the car seat, preparing to trash it. The cheerios that hid in the creases fell to the car floor and she was undone.

Camille fell to her knees, right beside the passenger side back door and started collecting the cereal like she had discovered a goldmine. She held the four or five circular bits in her hand and pressed them against her chest, then threw her head back in agony.

"Are you okay, ma'am?" a voice called out from the other side of the car door. "Do you need help?"

She couldn't speak but waved him away with her free hand.

"I can call someone if you'd like," the concerned stranger offered.

She swooshed him away, more vigorously this time. Backing away slowly, he left. She could tell that he would be trouble, so she decided it best to leave before the police came, or even worse, John was alerted by the commotion. She held on to the cheerios and started the car. With no place to go she called her best friend.

"Maria, please call me back," she sobbed into the voicemail.

It's funny that when you are your craziest, when you think your world is falling apart, and you just need somebody, anybody to talk to, nobody ever answers the phone. Camille must have called five people, but no one was available.

"This is Camille. Call me," she said, leaving messages on each person's voicemail.

How is it even possible in this day of instant access that not one of them is answering the phone, she thought. Maybe it was God telling her to breathe, to slow down, to go back and fix the mess that she had just created. If this was God, she couldn't hear her, she was too caught up in her feelings to hear anything reasonable.

The car seat stayed on her mind. Sammy loved its color-filled exaggerated animal caricatures. Camille practiced teaching Sammy each one, her way of keeping the child occupied when they traveled.

Camille couldn't keep the car seat, nor could she trash it, so she drove back to the dumpster, bent over the opening and pulled it out. The donation center was twenty miles away, but it didn't matter. That's where she was headed when her phone rang.

"What's wrong, Camille? You sounded like you were crying on the message," Maria asked, concerned.

Camille pulled over to the side of the road in hysterics.

"Calm down and tell me what's going on," Maria commanded.

Camille recoiled, her shoulders and head moving with each sniffle. All she could muster was his name, "John."

"What did that bastard do?" Maria asked furiously. "I'm on the next flight. I would ask you if you're okay but that would be dumb. So, I'll just tell you, whatever it is, whatever he did, you're better off without him." Maria paused. "No man should ever make you cry like this unless he died or something." Maria paused again. "Wait a minute, he didn't die, did he?"

Camille halfheartedly laughed. "No, crazy!"

"Then bitch, calm your ass down and talk!"

"I left him," Camille blurted.

"WHAT? What happened, and please don't be that person that makes me ask a question after every statement you make. Just start from 'a' and go in order to 'z' – Thank you," Maria suggested.

"Can I crash there for a couple of weeks, until I find a place?"

"So, you're just going to leave me hanging like that?"

"I can't think clearly right now," Camille confessed.

"Sure, come on. You know if I have a home, you have a home," Maria told her friend.

FOUR

....

best friends

CAMILLE had a campus map, but it didn't help. She had been wandering around disoriented for at least ten minutes before deciding to ask for directions.

"Excuse me, do you know where Stone Hall is?" Camille asked a girl standing at the 'Freshman Mixer' table that was set up near the pit. When students stopped by, rushing to class or wherever, the girl would coax a flyer in their hands, information about the mixer.

"Stone…that's where I'm going," the girl told Camille. "If you wait a minute until my backup shows, I'll walk with you."

Camille looked around as if this time she would know which way to go but was still confused.

"Matter of fact here comes my backup now," the girl said, pointing to the guy that was headed in their direction.

Camille stood off to the side and waited patiently.

"I'm Maria," the girl said, introducing herself between students. "Do you know about the mixer?"

"I'm Camille…my roommate mentioned it to me yesterday, but I don't really know about it," she told Maria.

"It's the most fun you'll ever have. I loved it so much that I signed up to organize this year's events," Maria said, handing Camille a flyer.

That's how Camille and Maria met, and they have been best friends ever since. Though time has a way of forging wedges, nothing got in the way of their friendship, even with the distance, their jobs, their relationships, and their busy schedules. They don't see each other or talk as much as they once did, but their bond is as strong as ever.

And although Camille had other friends, Maria was the first friend that she didn't seek out by design or manipulation. Aside from asking for directions the first time they met, Maria was the first friend that Camille didn't 'need,' her first chance at a real, honest-to-goodness friendship. Before Maria, Camille unconsciously formed need-based bonds, like the friendship she had with Mel, simply and instinctively for self-preservation.

Camille thought about driving through the night to get to Maria's but decided against it. She booked a flight from her phone through a last-minute discount site and before the night was over, she was on the short flight to DC.

Maria was waiting when the plane landed. When they saw each other, they embraced like the world was coming to an end, hesitant to let go. Maria was dying to know what was going on but didn't ask, knowing that Camille would tell her if and when she got ready to.

"Where's Sammy?" Maria asked first.

"She's with John," Camille's short and sweet response.

Fumes could be seen emanating from Maria's ears, but she kept her cool.

On the drive to Maria's house they stopped by the grocery store to pick up some breakfast food – eggs, sausage, corned beef hash, biscuits, cheese, grits, and Simply Orange. That juice was so good it always made Camille smile, but she didn't buy it unless she had company because she'd drink a whole gallon in two days if left to her own druthers.

Camille could throw down on breakfast and Maria thought that cooking might help to take her mind off of things. Plus, Maria hadn't forgotten about how delicious the scrambled cheese eggs were the last time Camille cooked her breakfast when Maria visited Kittery right after Sammy was born.

An hour after Camille's plane landed, they drove up to Maria's home. She lived just outside of DC, in Chantilly. Her house was way too big for one person, which is why she rented two of the five bedrooms out to her cousin and his quasi family.

Although Maria had prepared one of the spare bedrooms for her friend, Camille didn't want to be alone tonight and asked if she could sleep with Maria in her bed. There were no objections.

Maria was very particular. She was one of those people that woke up early just to make sure her bed was made and her house was in order before she went to work. Her style was simple. The walls were white, or cream or something in that family. She loved local black artist, which was evident by the Jenny Pickens and Shawn Etheridge originals throughout the home.

The master bedroom was the size of a studio apartment and exactly what Maria said she would have when the friends dreamt of their futures in college. Maria's mattress felt like it was made in heaven. It hugged her body in all the right places and felt like what you'd imagine love feels like, snuggly and warm. And even though Maria was almost six feet tall, she had step stools on either side of the bed.

The down comforter was enclosed in a paisley printed, bright, multi-colored duvet cover. There must have been ten pillows lining the head of the pillared bed, increasing in size and differing in shape the closer they got to the headboard.

Camille bathed in the oversized tub before getting into bed, trying desperately to scrub away the events of that evening, to no avail.

The friends lay beside one another and talked briefly about nothing of importance. The events of the evening had worn

Camille slam out, and within fifteen minutes, Maria was talking to herself.

The next morning when Maria awoke, she found Camille sitting at the dining room table sipping on a cup of OJ while typing on the computer. Cami was planning her next move.

"Good morning," Camille said when she heard Maria coming toward her.

"Good morning yourself. How are you this morning?"

"You know, I've been better," Camille said. "Thank you for letting me stay here."

"Girl, you know you're my ace," Maria told her, pointing at Camille, then pounding her fist on her chest.

"I'll cook in a minute," Camille said.

"It's up to you. No pressure. I was thinking we could go into town later and get a massage, a mani-pedi, and maybe even get our heads did," Maria said jokingly.

"That sounds like a plan," Camille agreed. "Are we alone?"

"I don't know. I'll check," Maria told her.

"Don't bother, this isn't top secret," Camille reasoned.

"You know you don't have to tell me a thing if you're not ready," Maria said pausing for a response. "But I'm dying over here, pretending that patience is a virtue I possess – just saying," Maria said, reluctantly prodding.

"I cheated on John," Camille blurted out.

Maria's eyes widened, but she said nothing.

"I've been cheating on John for some time now," Camille continued.

Maria made a circular motion with her hand as if to say – *come on, come on, spill the beans* – but she remained quiet.

"Sammy walked in on me," Camille said. The shame was evident in her confession.

Maria couldn't stop herself, she had to say something. "Dammmmnn!" She paused. "So, John found out?"

"No," Camille responded.

"Well, I'm confused," Maria said, scratching her head.

"I knew I wasn't going to stop," Camille admitted.

"Soooo – you fell in love?"

"Not with the man," Camille confessed.

"With what – his penis?" Maria speculated out loud.

Camille busted out laughing, while shaking her head. "No fool! With the excitement, the thrill of it all."

"Okay, I just have to make sure I heard you correctly." Maria paused. "You were cheating on your good, fine ass, successful, loves the ground you walk on, man with Mr. X because it was exciting, no strings attached. And your toddler, who can't talk yet, walks in on you. John knows nothing about it. And your solution is to leave your child and your great, to-die-for life?" Brief silence. "No judgment – but is that about right?" Maria asked.

"Yep," Camille said matter-of-factly.

"Let me see that damn computer," Maria demanded.

Camille slid the computer across the table. Maria started frantically typing like Tyler Perry playing Madea in *The Diary of a Mad Black Woman.*

"What are you doing?" Camille asked.

"Booking your flight back to Kittery. You had better come up with something to tell John. You need to go back and apologize. If you don't, you will regret it for the rest of your life."

"I'm not going back, Maria," Camille said.

"Now Camille, that's just silly."

"I don't want my daughter to go through what I went through," Camille told her friend.

"I have a great solution for that," Maria said sarcastically.

"What?"

"STOP DOING IT!" Maria demanded.

"It's not that easy," Camille confessed, she was weak.

"I don't pretend to know what you're going through, but what I know is that Sammy is innocent in all this. Whatever you're dealing with, you're going to have to suck it up, because she comes first now."

"I'm doing this for Sammy," Camille asserted.

"No! You're doing this for Camille," Maria countered.

"I love Sammy!" Camille insisted.

"Oh, I'm not questioning that, but…"

Maria was about to let Camille have it but was interrupted by her cousin. As the ladies changed the subject, Maria called the spa to make reservations.

"Think about what I said before you do anything else stupid," Maria added. Camille nodded, insincerely agreeing to reconsider her decision.

There wasn't enough time to cook breakfast, so they each grabbed a yogurt and banana from the fridge, which would have to tide them over until after their massages. There was a vegan spot not too far from the spa that Maria had been meaning to try. And although neither of them was vegan, they loved visiting new eateries. Besides, they were both trying to eat healthier.

The days flew by. Camille and Maria spent the week talking and making plans for the future. They didn't discuss Camille's situation again. They even got in touch with one of their mutual friends who agreed to meet them at Matchbox in DC later in the week. Camille had a love connection with their pepperoni pizza while in town for Obama's first inauguration and never forgot about it. When Maria had to go back to work, Camille decided to make her departure.

"You know I love you," Maria told her friend.

"It's the one thing I count on," Camille said.

"Keep in touch. I'll pray for you."

"Thank you, Maria. I need that. I love you too."

They hugged tightly, enough to last until the next time they saw one another. With that, Camille got in the Lyft and departed for the airport. Maria watched her friend drive away, knowing all too well what Camille was going to do, but accepted that it was her choice to make, a hallmark of unconditional love.

FIVE

....

no place like home

WHEN Mrs. Young picked her daughter up from the airport, Camille collapsed in a burst of tears in her mother's arms. An unfamiliar spectacle for either woman, one that Camille falsely attributed to her long and grueling work schedule.

A mother's concern drew them to the bench just outside the airport entrance, where Lynn swaddled her child in comfort like a warm plush blanket fresh out the dryer on a chilly winter's night. They embraced until Lynn's love diffused across the barriers that her daughter had built, a palpable osmosis.

There's something that always draws you home again, even when you fought so hard to leave and stay away, even when you have painful memories that fester like unwanted guests who stick around long after the party is over. Maybe it's the familiarity that brings you back, maybe it's the concentration of love that you know will surround you, or maybe you simply have nowhere else to go. It was a bit of all this for Camille. And although she had the financial means to have gone anywhere, there was no place she needed to be more, no place like home.

It had been years since she had seen her family, so long she couldn't remember now. This wasn't unusual, though. Camille had always been an adventurer. Even from conception she was trying to break away.

When her mom was two months pregnant, Lynn almost miscarried while teaching her second-grade class. All the students were in hysterics when they saw Lynn's bloodstained blue jean ruffled dress. From that day until Camille's birth, a month premature, Lynn was put on bed rest.

Camille has been persistent in her attempts to be anywhere other than where she was. So ready to leave her parent's house, she became one of the only students in Chimney Rock High School's history to graduate early.

Her baby sister, Tania, called Camille a gypsy because as an adult Camille never lived anywhere longer than two years. When she moved to Maine for a new job opportunity and stayed longer than usual, everyone was shocked. When questioned, why Maine, Camille would simply say, *I love the long winters.* And although a false statement, it was enough to put an end to the constant inquiries.

Some people envied Camille's independent nature. *Something must be wrong with that girl*, Ms. Loretta was overheard telling her hair stylist. *She's hiding something*, cousin Mikaela said to their grandmother, Bet. *She had better not be gay*, her father thought. And murmurs of *black people don't act like that*, were common amongst town folk.

Her mother didn't care for any of that gossip. None of it mattered. Lynn just wanted Camille to be closer to home, and of course, settle down and have a family.

Children had never before been on Camille's to do list. She desired a family on occasion but loved her freedom more than anything. Nevertheless, her mother held out hope that one day Camille would succumb to the callings of motherhood. And although Lynn's hopes had become a reality, it would be quite some time before Lynn would learn that her wish had come true.

Camille claimed not to care what people thought. On the surface, this may have been true. But deep down, in the places that take contemplation and truth to access, she had to admit that she was embarrassed about her situation.

And even though there wasn't a societal stigma attached to being an unwed mother anymore, Camille never wanted to be in that statistic. Not to mention, she could hear her father's voice drilling both his girls, *no sex before you're married* or his weekly mantra after they got their periods, *no child of mine is gone bring bastard children into this world*. His words were like a scratched record playing over and over again in her head from the moment she discovered her pregnancy.

Embarrassment wasn't a trait that plagued Camille too often but having a baby out of wedlock forced a feeling of shame so piercing that it unconsciously depleted the joy from her soul like a slow leaking tire. It was the apparent reason for keeping her personal life personal, even from the ones she loved the most.

She maintained a strict policy of 'if she didn't want it known, she didn't tell it to anyone.' Having learned long ago, that even the people closest to you, not meaning any harm whatsoever, will spread your business. So that's why everyone thought she was single. She never talked about John, much less Sammy.

She thought about getting married to ease the sting of her predicament, but she didn't want to be married. And figured John didn't want to either, because he never asked. Marriage wasn't even a topic of conversation between them. *He was probably still gun-shy from his previous engagement*, Camille had thought, relieved.

"Mom's cooking up a storm over here. What time are you coming?" Tania asked.

Camille had been home for a couple of days now. She settled into a two-bedroom townhouse rental not too far from her parent's home. Her realtor cousin found it for her at a reasonable price.

Even before Sammy was born, Camille made sure to rent a room whenever she came home. She didn't want to be around her dad's usual negativity. It was all the more imperative now, especially since she had this secret. She needed a place where she could have alone time to video chat with John and Sammy.

"Not sure, I'm just waking up," she told her sister.

"I think Marsha and the kids are coming over, and Aunt D, too," Tania told her.

Camille didn't feel like a family reunion today, she really just wanted to veg out around the house, get some business affairs in order, maybe workout or go to the spa for a treatment, and knock back a couple glasses of wine. But what she wanted more than all this was to see her baby girl, face to face.

The mind is a funny thing. It has its own personality. It may prompt you to do one thing or another, but your heart will always know the truth. Camille's heart was telling her she'd made a big mistake, and now she didn't know how to fix it. John wasn't taking her calls, still hurt by her abrupt departure. She couldn't talk to her mom or sister about this, only Maria, who had already made her opinion known.

It took John three weeks to accept Camille's calls again after she left Kittery. At first, she would call every day to talk to Sammy, but the child kept asking her mother when she was coming back home. The question broke Camille's heart each and every time. Cowering to the anguish she felt, Camille resigned herself to only speaking to her daughter when John initiated the call.

"I need to talk to Sammy, PLEASE," she read her text to John from yesterday again, then decided to resend it, hesitantly adding, "I miss you guys," on the end. Then she texted her sister, "I'm on the way." She decided, doing anything else would be better than sitting around moping about Sammy.

Upon entering her parent's home, Camille spoke to everyone with punctuated greetings, eager to see what was on the menu.

"Pork chop and mashed potatoes," her mom's abridged response.

"My favorite," Camille said, though she didn't really have a favorite. She loved everything her mom made except those stinky chitterlings, which were disgusting. She would leave the house every time her mom ventured in the pig intestines direction to avoid the offensive odor.

Her dad came in from his card game looking a little ragged, Camille thought, but passed it off as nothing. "Hi Dad," she said, standing to give his weakening body a hug.

"How are you, Camille?" he asked, voice stern as ever.

"Can't complain, Dad," she replied blandly.

After he washed up, Mr. Young joined the rest of the family in the dining room as they prepared to eat the feast that Camille's mother had cooked.

Lynn hadn't listed the whole menu when earlier asked. There were collard greens and cabbage, Camille's favorites, an apple cinnamon relish baked right on top of the peppered grilled pork chops, macaroni and cheese, garlic mashed potatoes, homemade lemonade with slivers of lemon floating about in a glass pitcher, and to top things off, two homemade cakes – carrot and a lemon glazed pound. They all set around the table, Marsha, Junior, Sable, and the Youngs, talking and eating until their bellies were full.

"Mom couldn't make it, she has an early appointment tomorrow," Marsha had told them.

"Tell D we miss her," Lynn chimed in after swallowing a mouthful of cabbage.

"I will," cousin Marsha said. "So, how is life in Maine?"

No one in attendance had ever ventured outside their small town for anything other than weddings, funerals or military service. Camille hesitated, because this was exactly what she didn't want.

"Everything was great but I'm not going back. My contract finally ended," she said, hoping the subject might change.

"I can't wait for y'all to meet Toni," Tania interrupted, trying to help, but Marsha was curious.

"You seeing anybody special?" Marsha asked her favorite cousin.

You could have heard a hair drop, almost as if the whole room shifted their attention to Camille. She felt like EF Hutton.

"No, I haven't had time," Camille told them.

The walls and everything contained within them exhaled.

"You not gay, are you?" her father blurted out.

"RICHARD!" Lynn snapped, embarrassed for her daughter.

"Yeah, Dad, that's my big secret," Camille responded sarcastically, his ignorance triggering an intense irritation. *Gay would be easy*, she thought, before turning toward her mother. "Thank you for this wonderful meal," Camille said, and got up to give Marsha and the kids a big hug. "It was good seeing you guys again," she told them. She retreated to the kitchen to get some of her mother's homemade cake before leaving.

She wanted to lash out at her father and tell him everything she had been hiding, but she held her tongue, sort of. *As a matter of fact, I've been having sex for years, I live with a fine ass lawyer, and we have a daughter, BAM!* All just thoughts she wanted to vocalize just to piss him off. Instead, as she walked toward the door she mumbled under her breath, "I see things haven't changed much around here."

SIX

....

one more thing before i go

IT seemed like only yesterday that Camille fled Kittery, but more than a year had passed now. Not too long after her departure, John and Sammy moved to New York. He was offered a partnership with his firm's thriving Manhattan office. John hired a nanny to care for Sammy in her mother's absence. And fortunately for John, Ms. Monroe was able to relocate with them.

Camille was the turtle, putting her business on hiatus, doing a lot of soul searching, reconnecting with family and friends, while Sammy was the hare, growing fast and forming adult words now. Her father taught her how to say 'ridiculous' and she's been saying it every chance she gets. When only a year ago she wore 3T, now she was well into the 5T's, and could even fit some 6's. Sammy's hair had turned a light shade of blonde and auburn in the summer and was fighting its way back to brown.

Sammy's infant sleeper was always with Camille, still tightly sealed in a bag. And on occasion, Camille would inhale the fading scent to help conjure those special moments in time. No mistaking it, Camille hadn't forgotten a thing about her baby. It's just that the smell heightened her emotion and somehow made her feel closer to Sammy. Sometimes Camille would even cradle the tiny garment against her chest at night and cry herself to sleep.

John was still struggling with the split and occasionally would want to talk about what happened. He couldn't fathom a plausible motive for her leaving, especially deserting Sammy. After each attempt at reason he was more confused than he had been before.

"Just talk to me. Was there someone else?" he'd ask, anguished.

"You don't really know me, John," she'd always respond.

"Is that your answer? I don't really know you." Her vagueness pissed him off all the more. "This is sooooo CRAZY!" he'd say, not needing a response.

"You're right, it is," she would say, calmly.

"I don't need your confirmation! Let me say this…until you get some help for whatever you're going through…"

She'd interrupt. "Until I get some help. WHAT? Are you threatening me?" she'd snap.

"Look, I can't do this. DAMMIT, Camille, you fucked this up! It was good. You and me, we…"

She could hear him choking back tears and assured him that there was no one else.

"Get some help," he faintly voiced through the sadness.

She argued no more, yielding to the pain she had inflicted. "I'm sorry, John," was her final offer before saying goodbye.

It was a beautiful autumn day. A slight breeze filled the crisp mountain air. A myriad of tangerines, gingers, crimsons, and golds adorned the fall foliage as it does during this time of the year. And the sun smiled on the rolling hills, just like every other morning.

Good news.

Although business had been slow, by design, Camille couldn't resist a new offer, an opportunity to work in Singapore. After all, she had been courting this contract for some time. Not to mention that the solace of being home and the healing power of time had their say once again, initiating the mending she so desperately sought.

When the doorbell rang, Camille was not ready. Tania was early. The robe hung on the bathroom door. Camille snatched it off the hook, quickly wrapping herself up, scampering to let Tania in.

"Come in. You're early," she said without even looking.

"Hello, sunshine," her sister sarcastically countered.

"Tania, you….," Camille couldn't finish before being interrupted.

"Girl just get ready. I'm not rushing you. I just wanted to move some stuff in before we left," Tania said.

"You're not wasting any time, are you?" Camille teased, "…the key is on the table."

Her sister chuckled, grabbed the key and went back out to the car to get her things. Tania would be staying in the rental while Camille was away.

Camille tried to rush but she didn't want to forget anything. An hour passed quickly. She was almost done, and so was Tania. They loaded the luggage in the car together. Taking a last-minute look at her packing list, she ran back in the house and grabbed her 'B.O.B.' from the nightstand.

"You're so nasty," Tania said.

"No, I'm practical," Camille said, adamantly. "Who knows when I'll get some again?"

They laughed together.

"I guess you're right about that," Tania said, and threw her hands up, shrugging her shoulders, as if to say, 'you've got a point.'

On the thirty-minute ride to the airport, the sisters talked about all the things sisters talk about – their parents, family, relationships, their plans for the future.

"You know Mel's pregnant again?" Tania said.

"WHAT! Again?"

"Yea, she got married about five years ago, she has a three-year-old daughter," Tania informed her sister.

A child around Sammy's age, Camille thought. "I really should get in touch with her," she said, though she didn't even believe her own words as they formed in her head.

When Camille left for college, she lost contact with everyone back home, some on purpose, but most just a casualty of leaving. It wasn't like she could just pick up the phone and call, Mel was deaf. Camille owed it to Mel, at least a card, or congratulations...something. Mel singlehandedly changed Camille's life, her after school playmate, and the impetus for her business.

At the terminal, the sisters said their sorrowful goodbyes, hugging one another tightly.

"I will miss you," Tania said, as tears filled her eyes.

Camille was tearing up too, though she was the tough one. "I'll only be gone for two years, it'll go by fast," she told her sister.

"We've just gotten close again," Tania said.

"I knowww…the timing sucks, but I love my job, and Singapore…well that's an added bonus," Camille bragged.

"Wish I was going with you," Tania admitted. "What time will you get there?" she asked.

"I wish you were too," Camille agreed. "Let's see…it's a sixteen hour flight. Sooo, maybe tomorrow around eleven, your time."

"Call us as soon as you land. You know Mom will be worried."

"I will...and I'll send pics every chance I get."

"You better!" Tania demanded.

"For sure munchkin," Camille assured, hugging her sister again. "Oh, I am expecting some very important mail, a check from the last training," she continued. "I spoke with Addison, the accountant, who said it should be here sometime soon. Please deposit it for me."

"Ok! I thought you had that set up on direct deposit," Tania countered.

"I did, but remember when my credit cards were stolen?" Camille said, reminding her sister. "I had to cancel my direct deposits. But all of my bills have been set up on automatic payment," Camille said. "There's no rush really, except the check is void after ninety days, I think."

Recently, Camille went to a weekend conference in Detroit with the American Foundation for the Blind. Not all the participants were blind, because ever since then someone has been on a joyride with her credit card, purchasing everything from videos to Gucci handbags. Camille didn't even realize the card was gone until last Friday when she tried to reserve a rental car and couldn't find it.

"I know, I know, I know, you've told me all this already, last night as a matter of fact, and the night before that, too. I know to check your mail and deposit your money. I will not forget! I promise," Tania said, agitated by the repeated instructions.

"Just making sure I haven't forgotten anything," Camille said as she rubbed her head trying to recall any last-minute details.

Though Camille didn't like flying all that much, she was really looking forward to this trip, it had been years since she traveled abroad. And as she contemplated about what else she should tell Tania, they heard the announcer call for all passengers for flight 478 to New York boarding at gate 12 in thirty minutes. That was her flight.

"Oh, shit!" Camille gasped, "This is it."

"For God's sake, don't say that when you're about to board a plane." Tania joked. "Anything but this is it. That's what MJ called his last tour. And we know how that turned out."

"You're so silly," Camille smiled. "Love you, munchkin."

"Love you back, gypsy. Send presents," Tania said in jest.

"Take care of my stuff," Camille poked.

"WHATEVER! Bye, girl."

"Bye T." With that Camille headed to the counter to check her luggage. She turned towards the window to watch Tania drive away, but she had already gone.

Camille had never been to Singapore before and was excited about the opportunity. Usually on business trips, a day of relaxation and time to shore up last minute details was calendared in. Unfortunately, this trip would be an exception. Camille's assistant, Jane, had to juggle plans in order to accommodate the employer, forcing Cami to have to hit the ground running not long after her arrival.

She slept the entire flight to New York, where there would be a somewhat lengthy layover. Once they were safe on the ground, she called John. The phone rang three times. She thought about hanging up but resisted.

Aside from FaceTime, Camille hadn't seen John or Sammy since she left Kittery, so she wasn't sure how the call would go. Their conversations were humdrum at best, awkwardly avoiding the usual 'whys.' Nowadays they only exchanged information about Sammy.

Every ring lasted a million years, allowing Camille's wayward mind to wander. She thought about how random and funny life was. How one simple decision can dictate everything. She couldn't have known that choosing the arduous women's studies class over the much easier nutrition class would change the course of her entire life. While waiting for the plane to come to a stop at the terminal, she smiled at the apparent randomness of it all.

John and Camille met her freshman year. They had one class together, women's studies. When she first saw him, she thought he was quite handsome. She also thought he was either gay or a player, because there were not many available men breaking down the doors to take women's studies classes, especially not Dr. Robin's class, where the A/D ratio was rumored to be 1:4.

On the first day of class he sat beside her. Cool as could be, he walked in the room like he was the one in charge. And surprisingly throughout the semester John proved to be a refreshing voice to the usual female tête-à-tête.

Sometime in the beginning of the semester John and Camille began seeing each other outside of class. At first it was just a friendship thing, but gradually the flirting and staring led to long, passion-filled kisses.

At that time, kissing was all Camille knew.

Three months into the friendship/relationship John began to get frustrated with the usual kissing and going home thing. Seeing each other daily gradually turned into five times a week, then three, then talking on the phone seemed to be a chore for him. When questioned about their diminishing time together, he passed it off as wanting to hang out with his boys, which suited Cami just fine because she missed her 'girlfriend' time, too.

Since this was her first 'real' boyfriend, she had no jaded relationship history of her own to make her think he was up to no good. Camille was a smart girl, and even though she had seen her father fool around, she was oblivious to what John was up to, just like her mother in this way.

One day, her afternoon lab was cancelled, so she decided to see what John was doing. When he didn't answer the phone, Camille went to his dorm room. As fate would have it, just as she arrived, the door opened. To her surprise John was standing there half naked ushering his 'new thing' out the door. 'New thing' and John were so busy kissing and groping one another in inappropriate places that neither one of them noticed Camille standing there.

Camille had seen John with this girl before, but he told her that she was just a friend. Frozen, Camille stood there for what seemed like a lifetime. Flashbacks of all the times she couldn't reach him came bouncing to memory like ping pong balls. Every time he wanted to hang out with Jason or Tim, or when he was too sleepy to come over to play spades in her dorm lounge, now all made perfect sense.

The thing that pissed Camille off more than the kissing and fondling was that the girl knew she and John were in a relationship. Just last week, 'new thing' stopped Camille on the yard to, as 'new thing' said at the time, just shoot the breeze.

The two young ladies had a somewhat lengthy conversation, where 'new thing' asked Camille, among other stuff, how long she and John had been together. And unfortunately for 'new thing,' this encounter flashed fresh in Camille's mind.

The next fifteen minutes were a blur to both her and John, which to this day made them laugh every time they reminisced. What happened next was so out of character for Camille. She totally came unhinged and lost her cool. She gave that girl an old-fashioned ass whooping like 'new thing' had talked about Camille's mama – pulling hair and ripping clothes. When all was said and done the 'new thing' had a Janet Jackson like wardrobe malfunction.

John tried to break up the fight by grabbing Camille's arms, which was a huge mistake. Camille head-butted him so hard that it broke his nose and blackened her right eye for weeks.

Needless to say, that was the end of act one of the John and Camille saga. He begged and pleaded with Camille throughout the semester, even so bold as to bring it up as a topic for debate in their class. Cami was numb to any of his attempts. And finally, when freshman year ended, so did his fruitless efforts at reconciliation.

Camille's memory of these events was as fresh as her last breath. And for the briefest of moments, she thought her abandoning John in Kittery might have been some type of unconscious retaliation for freshman year. Then she shook those thoughts off as utterly absurd, knowing she would never hurt her baby girl to get back at some man, especially for something that happened a lifetime ago.

John's phone rang once more before going to voicemail. Camille contemplated her recklessness for the millionth time, if there was any reason good enough to leave your child, to not see her for over a year, or not be there to help her learn the alphabet, or not teach her how to count to ten, or not take her on play dates.

And just as swiftly as those thoughts formed, they were replaced, as she prepared her bogus, 'all the world is happy' voicemail message. She was relieved when he didn't answer, but as she began speaking, her phone rang. It was John calling her back. She thought about not answering, but had no reason other than guilt, so she clicked over.

"Hold on, John, I have your voicemail on the other line." Camille clicked back over and uselessly proceeded to leave the message she had prepared. "I'm in town for a bit. Calling to see what you are up to. Tell Sam I love and miss her. Call me." With that she clicked back over to John. "Hey, baby. What have you been up to?" Camille said, a fake cheerfulness.

"Not much, Cami. What about you?" John returned the emotion.

"Well, I know we haven't talked in a while, but I am in town, at JFK on a layover. I have three hours. Are you free? Where's Sam?" she said in nervous breathlessness.

"You are funny! Really, three hours," he replied.

"Yeah. I would love to see you guys! What's wrong?"

There were many valid comebacks he could have rattled off — *why didn't you let me know ahead of time, or you're going to spring this on Sammy like you're just a friend dropping by for a visit, or have you ever driven in NYC traffic before*, were among the many unspoken thoughts going through his head, but instead he just said, "You know three hours in New York is more like thirty minutes with the traffic and all. Next time give me a heads up. We would have been there waiting on you."

"…it was last minute and rushed, totally slipped my mind. And I didn't even think about the traffic, just thought about seeing you guys. Well, maybe next time," she admitted.

"Yeah, I guess so," he sighed, "I'll tell Sam you called. She's not here right now."

There was a definite awkwardness to the conversation, so much that needed to be said, but a void had wedged a space so vast between them that all the necessary words had been swallowed up in a blackhole of neglect. Camille sighed deeply to herself, her mind consumed with heaviness, both of them avoiding any real topics, instead opting to talk about work and family, but only briefly until the intermittent quiet became deafening.

"It was good to hear from you Cami. Don't be a stranger," he told her. "You know we both miss you."

"…good talking to you too, John," her final words, the rest stuck in her throat waiting for the courage to conquer thinking.

They were both quiet now, neither certain of what to say next. Thinking it meant goodbye, John hung up, as Camille choked back an apology.

"John," she said, mustering the nerve that had taken months to gather. When she realized he was gone, she thought about calling back, but pride prevailed again.

Fresh from their conversation, the plush sofa lent itself to feckless contemplation. A smile surfaced on John's face remembering their first snowball fight, the birth of their daughter, the first time they made love, the time Camille fought the girl in the dormitory hallway. Too deep in thought, he didn't hear the alarm chime when the front door opened.

"Hello, Mr. John," the nanny said, carrying the sleeping child into the bedroom. She didn't want to disturb him but was rushing to beat the afternoon traffic.

His eyes now closed. The couch tightened its grip. *I could have made it to the airport*, he thought.

"Mr. Sabourn, I put the baby down in her room. She's knocked out," Ms. Monroe said more forcefully, tapping him lightly on the shoulder.

He flinched, turning to face her. "Ooooh, I'm sorry – just thinking."

"Musta been kind of important," she muffled and reminded him that Sammy was asleep in her bed. Scrambling toward the door, she said her goodbyes until the next morning.

He responded in kind. The computer sat idle on the coffee table for nearly an hour now. He had been responding to work emails when Camille called.

Sammy woke up and ran into the living room looking for her father. She smelled of cotton candy and chocolate. John beamed and pulled the child onto his lap.

Every time he looked at their daughter, he fell in love all over again. Sammy's gray eyes and long eyelashes were identical to Camille's. When Sammy slept, she would somehow wind up diagonal on the bed just like her mother. Their child even folded her arm and slept on them like a pillow, exactly like Camille.

"I lub you Daaaddy," Sammy told her father, out of the blue.

"I love you more, baby girl," he said, and kissed her on the neck. Sammy giggled. Then he realized that he hadn't even ask Camille where she was jetting off to. "Mommy loves you too," he told his daughter, squeezing her tightly, afraid she might disappear if he let her go.

And in no time at all Sammy fell back to sleep, in his arms. Instead of putting Sammy back in her bed, John gently placed her on the couch beside him. The work briefs would have to wait while he watched his daughter's every breath. He was saddened by the circumstances, but amazed that she was his.

There they were, John firmly anchored on an old familiar piece of furniture, nuzzling his favorite girl. Camille, who still clung to her shame like a spider dangling from its web, was indelibly lost, waiting to board her flight to Singapore.

Both parents, for the moment, hopelessly daydreaming.

SEVEN

....

is that you?

WEATHERVANE'S Bistro was a quaint seafood bar and grille, popular amongst Kittery locals and tourists alike. Reservations were hard to come by, which might suggest stuffy and sophisticated, but to the contrary, the bistro was a warm and welcoming place. This was John's first stop after checking into his room, a recommendation from one of the flight attendants.

John, an accomplished corporate lawyer, was in town for an interview prompted by an old college chum. He made his way to the bar, ordered a beer and waited for an open seat.

Always impeccably dressed, he sported a pastel pink button-down dress shirt that appeared professionally pressed. The collar and the cuffs were paisley print, in various shades of pink and blue. The first two buttons on his shirt were unfastened, exposing his smooth chocolate skin. The blue suit that decorated his frame looked tailor made. A small pink square scarf winked just slightly from his jacket's left chest pocket.

Of course, he didn't expect to see anyone he knew, but across the room, Camille, who looked like a million bucks herself, was on a blind date with Mr. Oh So Fine, never been anywhere, never done anything, simple, and boring as hell.

She did a double take when she saw John standing at the bar. They hadn't kept in touch and only saw each other in passing on occasion at alumni gatherings or college sporting events.

She admired his sunglasses, which fit his freshly shaven face precisely and helped accessorize his tightly trimmed mustache and beard. Her eyes were entertained, a relief from the agony she was experiencing on her date. She went into action immediately.

"Oh my God!" she blurted without warning, just loud enough to shock Mr. Oh So Fine, his eyes widening over her sudden outburst.

"What's wrong, sexy?" Mr. Oh So Fine questioned.

"Oh my God, it's my ex-boyfriend! HE'S CRAZY FOR REAL!" she exclaimed.

"He's your ex, right?" Mr. Oh So Fine asked.

"Yes, but you don't understand," she told him. "I have to go talk to him before, before…I don't know what he will do."

Camille sprang up and walked over to John, leaving Mr. Oh So Fine sitting at the table, telling him to wait, so she could smooth things over with her ex.

"Dukes," John teasingly bellowed, surprised but glad to see a familiar face.

Her abridged chuckle and sharp side eye spoke for itself. Camille didn't know how John would react when she asked him to play along, but it didn't stop her from asking.

"John, I need your help," she said sharply, dismissing his waggish welcome. Not exactly the first thing you say to someone who you haven't had contact with, which explained John's confusion.

"I am on the date from some place worse than hell and you're my out – my crazy ex-boyfriend," she told him, speaking almost at a whisper. In Camille's eyes, her story wasn't that much of a stretch. John was her ex-boyfriend and he was crazy for messing up the way he did back in college.

She gave John a brief synopsis of the date and told him exactly how she wanted him to act. Having nothing else to do, or nowhere to go, he agreed. Maybe he wanted to catch up or see what would happen. Thinking back on the whole ordeal, he should have politely declined, giving her a business card and jetting, but that's ancient history now.

"Feel free to pace the floor and look a little angry," she whispered, and walked back to the table where Mr. Oh So Fine was seated.

John jokingly commented, "Come on now, I don't exactly look the part," and semi-smiled.

He was reluctant but consented to play the role as assigned. As part of the plan he stayed back by the bar and waited for her to return. Per instruction, he gave a stab at pacing and began to sway side to side, which was his best attempt at angry, considering the circumstances.

"I am very sorry for this, but I have to go. I don't want any trouble," Camille softly whispered to Mr. Oh So Fine. She went into her purse and pulled out four twenty-dollar bills and laid them on the table. "This one's on me." Camille said, extending her hand to shake with Mr. Oh So Fine. "I'm so sorry," she told him, *sorry you're so fine and stupid at the same time, sorry you have no talk game, sorry I wasted my night when I could have been doing anything else.*

"Are you going to be alright?" he asked in the same murmured manner, while simultaneously scooping up the cash she offered.

"Yeah, I will be, just as soon as I get out of this place." And that too was the truth. Camille couldn't wait to call her so-called 'friend' who set her up with this loser.

She walked to John, who was still 'pacing' at the bar. Whew, she motioned, her right-hand swiping across her forehead in relief as she stepped out of Mr. Oh So Fine's view. "And by the way, what the hell was that? You call that pacing?" she softly chuckled, still clinging to the hoax.

"He can't see you," John said in a 'whatever' tone. "Woman, what have you gotten me into?"

"Let's go!" Camille motioned for John to grab her by the elbow. John obliged with one hand, tickling her with the other. Once outside, they hailed a cab.

"Soooo….," she exhaled, semi-exhausted from the performance, "John Sabourn, how have you been?" she said, situating herself inside the taxi.

"Maybe I should be asking you that, Ms. Dukes."

"Stop calling me that!" she said, shaking her head.

"You'll never live that one down, so get over it," he laughingly told her.

"Anyway, thank you for rescuing me. What can I say? Men lie on their profiles too! There's absolutely no way my friend would have done that to me." Cami laughed hysterically in disbelief.

John couldn't help but join in.

"Waaait, wait a minute. Noooo, wait a minute." She said skeptically. "Where's Ashton Kutcher? Am I being punk'd, or something? First, the date from the pits of hell and then you just so happen to show up in Kittery, of all places, at the exact restaurant, just in time to witness the fiasco," Camille thought out loud. "Someone must be playing a big joke!" she exclaimed, shaking her head.

John was amused, the whole situation was funny to him. But when he saw that Camille was really getting into conspiracy theory mode, he decided to coax her back to reality. "DAMN, that dude must have really been horrible!" he said.

"You think?" she said, sneeringly.

"But no, you're not on *Candid Camera*," he assured her. "And yes, that was your friend that set you up with that joker. I use the term 'friend' loosely. If I were you, I would reevaluate that friendship!" he said, with an 'I'm smiling but I'm serious' smirk on his face.

"Who wears an ascot to a seafood restaurant, in Kittery? What straight man does that?" she questioned, still flummoxed.

"You've got a point. He might be suspect," John agreed.

"I'm so done with that. Why did he have gold and silver caps on his teeth? What's that about – ran out of money or something? Believe me when I tell you, Shannon left that out! Yuck!!!"

"To ease your paranoia, I'm here for an interview at McEachern & Thornhill."

"Really?"

"Do I detect a bit of sarcasm? Really. You remember Ian from college?" he asked.

"Red-headed Ian, who dated Randi, Ms. Kappa Kappa Gamma?" she questioned.

"Yeah. Mr. Kappa Kappa Gamma himself. Well, his father is one of the partners at McEachern & Thornhill," John told her.

"What's Ian up to?" Camille asked.

"He lives in Virginia with his family."

"Family? That word is so far off of my radar!"

"Annnyway, I was talking to him a while back and told him I was interested in relocating. He remembered our conversation and called me when he found out about the opening. I'm a shoo-in for the job. The interview is just a formality," John said confidently.

"Well, that sounds great!"

"Yeah, I came here a couple of times with Ian when we were in college and fell in love with the place."

"…fell in love with Kittery? Now I know you're playing," she said. "Winter lasts thirteen months, too much snow for me."

They both chuckled.

"Yeah. It's perfect. They actually have seasons here, unlike in Miami, where I grew up."

"I know what you mean. In the south, unless you lived in the mountains, the only time you saw snow was on TV. It wasn't until we visited family up north, that I saw snow for the first time," Camille told him. "Where are we going?" Camille asked, ten minutes after she and John got in the cab. They had been wandering around aimlessly.

"I have no idea," John replied. "You're the one with all the plans. I'm literally just along for the ride."

"Cute! Real cute," she said, looking at John cynically. "Driver could you please drop us off at the Little Brown Jug?"

"Yes, ma'am," the driver replied.

"I think you'll enjoy this spot, John. They have a nice atmosphere, a live acoustic band, and we can get some dessert or wine or…oh my God, that's right, you're probably hungry," she said, placing the palm of her hand to her forehead. "You didn't get a chance to eat anything, did you? I'm so sorry. They have a good entrée selection at the Brown Jug too. It's no Weathervane's, but it's nice all the same," she told John.

The cabbie nodded in agreement.

"You know me," John said. "I'll try anything once."

Ten minutes later the driver pulled up in front of the Little Brown Jug. There was a good-sized crowd inside from what they could see through the window. John pulled out his wallet to cover the thirty-dollar cab fee. Just as the cabbie was poised to reach for the money, Camille interrupted and pushed John's hand back, motioning him to put his wallet away.

"No, John! No, I have this," she insisted. "This one is definitely on me," she said, adding in a twenty-dollar tip.

The aimless driving didn't trouble the cabbie at all. Besides, he enjoyed the conversation, listening to Camille's crazy date and subsequent rescue.

When they entered the pub, the hostess informed them that there would be a thirty-minute wait. They had a lot of catching up to do, so they didn't mind, sitting at the bar until a table was available. The bar was crowded, only one stool was available. John, always the gentleman, pulled the seat out for Camille. She thanked him with a wink.

The noise level in the bar was minimal, considering the size of the crowd. Camille situated her barstool so that she faced

John who stood to her left, making it much easier for them to talk over the crowd.

"So, you're in town for an interview?" Camille began.

"Yes. But as I said I'm almost certain the job is mine. So, I would say I'm in town for a new job. What are you doing here?"

"Well, as a matter of fact, I'm here on business, too," she responded.

"Really? If I may ask, what do you do?" John inquired.

"I have my own company," Camille explained. She went on to tell him about her business and the travel opportunities it afforded her. He was fascinated. She had recently returned from Turkey with a group of touring deaf students. "Turkey is beautifully rich in tradition, it was amazing. All my expenses were paid in full, which made it even more beautiful. Not to mention, I was well-compensated."

"How much do you bill for something like that?" John was curious to know.

"Whatever I want to," she said matter-of-factly.

"No, really?"

"Well, I've been doing this since I left college. It is all outlined on our website," she explained. "At first it was difficult getting my bearings as far as billing was concerned, but now it's second nature."

She went on to tell him that all her expenses, including travel and lodging, were paid in full by the client. When she first started her business, she was surprised at how much people were willing to pay for her expertise, practically anything she asked.

He was intrigued, especially when she explained how she helped her clients secure government subsidies that cover her services.

"It all sounds so interesting," he told her. "I would assume that you meet a lot of people."

"I definitely do. Many times, my clients give me great referrals. In fact, I got this current job because the teacher of the class that I traveled to Turkey with is the cousin of Walter Shapleigh," she told John.

"Who is Walter Shapleigh?" he asked.

"Only the richest man in Kittery, and the principal owner of the company I currently work for."

"Oh, okay," John nodded, just as the bartender greeted them.

"Good evening," she said. "I'm Nicole. Is there anything I can get for you?"

Camille looked back at John to see if he was ordering anything.

"Let me have a Bud," he said. "Are you having anything?" he asked Camille.

"Yes, just some ice water, please. I'll get some wine when we're seated," she told him.

"Ice water and a Bud," Nicole said, repeating their orders and placing coasters on the counter in front of Camille.

"Well…are you married or in a relationship?" Camille asked abruptly as the waitress walked away.

John smiled, liking her directness. "Now that came from out of nowhere," he said.

"Well?"

"As a matter of fact, I am engaged," he told her.

"Are you now?" she said, silently begging for more.

"Yes. My fiancé's name is Mia," John said.

"Tell me about her."

"What do you want to know?"

"…I don't know – everything," she said, smiling slyly.

EIGHT

....

reunion

JOHN was reluctant to discuss his relationship while standing at the bar. Instead, he changed the subject and told Camille that he would wait until they were seated to continue. She understood. Besides, he was curious to find out her relationship status, although he was already somewhat acquainted with it.

They continued to drink and talk and within twenty-five minutes they were seated at a table near the window. Camille loved window seating, especially when alone. She would look out in boredom, making up stories about the passersby.

On one such occasion, she noticed two couples as they shuffled down the street, the ladies walking in front of the men.

By their manner, Camille reasoned that they were all well acquainted.

The couples were laughing, smiling and enjoying one another when Camille saw the tall tan man reach out and tap the brunette on the bottom, just as the man who Camille had designated as the brunette's boyfriend turned to check out the commotion of the passing motorcycles.

The tan man's designated girlfriend, a fiery red head, was oblivious and never stopped talking, even though no one was paying her any attention. Once the motorcycles passed, they all continued in their previous manner, no one the wiser, except the brunette, the tan man, and Camille.

Camille wondered endlessly about the couples as she ordered and ate her lunch at the café that afternoon. By the time she was finished conjuring up stories about them, the tan man and the brunette had run off to Las Vegas together. When they married at the same wedding chapel as Brittany Spears, the brunette was five months pregnant.

An active imagination was one trait that, at times, did not serve Camille well, often landing her in a lot of trouble. Had she not been interested in John's relationship she would have fabricated a story about the Amazon woman, who looked like she used to be a man, and the man who looked like her son, who were canoodling at the table next to them.

"Tell me about Mia," Camille said, her nosiness getting the best of her.

"You don't mince words, do you?" he said.

"What's the point of doing that?" she questioned.

"Her name is Mia Lee," he told her. "I met her while I was in law school."

"Is she a lawyer, too?" Camille asked.

"No. Actually, she's a physician."

"Wow, the Huxtables in reverse," Camille teased.

As John began to tell their story, he pulled his phone out to show Camille a photo. "Here's a picture of her with her daughter," he said.

"Daughter?" Camille questioned, shocked.

"Yes, she has children," he confirmed.

"Children?"

"She was married before," he told her. "Her husband was tragically killed in a car accident the week after their youngest child was born."

Camille took the phone, staring at the picture. "She's gorgeous!"

Mia was a beautiful woman. Her Halle Berry in *Jungle Fever* cut suited her well. Her hair was jet-black and rippled like soft rolling waves, her skin was like Hershey's milk chocolate. In the picture, Mia's daughter was a toddler, and although that was a long time ago, Mia still maintained her curvaceous figure and youthful allure. Good thing Camille was a confident woman, Mia was the type to arouse envy.

"Thank you," John said.

"Wow, that's crazy. That must have been really hard for her," Camille commented, appearing sympathetic.

"It was," he confirmed. "She was in the middle of her residency and had to drop out."

"You knew her husband, too?" Camille asked.

"Yes. Like I said, we met when I was in law school. We've been friends for some time, only reconnecting when she came into the firm seeking legal advice."

Camille impulsively started swiping through the photos on his phone. When she realized what she was doing, she snickered shamelessly and apologized. "I'm sorry. I'm just nosy. You don't mind, do you?"

He shook his head and told her he didn't, inwardly agreeing with her. Camille had heard enough of the John and Mia story, though she continued to prod him for information. By the time the waitress returned with their food, Camille knew so much about John's fiancé that she could have passed herself off as one of Mia's family members.

"What's going on with you?" John asked once realizing he had been carrying on way too much.

"Sad," Camille began, "...there's not really much to tell."

"What do mean?" he questioned, "You're beautiful, smart and successful. I'm sure you have men lined up to sweep you off your feet."

"I will graciously accept that compliment. Thank you. But if beauty and brains were the only requirements to be in a great relationship, a lot of women would be off the market," Camille remarked. "...the reality of my career is that it's not conducive to sustaining any type of long term anything. And frankly, right now, I like things this way," she told him. "Sadly, most of the men I meet are just as corny as the blind date guy – just nice to look at."

"You don't want a family one day?" he asked.

"Why are you so shocked by that? I don't subscribe to the societal pressures that say I'm supposed to want a husband and kids," she pounced. "Like I told you earlier, that family thing is way out of my stratosphere. And considering my history, it's probably for the best."

"What do you mean by that?" he persisted. "No one is ever really ready. Before Mia, I was adamant about not dating a woman with kids," he confessed, "…but look at me now."

"That's real nice of you," she said snidely. "I have my reasons. It's a long story that I'm sure would bore you, take my word for it."

"Okay," John said, hastily moving on to the next subject. "Do you remember Sabrina Long?" he asked.

Camille didn't, but told him the name sounded familiar. John recounted numerous stories to help jog her memory, and eventually she had a vague idea about who he was speaking of.

John continued recounting stories about Sabrina and other classmates they knew in common. And although they both frequented annual alumni events, John was more committed to keeping up with everyone.

When Camille asked him how he had the time to keep up with everybody, John said, "You never know when you might need to network – Kittery job."

John ordered another beer, a well-done cheeseburger and some potato wedges, while Camille sipped on a couple glasses of wine. Camille and John talked for hours. They were the last patrons to leave the Little Brown Jug that night. When John finished the last bite of his burger Camille convinced him to have dessert.

"You have to try their walnut cake," Camille insisted. "People come from all around coveting the Little Brown Jug's cinnamon walnut bake. It's served fresh out of the oven with a scoop of the best homemade French vanilla ice cream I've ever tasted," Camille testified.

The waitress, overhearing Camille's testimony brought each of them a slice, on the house. And good thing she did, because Camille wasn't sharing. And after tasting it, John understood the hype.

As they were leaving the restaurant John chuckled.

"What's so funny?" Camille asked.

"Tonight," he said. "I was just thinking about our night. I really enjoyed it."

Before he could finish, Camille chimed in, agreeing.

"...I have to say it, and please don't get mad, but the last time we were together, it was quite different." He laughed.

"I was hoping you wouldn't bring that up, again. How long ago was that?" she asked.

"Don't try and wiggle your way out of it," he told her.

"What do you mean? Why wouldn't I want to talk about it...again?" she said sarcastically.

"You whooped that girl's ass, if I do say so myself."

"She was wrong. She knew we were together. No, you were wrong – that troll!" Camille jokingly erupted.

"…then you head-butted me and whooped my ass, too," he said, still laughing.

"Well, I was pissed. Y'all got what y'all deserved," she said, rolling her head and pointing her finger, ghetto fabulous Cami making an appearance. "That's the way I thought about it back then. Hopefully, I would handle things differently now. But you never know. Let's just say, I don't want to find out."

"We can laugh about things now, but seriously, I'm sorry that I hurt you. I never forgot about you, Camille," he confessed. "I never said this to your face, mainly because you refused to see me, but I am truly sorry. You were my first love. I was just young, dumb, and full…."

Camille interrupted. "Do not finish that sentence!" she said emphatically.

"All I was going to say was, full of curiosity," he told her, winking.

"Oh. Okay. That's nice to hear now – ESPECIALLY SINCE YOU'RE ENGAGED TO SOMEONE ELSE!" she exclaimed, jokingly, but she was serious. She hated useless rhetoric. While John was carrying on with his 'I loved you', 'wish it could have been you', nonsense, she rolled her eyes, it perturbed her.

"I know it really doesn't matter now, but I promised myself if I ever got the opportunity to apologize to you in person, I would," he said sincerely.

"Thank you, I'll let you know when I forgive you," she laughed. "No, that's valiant of you, especially after all this time."

They walked to the corner of Remington and Duke, where they stood watching the cars drive by. The taxi that they called for John twenty minutes earlier still had not arrived. Camille's place was only a block away, but she wasn't in a rush. She really enjoyed John's company more than any of the men she had dated in the recent past.

"I'm just around the corner," she told him, pointing in the direction of her home. Since the taxi still hadn't arrived, they began walking toward her brownstone.

"What's just around the corner mean to you?"

"…umm, a five to ten-minute walk at best. You're welcome to come over and wait for the taxi at my place, or I could give you a ride to your hotel," she told him. "If you'd like, you could even crash tonight. I have two guest bedrooms that have never had guests in them."

"I have a room downtown. I'm sure your place would be much nicer," John said, contemplating the offer.

They walked the two blocks down Remington until they reached Maddox. The night air was cool, and the sky was clear. The light from the stars seemed to illuminate their path as they told tales that neither one of them had thought about in ages.

"How long were we together?" Camille asked.

"Not long enough," John replied much too quickly, before realizing the implications of his words.

Camille, indifferent to inconsequential words, acted as though he had said nothing and countered with, "I know it wasn't long, but I remember when you went home with me. I think I even went home with you once, too," she said. "Where are you from again – Opal Local or something like that?" she said, joking.

"Opa Locka," he corrected her.

"Yeah, that's right. How are your parents? And what about your brother and sisters? What are they up to? I remember that Cassie being a trip," Camille recalled.

"Everyone's doing well, and Cassie is still crazy as ever. She married that guy she kept on telling everyone was just her friend," John said.

"I know. We kept in touch for a while. She sent me an invitation to the wedding. Everyone thought it was a shotgun wedding because she insisted on a justice of the peace ceremony."

"She fooled us all, didn't she? You know she has twins now? Why did that nut go and name them Phinneaus and Hazel."

"*Pretty Woman* was her favorite movie," Camille said, laughing riotously.

"…you remembered that? We had some good times, didn't we?"

"…we did!" she agreed.

"How is your sister doing?" John questioned.

"She's doing well. Still at home with mom and dad, milking it for all she can," Camille said with a smirk. "Tania isn't moving out until she's saved enough to pay cash outright for a house."

"She did something big in microbiology, right?"

"…something like that. I'm not sure, that mess is way over my head."

"How are your mom and pops?" John asked.

"Mom is feisty as ever – always on the go. And Dad, well that's another story altogether. He and I never really got along," she reminded him.

"I remember," John paused. He recalled that Camille and her father's relationship was touchy, but never really understood why. She never wanted to talk about it.

"I do, too," she said, a gloomy sadness overtook her. "I do too," she repeated.

John quickly diverted attention to another topic, cued by the sudden change of mood. "You know Angela is a published author now."

"Angela?" Camille asked quizzically, not yet fully reengaged in the conversation.

"You remember my baby sister, Angela?" John asked.

"Dodi?"

"Yeah, Dodi. No one has called her that in years," he commented. "She's an author."

"What has she written?" Camille asked.

"She has a lucrative line of children's books. Have you heard of the *Where Does That Come From* series?"

"No," Camille answered.

"So far she has fifteen books in circulation and is contracted to write ten more. She self-published her first three books. When the publishing company got wind of her success, they offered her the deal of a lifetime. Her most successful one so far is her fifth book, *Boogers and Ear Wax*."

"That's great!" Camille said, her praise sincere.

They talked and walked, and time flew by as it does when you're having fun. As they approached the brownstone, John and Camille looked at one another with wonder. They speculated silently about what might have been. For the first time that evening the air was saturated with tension. The awkwardness of the moment caused them both to ramble nervously, which was unusual for either of them.

"We're here," Camille said.

"Oh, this is nice, Camille," John said. "If I'm not mistaken, McEachern & Thornhill is not too far away from here."

"What street are they on? I haven't been here long, but I do know my way around," Camille braggingly commented.

"Strouss and Main," John said.

"You're right. You could walk to work from here. It's about five blocks north."

John followed Camille up the short flight of stairs that led to the front door.

"You know you're welcome to stay," she reiterated, as she unlocked the door.

"I'll take you up on that," he told her.

NINE

....

friends with benefits

CAMILLE woke up early, just as the sun was making its appearance. She had kicked the goose down comforter off the bed during the night and was cold. Instead of grabbing it and going back to sleep she decided to get up and take a shower. Before going into the bathroom, she looked at her phone and saw that she had a text from Maria. She waited until after she showered to call her back.

"Heeeyyy girl!" Maria said cheerfully.

"What's going on, ladybug?"

"You know I hate that ladybug shit."

"Oh girl, get over yourself."

"Ok, Dukes, I will," Maria countered.

"I should straight hang up on you," Camille joked.

"You better not," Maria said.

"You won't believe who's here," Camille whispered.

"You're right, I won't. Who?"

"Guess," Camille prodded.

"Just tell me. The list is entirely TOO long," Maria said in jest.

"You are so wrong for that."

"But I'm real, though," Maria said and paused just briefly trying to come up with a name from Camille's past. "Okay, I'll take a stab at it – Rachel?"

"No, fool. That was just that one time. And I was white girl wasted," Camille said, laughing.

Maria chuckled too. "That's what you say. But y'all were way too cozy that one time we were all together for it to have been a hit and run, 'I was white girl wasted' thing – just saying."

"Guess I'm busted. But don't ask cause I'm not talking about it. And no, Rachel's not here."

"I give up. Who then?"

"John, from freshman year," she said, enthusiastically.

"WHAT? Oh, so that's why you're whispering. Speak up, Camille! Speak up!" Maria joked. "I didn't know you kept in touch with him."

"I don't," Camille tried to convince her friend.

"Right…right. But he's in your house and you're whispering. My name is Maria, not Boo Boo, sweetie."

They laughed together. Maria was crazy, she kept it all the way real. She's the kind of friend that everybody needs. Camille told Maria about her date with Mr. Oh So Fine and running into John at Weathervane's. Maria first thought it was *Candid Camera* too. She couldn't believe that they just happened to run into each other out of the blue, but she played along anyway.

Before Camille could finish her story, Maria rushed off the phone. It seems Maria was with her very own blast from the past. That's why she texted Camille in the first place. She didn't get a chance to tell her story. But a male's voice could be heard in the background.

"Girl, don't let that fine sip of wine go to waste! I gots to go!" Maria said and hung up without giving Camille a chance to say or ask a thing.

That's my Maria, Camille thought. For some reason, their conversation inspired her to make breakfast. So, when John woke up, they sat at the dining room table and talked over a homemade meal. He loved the brownstone and suggested that the space was entirely too big for one person.

"It is huge," Camille said, oblivious to his overture.

"Have you considered getting a roommate?" John asked.

"No," she said without hesitation.

"Why not?" he asked.

Overnight the notion of renting a room from Camille popped in his head. Her negative response didn't deter him from pursuing the matter. Not to mention, he had run the idea by Mia late last night, and although she had reservations, she trusted John wholeheartedly, with good reason.

Mia and John were truly a team. So, before he left Dallas for the interview, they thoroughly discussed all of their options and concluded that the distance would not be a deterrent to the stability of their relationship. John told Camille all of this in an effort to sway her.

It would be some time before she and the kids could join him in Kittery. In fact, she began a new partnership with Roberson Medical Family Practice around the same time that John got the call from McEachern & Thornhill.

"Well, for one, I like walking around in my birthday suit," Camille said, attempting to be humorous. "Secondly, it's not my place to solicit for a roommate. I don't pay a single dime to stay here. Did I mention that it's not my place?" she reiterated. "I don't have time to make sure someone else would care for things like I do," she continued. "Shapleigh-Small was very clear in their contract, page five, no parties, no subletting, no roommates, etc., etc., etc."

"I'm not talking about just anyone," John said.

"Who are you talking about then?" she questioned, feigning confusion.

"I'm talking about me," John said with a smile. "I would love to be your roomie."

"I knew you were frugal but, WOW!" she said.

"That's not it at all," he said, "I'm not being frugal. I'm being practical. I'll even pay you rent and utilities. We could negotiate a contract, of sorts, if that would make things better."

In a million years, she would never have fathomed this as a possibility. And although she heard him, she was still in disbelief. She contemplated the idea over and over and couldn't get past the fact that he was her first love, who happened to be engaged to another woman now. All these thoughts circulated in a split second. Then reality and reason surfaced.

"Why would you want to stay here?" she questioned.

"For starters, I don't have anywhere else to stay," he said.

"Aren't you in the hotel downtown?" Camille questioned.

"I'm talking long term," John petitioned.

"Long term what?" Camille said with an attitude, probing to see what John had on his mind.

She wasn't completely opposed to the idea of him moving in, but she didn't want to seem desperate by any means, so she continued to make him think she really didn't want the hassle of a roommate, especially one with a fiancée who had children.

"Well, I was thinking maybe I could stay in the penthouse bedroom until I found a place. I don't know how long that will be, but we can negotiate all of that," John said, prosecuting his case.

The fourth floor of the brownstone had an entertainment room, a guest bedroom and an open roof terrace. He slept there last night. When Camille showed him the space, she told him that she had only been upstairs, at most three other times. *All those stairs*, he thought last night but when she showed him the elevator, he was all in.

"You've really thought this one through, haven't you?" Camille asked.

"As a matter of fact, I have. I even discussed it with Mia."

"What did she think?" Camille was anxious to know.

"I told her everything about us, that you were my first 'real' girlfriend, that we've never had sex, and why things ended – everything."

"What did she say?" Camille's eyes widened with curiosity.

"She really didn't have much to say. I told her that we hadn't maintained contact and that I just happened to run into you at Weathervane's," John continued. "I even told her about the wonderful date that you were on," he said, grinning.

"It's a funny thing, isn't it? You and I have barely said hello to one another in the past ten years, and out of the blue we run into each other, and now we're talking about living together, being roommates. Who woulda thunk it?" she said.

"It's wild, I know."

"Do you think Mia would have any reservations about the arrangements, and wait a minute what about when she comes to visit? And the kids?" Camille questioned.

"I thought about that, too. You should meet her first and we can work all of those other minor details out," John said.

"Wife and kids, that's minor to you?" Camille said facetiously.

"No, they're not minor, but I know it will all work out."

"I hear you, John. The last time someone told me things would work out, I was headed to LA with my family on the redeye to beat the crap out of some jerk for hitting my Aunt Lizze up-side the head. Things working themselves out doesn't rank too highly in my book."

"Apples and oranges, Camille. That's a totally different story," he said. "Okay, how about we arrange for Mia to come and meet you or better yet we can both fly to Dallas to meet Mia and the kids," John said enthusiastically.

"That sounds like way too much for me," she said. "You may be right."

"…about what?" John questioned.

"Right about things working themselves out," she admitted.

"I don't believe it. So…, that's a yes? I can move in?"

"I guess so," she said, still skeptical. "We have a lot to discuss first, but right now let's just please change the subject."

"No problem," he conceded.

"What time is your interview?" Camille asked.

"Oh, I forgot to tell you, they emailed me early this morning to say that the interview was postponed until next week. Ian's wife gave birth to their fourth child and first granddaughter. Mr. Thornhill is big on family and hasn't missed the birth of any of his grandchildren," John said with pride. "Family values is one reason the job was so attractive."

"You mean the one that hasn't been offered to you yet?" Camille said snidely.

"That very one," John said with confidence.

With the interview delay caused by the unexpected early arrival of little Abigail Thornhill, John planned a surprise trip to Dallas to see Mia and prepare some of his belongings for the move. Mia told him that she would handle all of that, but he decided to take advantage of the extra time.

The week passed quickly, but by the time he left Dallas the majority of his affairs were in order. By Friday afternoon John was back in Kittery. Late that evening he received a call from Mr. Thornhill who gave him an interview over the phone. Mrs. T wanted to spend more time with the grandkids, and the Thornhills wouldn't be returning until the following week.

"John, the job is yours if you want it," Toby Thornhill offered.

"Thank you, Mr. Thornhill! You won't regret it," John said, still in interview mode.

John was standing in the middle of the penthouse bedroom unpacking. Mr. Thornhill told him that he would start on Monday at noon in order to get all of the formalities out of the way – paperwork, company policies and regulations, etc. One of the finest legal assistants in the business, Halle Greyle, would guide him through the whole orientation process.

Halle handled scheduling, among other things, for the Kittery office. John could tell that she was held in high regard. And although 'finest' referenced Halle's business expertise, when John laid eyes on Ms. Greyle the adjective applied to her appearance as well.

After the phone interview, John took the elevator down to the first floor where Camille was quietly seated at the dining room table reading one of her many spiritual self-help books. She was startled when he approached. It was clear that the roommate thing was something she was still getting used to.

"I got it!" John said.

"You got what?" Camille questioned.

"I got the job at McEachern & Thornhill."

"I thought the interview was on Monday."

"It was, but Mr. Thornhill called and offered me the job over the phone, because he was extending his vacation," John said, with 'I told you so' on the tip of his tongue.

"I guess you were on your 'A' game," she responded. Camille's way of saying that John had been right all along.

"It's all about networking," John jabbed.

Camille and John sat at the dining room table and talked for hours. John told her that Mia rearranged her schedule to come and visit in three weeks.

"That's great timing," Camille said.

"Oh really? I'm glad to hear that." John was more than excited about her response.

"I will be out of town on business. Shapleigh-Small is sending me to a three-day conference in Houston."

"Houston?" he questioned. "Houston, Texas?"

"Indeed."

"Why didn't you tell me?"

"Tell you what?"

"That you were going to Texas?"

"I didn't know I had to report to you."

"Come on, Camille, work with me a little here. You know I was trying to introduce you and Mia. Why wouldn't you tell me about your trip to Texas?"

"I'm not going to have time to socialize or anything like that. It's a business trip," she reminded him.

"Like what – dinner?"

"Schmoozing."

John didn't know how to react. He assumed that Camille was open to the idea of meeting Mia, but from the way she was acting he began to doubt it. He sat there beside her, contemplating how they could reconcile this situation, while Camille returned to reading her book.

When he got up, Camille couldn't resist giving him a compliment. "You are quite handsome, John. I'd forgotten how dapper you were," she said as if shocked by his charm.

Not only was he well-dressed, he always smelled good too. He favored Mambo, something Mia purchased for him last Christmas.

"Thank you," he said and walked away, disgusted.

TEN

....

out of town guests

THREE weeks passed quickly, and the roommate arrangement turned out to be beneficial for both Camille and John. The agreement was for John to pay six hundred dollars a month, which covered Camille's phone bill, the only expense she was responsible for under her contract with Shapleigh-Small, plus left her with a substantial revenue, all of which she banked. He originally offered her a thousand dollars, which still would have saved John considerably, being that he couldn't find any suitable accommodations under fifteen hundred dollars a month within the city limits.

They both appreciated sophisticated dining establishments and took turns finding the hot new restaurants to critique. It was John's turn to choose tonight, but Camille was tired and wasn't really up to getting dressed to go out. When John came home, she politely declined his invitation. His efforts to persuade her were fruitless.

John left out saying he would return shortly. When he came back to the brownstone a little after 7 p.m., he surprised Camille with take out from the Asian Bistro, which was one of her favorite places. He even went by the Wine Cellar, which imported some of the world's most exquisite fermented beverages and picked up one of their favorite wines.

"Camille, I'm back," John called from the doorway. He placed the bags on the table, pulled his phone out his pocket and proceeded to dial her number. As the phone rang, she appeared in the stairwell. "I was just calling you," he said.

Camille was busy finishing up some last-minute packing in preparation for her trip to Houston. "I heard you come in," she said.

"I picked up something from your favorite place. You looked a little tired so…" just as he was finishing his sentence she interrupted.

"That was nice of you, but I'm not that hungry."

He prepared the table for both of them anyway. The plates were in the cabinet to the right of the stainless-steel sink and the wine goblets were in the cabinet next to the plates. He folded a couple of paper towels as though they were fine linens and placed the silverware on top of them.

Camille didn't feel right about excusing herself, she saw the effort that he had extended on this impromptu dinner. When he finished setting the table, he pulled out her chair and asked her to be seated.

John had ordered ginger chicken and spring rolls. Camille loved the Bistro's spring rolls and couldn't resist. So, instead of letting John dine alone, she poured herself a glass of wine and indulged John by eating a couple of the spring rolls. They were delicious as usual.

"Are you excited about the conference?" John questioned.

He really wanted to see if he could convince Camille to meet with Mia while she was out west, but he didn't think she would agree to any of the ideas that he came up with. And since everything else was going smoothly between them, he didn't want to ruin it by backing her into a corner. Besides, he knew Camille wasn't the type to conform under pressure.

"…umm, I'm looking forward to getting out of town, but I wish I had more time to do some touristy stuff and actually relax," Camille told him.

With that, and similar responses at every turn, John knew not to even mention Dallas, or Mia. John resigned himself to the fact that Camille and Mia wouldn't be meeting any time soon.

The two roomies bantered back and forth about the plans for the morning commute. She had previously arranged for John to give her a ride to the airport the morning of her Houston trip. Because they spent most of their free time together, he was the obvious choice.

"Can you tell that I'm trying to butter you up?" John asked, with cautious amusement in his voice.

"I was wondering," she said. "What's going on, John?"

"I can't take you to the airport in the morning," he told her.

"Okay," she said, irritated. "When were you going to tell me?"

"I just found out tonight. Halle scheduled a last-minute briefing first thing in the morning that I have to attend," John told her.

"I guess I'll just have to leave my car at the airport, but I really didn't want to pay for that."

"I can arrange to pick your car up," John offered a solution.

"That's not necessary," she said. "Thanks for the dinner. I better go finish packing and go to bed. I have an early morning. Goodnight," she told him, sighing. She hated surprises, even when they were good, which this wasn't.

"Goodnight," he returned, sensing her frustration.

Camille got up from the table and went to her room. John finished eating his ginger chicken, tidied up the table and started riffling through the documents in his briefcase. He arranged them on the table in preparation for tomorrow's hearing. While reading over his client's tax records his phone rang. It was Halle.

"John Sabourn," he answered in full business mode.

"Hi, John. This is Halle."

"What's going on, Halle?" he said, not expecting to hear from her. It was well past 9:00 p.m.

Just as he was beginning his conversation with Halle, Camille came back into the kitchen to get a glass of water. She started talking to John without realizing he was on the phone. "It is so hot in my room. I had to get some water! I am parched," she said.

"Yes," he said, responding to Halle.

"You're hot too?" Camille asked.

"I have that," he said.

"What are you talking about, John?" Camille questioned.

John looked at Camille and mouthed, "I'm on the phone with Halle."

Camille quietly laughed. "Sorry," she said, "I didn't realize."

"Okay, Halle, I think I have everything I need for in the morning. I'll see you at 7:00 a.m., at the office. We can go over any last-minute changes then." He paused to listen. "Okay. Have a good night." He paused again as Halle finished up on the other end. "Okay," he said and pushed the button on his Bluetooth to hang up the phone. "That was just Halle calling to confirm last-minute changes I need to address in tomorrow's briefing," he told Camille.

"Halle, again?"

"I know. She's thorough."

"Oh, that's what they're calling it nowadays."

"Jealous, huh?" he said jokingly.

"I'm not you're fiancée. I don't have anything to be jealous about," Camille snapped. "I know women, and I can tell you Ms. Halle is interested in more than just work."

"Please, not Greyle!" he said, dismissively.

John didn't think twice about Camille's comments because Halle's interactions with him have always been professional. Even when John tried to lighten the mood by making lighthearted jokes, Halle always maintained a steadfast business demeanor.

Nevertheless, the seed had been planted.

"Alright, I'm just saying you might want to be careful with that one," Camille reiterated as she walked over to the sink. After filling her glass with the filtered water, she went back upstairs to her bedroom.

Although John had cheated on Camille before, she sensed his commitment to Mia and was sure that he would keep his relationship with Halle strictly professional. The only reason that she pressed the issue, aside from being pissed that he waited to the last minute to let her know that he wouldn't be able to take her to the airport, was because although she didn't know Halle, she knew women. And John was the perfect target for thirsty women – single, wealthy, successful, handsome and upward bound.

He was the perfect target for Camille.

The tickling sparked by a chance encounter, that blossomed into effortless conversation that night outside the Little Brown Jug had mutated into an orchestrated chaos. And albeit unconscious at first, Camille became consumed with hashing out plans designed to forge a wedge between lovers.

Life moved steadily along as it does. Camille had come and gone from the conference in Houston months ago. She busied herself with work, which kept her schedule full. Shapleigh was hiring new employees that required her expertise, a benefit that Camille brokered to her advantage.

John excelled in his new position with McEachern & Thornhill. Increased business kept him traveling back and forth to the New York office, more alone time with Ms. Greyle.

Mia's practice also saw a dramatic increase in clientele, a direct result of the exposé done on Roberson Medical Family Practice, naming it as one of the best private medical facilities in the Dallas metro area.

Every time the couple planned to see one another, business interceded. On the recent occasion when Mia planned a visit, around the time of Camille's trip to Houston, John unexpectedly had to go to New York for two weeks to handle the Madson account. Madson was a loyal and profitable client of McEachern & Thornhill. They alone were responsible for eleven percent of the practice's gross income last year.

One week, John would be called to New York to negotiate important deals with long-standing customers, the next week the medical practice would hold free clinics, prompting local media coverage and garnering publicity for the practice.

Something, it seemed, was always getting in the couple's way. Months flew by, Mia and John hadn't seen each other in person. They stayed in touch, constant conversations over the phone, texting, or video conferencing. This proved to be taxing on them both and totally different than what they planned when John relocated.

When it appeared that they would finally get the opportunity to be together, Mia booked the first flight to Maine for her and the kids. And John made false assurances that he would clear his schedule.

Mia and Camille had come to know one another quite well through their many conversations over the phone during the time Camille and John shared the brownstone at 331 Mary Belle Way. And although they began to regard one another as friends, today would be the first time that they would actually meet in person.

When Mia arrived in Maine, Camille was the one who picked her and the kids up from the airport. John had a last-minute scheduling conflict that he was obligated to keep. And since this was the first opening on her calendar, Mia decided that rescheduling was not an option.

Mia knew Camille immediately, admiring her casual chic look from a distant walkway, the photo and occasional video conferencing back and forth assured recognition. Camille had on form-fitting dark blue jeans with a thick brown belt. An over-sized black suit jacket covered her mock button-down white shirt. The bright red toenail polish poked out through her open-toed mules. And her hair was neatly placed in a bun, crowning her head. Camille was looking through her large handbag when

Mia called out her name, softly yelling down the baggage claim corridor.

"Hi Mia," Camille said with as much excitement as she could muster. "You look just like your pictures," she announced.

"It's good to finally meet you," Mia said sincerely, reaching out with arms wide open for a hug.

They embraced one another as if they were long lost friends. They waited patiently for Mia's luggage to make its way around the conveyor. Camille admired Mia's red, white and blue Kate Spade garment bag and suitcases. *We have similar tastes*, she thought. That was true about many things.

"I have everything," Mia confirmed.

"Are these the beautiful children from the photos?" Camille said, playing her excitement to the hilt. "…and you must be Joshua," Camille continued, the boy shaking his head in affirmation. "Hi Shelly," Camille said to the young girl standing in front of Mia.

"Hello, Ms. Camille," the tween said in response. Camille smiled at the little girl's reply while inside cringing.

Had Mia known the woman before her, she might have recognized Camille's disdain, but no one really knew Camille at all. A phony smile hid Camille's contempt. The southern hospitality bestowed upon the out of town guests concealed Camille's true intentions. The feigned interest in all things Mia, masked Camille's deceitful objective, while at the same time luring Mia closer and closer, like a fish enticed by a worm dangling from a hook.

Just outside the airport they loaded the luggage in the vehicle. The children took their positions in the back seat as the women got comfortable in the front.

When they arrived at the brownstone, a gorgeous bouquet of flowers was waiting on the dining room table. Wanting eyes gleamed with surprise.

"That is so sweet," Camille said.

"Isn't he a wonderful man?" Mia remarked, opening the card that was attached to the two-dozen vibrantly colored magenta roses. Camille smiled as Mia read the attached card. It began with, 'Hi Doll'. *Doll*, Mia thought. John never called her that, but the beautiful arrangement beckoned her to read on.

> *I am so sorry I couldn't be there with you. I will make it up to you when I get back. Getting to know you has been amazing.*

Mia was reading the card aloud until she got to the 'getting to know....' part. She thought, *these can't be for me.... 'doll' and the 'getting to know you'*. Mia and John had known each other for years and was way past the point where the relationship was new, although at times it still felt that way. All this didn't stop her from reading on.

> *I've never been here before with any one and I love every moment with you. Hope this makes you smile! Looking forward to Wednesday when I can see you again!*

The card was signed, 'J'.

"What's wrong?" Camille asked, seeing the expression on Mia's face change drastically.

"I don't think these are for me," Mia said, handing the card to Camille.

Camille read the card aloud, Mia looked visibly awkward. "Hi Doll, I am so sorry I couldn't be there with you. That John is something else," Camille said, continuing. "I will make it up to you when I get back." As she read the word 'back', she looked at Mia to gauge her reaction. "Getting to know you has been amazing. He's acting like you guys just met. That's cute. I thought John was coming back in the morning."

"He is," Mia confirmed. "Those are not from John."

Camille shook her head, pretend ignorance. "I didn't read the card when they arrived. I just assumed they were from John. I'm so sorry."

"That's okay. You didn't know."

"Now, I am in shock," Camille said. She wasn't dating anyone. She wasn't shocked at all, but Mia couldn't tell.

"Who's the lucky fella?" Mia asked.

Luckily, right on cue, the phone rang. Once again Camille was able to wiggle her way out of an awkward situation. "That must be John," she told them, running to answer the phone. "He's the only one that calls on that line. Hello, Young residence," she said.

"Camille, did Mia and the kids arrive?" John asked.

"Yes, they're right here," Camille said, handing the phone to Mia.

John assured Mia that he would be back in the morning. They chatted briefly before she passed the phone to the kids to say a quick hello. Sensing that the conversations were coming to an end, Camille asked if she could speak back to John. Mia handed her the phone without hesitation.

Unbeknownst to Mia, John said his goodbyes and hung up, like Camille hoped he would. But she commenced to hold a conversation with him, pretending that he was still on the phone. "Did Ms. Greyle go with you again?" Camille said, knowing Mia was listening. Camille paused briefly as if listening to John's response. "Oh, she did," Camille said, shaking her head in a faked disappointment. "She keeps you busy! That's for sure."

Mia wasn't worried about John being unfaithful and only listened to the conversation because of her proximity.

Camille paused again. "You're right, it is good for business," she said and paused. "Did Mr. Thornhill say that for real?" She paused. "I totally agree with him," Camille said, "Halle is keeping your schedule full," she said with emphasis.

Camille wouldn't dare say anything directly to Mia about Greyle. Knowing if she did, it would be 'Camille said this' or 'Camille said that'. She simply allowed the insinuations to marinate, knowing there would be plenty of opportunities and many more trips to New York for John. She would make sure of it.

Mia was listening intently now. Camille could feel her peering and decided to end the farce, just in case Mia asked to talk to John again.

"Okay John, we're all tired. We'll see you in the morning." Camille paused one last time, just because. "Okay, I'll pass that on," she said, turning toward Mia. "He wants me to tell you goodnight," Camille told Mia. "Mia says goodnight, she loves you," Camille spoke into the receiver, before abruptly hanging up. "That Greyle is something else," Camille said under her breath but just loud enough for Mia to hear.

Mia tried to remain calm, but the more she thought about all the cancelled plans and extended trips to New York, the more doubt crept in. She chose not to address it with Camille, though. But words were unnecessary. Camille could sense Mia's uneasiness sprouting like unattended weeds.

John had purchased two air mattresses for the kids, who would be sleeping downstairs in the basement, which was a fully finished functional area. Shapleigh's designers turned it into a recreation room. And it was evident that no expenses were spared. All the latest game systems from Xbox to Wii were available and could be played on the fifty-four-inch flat screen television that made its home on the room's longest wall, closest to the restroom.

A cozy looking burnt tan couch was ideally placed to aid anyone who wanted to enjoy a movie or play a video. A nicely built, darkly stained wood grain pool table also shared this large space, along with two pinball machines, all conveniences for the kids to enjoy.

It had been a long day for everyone. John had been in council all day handling one of the numerous new Manhattan accounts, Mia and the kids had been in various stages of travel from the moment they awoke, and Camille, not to be outdone, spent her day acting out the role that had been planted well in advance of Mia's visit to Kittery.

Camille showed Mia to John's room on the fourth floor via the elevator, too tired to walk up all those stairs.

"This is a beautiful space," Mia said. "I can see why John wanted to stay here."

"Thank you. I love it!" Camille replied.

"Camille, is everything alright here?" Mia asked in the best way she knew how. She simply couldn't resist.

ELEVEN

....

the kids

THE visit was going well. John, Mia and the kids got a lot accomplished, visiting schools, securing a place to live – a condo because neither John nor Mia liked yardwork. The homeowner's association would handle this in the community they chose. They also applied for their marriage license, taking care of all the last-minute things that they needed to handle together before Mia returned to Dallas, just days from now.

To Camille's delight, she barely noticed the guests. Aside from the occasional living room chats with Mia about the wedding, Camille enjoyed her solitude, even more so now than before the out of town guests arrived. And despite the fact that Camille had grown fond of Mia, she intended to make Mia's first visit to Kittery her last.

Something about the impending wedding was irking Camille today. Could have been John's enthusiasm that she hadn't noticed before, or the fact that Mia and John's happiness made her jealous, an uncomfortable emotion.

Her mood coaxed her to work from home in her pajamas today, but she refused to play the gracious host. When asked, Camille claimed to be bogged down with work, which Mia understood.

The Dallas clan relaxed the day away, watching TV and playing videos while patiently waiting for John. When he got home, he checked on Camille to see what she had planned for the evening. Camille intended to chill at home, just as she had done all day long. John thought that was a brilliant idea, so that's what everyone did. He also clued Camille in on the big surprise he had for Mia. John wanted to make Mia's last day in town special.

"Can you watch the kids for us?" he asked. "I have something exciting planned."

Begrudgingly, Camille was persuaded, but not without first playing the investigator, though John was determined to keep the details to himself. He thanked her, handing her some spending money. After talking a minute or two longer he went back downstairs.

The short workday turned into a gorgeous afternoon. Kittery was a beautiful place to be in the fall. At night, the sky was so clear that you could count each and every star. The autumn air was crisp, but pleasant enough for Mia and John to relax on the patio. They moved between the patio and the living room, alternating to the plush couch when the TV programming suited their liking. The kids played in the basement, surprisingly keeping distractions to a minimum.

Camille sat quietly in her room reading or writing or whatever she could do to occupy the lackadaisical day. Secluded, the day lingered. She hadn't seen anyone but John since yesterday. Famished, she hadn't eaten since breakfast. It was now approaching early evening. It was her intention to finish what she was working on, but as the pangs of hunger became unbearable, she had to get something to eat.

The Boar's Head mesquite turkey was summoning her from the refrigerator, so she decided to take a break from the self-imposed hibernation to make a sandwich. Besides, she wanted to be nosy.

Descending the stairwell, she noticed that the lights in the house were dim. She wondered where everyone was. When her bare feet touched the coldness of the stone kitchen floor, she flinched.

From the cabinet beside the refrigerator she retrieved the honey wheat bread. As she was placing the bread on the counter, she saw something moving out of the corner of her eye that caused her to wince. She was relieved when she realized it was Mia peering over the balcony.

A slight breeze filled the living quarters and Camille could smell the impending rain. John and Mia gathered their belongings from the patio and made their way into the living room where they reclined on the sofa.

"Everyone was so quiet, I didn't know you were here," Camille said.

"I know. It's so peaceful, isn't it?" Mia replied.

"Yes, it is."

"We've been running, running, running ever since we got in town. Tonight just seemed like the perfect night to relax," Mia continued.

"I HAD to get out of that room!" Camille said emphatically. "I was getting so hungry, but I got a lot done."

"Good for you. You have been tied up all day, couldn't even tell if you were here or not," Mia said.

Camille smiled at the comment. She had a lot of work to do but the work she did today could have waited. The assignments were for new clients who wouldn't be starting for three months. Mia and her family would be long gone by then.

The women continued to chat while John anchored himself in front of the television. Football season was in full swing and he was a diehard Bears fan from way back, even before they won the Super Bowl in the '80s. He tuned into ESPN, of course. And the women chuckled with one another about what they lovingly referred to as 'Every Sista's Pain in the Neck.'

"MY STOMACH IS TOUCHING MY BACK! I better eat," Camille said, returning to her sandwich making activities.

"I'm sorry. Go ahead. I know you must be hungry!" Mia sympathized.

Camille shook her head in affirmation and simpered to mask what she was really thinking. *Being in my room all day starving was much better than listening to you talk about that damn wedding and John, ALLLLLL DAYYYY LONGGGG.*

She remembered a bag of chips in the cupboard and turned around to get them. And although eavesdropping was not beyond her, Camille's intentions were purely innocent when she overheard Mia and John discussing their plans.

"The invitations haven't been printed yet," John said.

Camille tried not to ruffle the bag of chips, gently placing them on the counter. She opened the refrigerator as fast as she could without appearing too obvious, taking out the Miracle Whip. Camille also retrieved the turkey, Swiss cheese, romaine lettuce, and sprouts.

On the counter was a bowl of apples and oranges. Someone had placed a tomato in there that was perfectly ripened to Camille's liking. *My house, my tomato*, she thought, removing the tomato from the bowl. She grabbed the serrated knife from the knife block and sliced four thin slices from the Porterhouse. She moved to the counter that was closer to the couch where Mia and John were seated.

"Yeah, I know. But the Save-the-Dates have already been sent out. Do you think it would be too confusing for everyone?" Mia questioned.

"Well…probably. But this is our wedding and the guests will just have to understand, or not come," John said matter-of-factly. "I guess we'll just end up having a smaller wedding than we had originally planned." He smiled shrewdly, mentally calculating how much money he could save.

Camille stood at the counter breathless. She couldn't believe what she was hearing.

"I guess so, John. I don't mean to worry but…."

Just as Mia was about to finish her sentence Mia's daughter, walked into the living room from the basement. Shelly walked past the couch where the couple was seated, noticing the paper on the coffee table that Mia had been doodling on. In her nosiness, the child asked what all the dates on the paper were for.

"Shelly, we're moving the wedding date up, getting married this summer instead of waiting until next fall," Mia told her daughter.

"Really Mom?" Shelly said with excitement in her voice.

"I'm glad you're happy about it, Shelly," John said.

Camille couldn't believe her ears. "Wow, that's just around the corner," Camille interceded, hunger on the back burner.

"Yeah, we know. We're going to need a little help getting this off the ground if you're willing to be my go-to person in Kittery," Mia said, winking at Camille.

"Of course, if John's okay with that. Whatever you need," Camille said, winking back. "Are you expecting?" Camille asked candidly.

"Whatttt? No!" Mia and John said in unison, surprised that Camille would be so tactless in front of the child.

Eagerly, Shelly chimed in, "Mom, are you?"

"No, dear," Mia assured.

"What's the rush, then? Shotgun wedding – that's what they're called, right?" Camille continued her vindictive assault.

John and Mia attempted distraction, not wanting to alarm the child. "Wish I had a shotgun right now," John joked. "Mia's not expecting, Camille."

"We just thought the sooner we get married the sooner we can be together," Mia added.

"Worried about shacking? I understand…with the kids and all…," Camille said, resuming her underhanded spasm.

"Shelly, go on back downstairs," Mia said, steering her daughter toward the basement, Camille's cue to depart.

Camille nibbled on her sandwich, having gotten all the information she could squeeze out of the happy couple. She excused herself and returned to the bedroom. Camille's mind was too occupied with the changed wedding plans to do any more work. She reclined on her bed and tried to sleep.

Two hours later, John finally grew tired of the repeating sports coverage. He and Mia retired to his bedroom. The kids rumbled in the basement until dawn.

Restless, Camille listened as Mia and John made love upstairs. Lying on the bed she wondered about the acoustics and if John had ever heard her before, especially when she was alone. A half grimace, half smile accompanied the thought. She wondered if the door was open, or if Mia was just that loud. Regardless, the moaning affected Camille in ways she never experienced before, making her body long for what Mia was getting.

The sunrise was an amazing sight to behold this time of the year in Maine. Today was no exception. Mia and the kids were almost finished packing for their return to Dallas. Tomorrow would be the last full day in Kittery.

Camille laid quietly in her bed staring at the walls, wondering how to get out of the promise she made, but couldn't think of a way that wouldn't completely spoil John's plans. She peeled herself from her bed, showered and dressed. When she heard the children laughing in the living room, she decided to make her appearance.

"Good morning," she said making her way down the stairs. Although it was afternoon, she always found herself saying good morning regardless of the time.

"Hello, Miss Camille," Joshua said.

Shelly followed with the same greeting. Camille cringed every time the kids said this. And although it was the polite thing to do, the salutation made her feel a thousand years old.

"Are you guys ready to have some fun today?" she asked cheerfully.

They both shook their heads in affirmation, followed by a 'yes ma'am' from the boy. Then they sat on the couch, watched TV and waited for John and Mia to come downstairs. It seemed like hours passed before the couple emerged, but it always appears that way when you're waiting.

"How's everyone this afternoon?" John asked.

"We were just waiting for you guys before we headed out," Camille said.

"Sorry to keep you waiting but it wasn't necessary," he said.

"Well, I wasn't sure. We found some things to do that seemed like fun," she told him.

"That's great!" John said.

A movie along the lines of *Shrek* or *Toy Story* was playing at the local theater. John made sure they had everything they needed before sending them on their way.

It was a short drive to the theater, but Camille decided to use the time to ask the kids some questions. *Joshua was the youngest and could be easily persuaded to talk,* Camille thought. *But because she was older, and a girl, Shelly probably knew more details about her mother's day-to-day goings-on.*

Camille thought it wisest to question the boy first, she had a way with boys, a power of persuasion. She knew that Joshua would disclose more info just in casual conversation, material that Shelly would naturally guard. And if Joshua said anything that was wrong, Shelly would surely correct him, not just because she was a smart ass, but because he was the kid brother.

"Are you guys hungry?" Camille asked.

"Not really," Shelly spoke first.

"I am," Josh replied.

"Can you wait until after the movie?" Camille asked Joshua. "We'll get some snacks to tide us over."

"Ok," he and his sister said in unison.

"We have some time until the movie starts. How bout we go check out the carnival? I think you guys would enjoy it."

"Ok," they both said, again.

"Joshua, I hear you love football," Camille began.

Shelly laughed out loud. "That's a joke," she said. "He can barely hold the ball and stay on his feet."

Camille chuckled quietly. She didn't want Joshua to be embarrassed.

"Shut up," Joshua snapped at his sister. "I tried out for the team but didn't make it," he told Camille.

"You guys live in Dallas, right?" Camille asked as if she had forgotten.

"Yes ma'am," they said together.

"Well, I have a good friend who coaches football. He works at the YMCA in Dallas. I'm sure he'd be happy to give you some pointers. I'll give him a call if you're interested."

Shelly was not mistaken when she said her brother sucked at the sport and Camille knew it. She overheard Mia talking to John about how hurt Joshua was when he didn't make the team. Camille looked at Joshua through the rearview mirror. She could see the happiness her offer ignited.

"What do you think? Should I talk to your mom about it?"

"Yes ma'am," Joshua quickly responded, pulling his PSP out his jacket pocket to play with.

Shelly sat quietly beside him and texted on her phone. Camille turned on the radio. She made sure the volume was low enough that she could hear the children if they decided to talk to one another.

Shelly was a teenager, and like many kids her age, she didn't let the phone out of her sight. The noise from Joshua's PSP was clearly irritating her, but she just kept right on texting. Then, out of nowhere, Cyndi Lauper's, *Girl's Just Wanna Have Fun* rang out over all other noises in the car. Shelly quickly answered.

"Wuz up?" she bellowed. It was obviously a boy on the other end by her change in octave. "Can you turn that stupid game down?" she barked.

Joshua ignored her ranting, his play more animated now.

"Joshua!" she yelled. "I can't hear!"

"Maybe if you were a little nicer about it, he'd respond," Camille said from the driver's seat.

Shelly's face showed everything that she wanted to say but couldn't. "Hold on, please," Shelly said to the person on the phone. "Joshua, can you please turn that down so I can hear?"

"Hiiii Mason," Joshua blurted out in a drawn-out exaggerated smear, lowering the volume on his game at the same time.

Shelly returned to her phone call without skipping a beat.

"I'm sure your sister wants to thank you," Camille said to Joshua, staring through the rearview mirror directly into Shelly's eyes, "...but she's being rude," Camille continued, knowing all too well this would stir things up even more than they already were, as evidenced by Shelly's glare.

When the trio reached the carnival, Shelly was still on the phone, Joshua sat beside her, still playing his video game. The lights, the rides, the food, the crowd all but assured that they wouldn't make it to the movie on time.

"What movie are we seeing, again?" Joshua asked.

Camille told him, and he sighed. Shelly still on the phone, was clueless. She was so engrossed in her conversation with Mason that she couldn't appreciate what was going on around her.

Joshua had been trying to get her attention from the time they entered the gate. He saw fried Snickers and wanted to try one. And the corn dipped in the most succulently fragrant melted butter was covered in cheese. The aroma alone teased the nostrils and courted lines of twenty or more.

There was a game of miniature hoops that caught Joshua's attention. The winning prize, a gift certificate to the game store, enticed him all the more. He even recognized a couple of kids from Camille's neighborhood off in the distance and asked if he could go talk to them. When Camille consented, Joshua took off running.

Camille and Shelly followed the boys around as they moved from one attraction to the next, thoroughly enjoying themselves. Every now and again Shelly saw something that sparked her interest, temporarily easing her out of the phone-induced trance.

Four hours skated by. Stuffed and tired, they were all ready to go. They missed the movie, as expected. As they walked back to the car, Joshua's eyes where teetering, fighting for an open stance, but he still asked if they could go to the movies. The same movie that hours earlier he abandoned like trash, for the carnival.

Camille, who had long ago released her kid-sitting angst, grinned at the request and texted John to let him know that they would be a little late, but got no reply. Way too busy courting, John knew they were in good hands.

Shelly had been on and off the phone with Mason the entire time they were at the carnival. By the time her conversation concluded, Camille's mind was churning. The young lovebirds were on their school's cheering squad. Camille established that that's how they met. Shelly casually flaunted her intentions to become a Texas Longhorn cheerleader. She spoke as if a full scholarship were a foregone conclusion. The child's confidence reminded Camille of herself, forcing her to disguise a smile.

"You remember Sarah McNeil and Candy Brannon?" Shelly asked, pausing to give Mason a second to think about it. "They both got cheerleading scholarships. Sarah's at MIT and Candy is somewhere in Florida."

Mason must have questioned what she said because she repeated it, more emphatically the second time.

Camille and the kids rushed back to the car in pursuit of their original plans, the movie turning out to be a good choice. Even Shelly made a rare positive comment about it.

Tired and ready for bed, Camille raced home. They had been gone away from the house nearly eight hours. Once they arrived, Camille inspected the car, making sure the kids had all their belongings.

There was total silence in the brownstone, no sign of John or Mia anywhere. Camille told the kids to finish packing, wash up, and prepare for bed. Before they went off to follow her instructions, they thanked her.

Hours passed before Mia and John showed up. John had secretly planned a mini getaway for the two of them. He left no room for another man to move in on his territory. Turns out, soon as Camille and the kids left the house, John whisked Mia off to the airport. He had secretly chartered a plane to take the two of them to New York City, two tickets to the Metropolitan Opera. The opera was on Mia's bucket list. She was thrilled, to say the least.

That night, struggling to sleep, Camille listened again with forced intent to the sweet moans of a couple obviously in love.

The next morning Mia bragged and bragged with her smile, as Camille made her best attempt to sound enthusiastic about her day with the kids. "You have some of the most well-behaved children," Camille commented.

"Thank you," Mia said, unintentionally beaming. *He must have really put it on her good*, Camille thought. Mia was acting like an infatuated schoolgirl.

"Is everyone packed and ready to go?" John asked, descending the stairwell.

"Yes," they confirmed.

John loaded the Range Rover with their luggage. One by one they hugged and said their goodbyes to Camille.

"I'll be calling you soon about the wedding," Mia assured.

Camille watched as John drove Mia and the kids down the street away from the brownstone, waving goodbye until they disappeared out of sight. She went back in the house, intending to go immediately into action, but tripped on her way up the stairs, a disregarded sign. In so much pain from the fall, she took a nap, delaying her plans 'til another day.

TWELVE

....

planner extraordinaire

CAMILLE'S 'friend' that worked at the YMCA, wasn't actually a coach like she had said, but he did know the ins and outs of football. In fact, he was slated to be one of the top recruits for the University of Michigan the year he graduated from high school. Three weeks prior to the start of his freshman year he found himself in the back seat of a SUV that collided head on with a minivan. The accident killed two of their classmates and permanently damaged his right knee, ensuring that he would never play competitively again.

Camille kept in touch with him through the grapevine and on social media. She knew all Henry's business because his wife Barbara, who had also gone to high school with them, was way too personal with her posts.

Every now and then Camille would shoot them a, 'Hello, how's Dallas?' when the posts revealed more than anyone should know. Henry would respond as he always did, 'Dallas is Dallas.' Camille interpreting that to mean, *I know my wife is looney, I married a crazy b**ch.* Camille would always respond, 'lol'.

This time however, Camille didn't wait for wifey to post something ridiculous. Instead, she sent Henry a private message, leaving her number for him to call at his earliest convenience. The next morning, she was awakened at 6:00 a.m. by his wife.

"Hello," Camille said groggily.

"This is Barbara Mitchell. You left your number for my husband to call you."

Camille's profile was a picture of her fish Barney and her nickname. And even after looking through all her posts and google, Barbara didn't recognize Camille.

"Barb," Camille said.

"Barb? Who is this?" Barb questioned.

"Camille Young, from CRHS."

"Camille, from Chimney Rock?" Barbara questioned.

"Yes. Remember my sister Tania? You guys wrote on the newspaper together."

"Camille?" she questioned again.

"Yes, Camille."

"Why are you messaging my husband?" she asked apathetically.

"Let me start by asking how you've been?"

121

"Fine," Barb said sharply. "Why are you messaging my husband?" Barb repeated.

"How is Henry?" Camille asked, realizing it was going to be tough getting past this one.

"We're fine. What do you want?" Barbara asked sharply.

"I would love to talk to Henry. I have a business opportunity to discuss with him," Camille said, trying to calm crazy down.

"Business? What kind of business opportunity? Henry don't know nothing about no business," Barbara said ignorantly.

"A coaching opportunity," Camille told her.

"Coaching?"

"There's a good deal of money involved."

"How much?" she questioned. Barbara was intrigued now.

Camille hadn't even thought about how much money she was willing to pay, but she knew she had to come up with something substantial with his wife acting like this.

"Please have him call me. I'll let him discuss that with you," Camille told Barbara.

Barb passed the message on quickly. Not even thirty minutes passed before Camille's phone rang again. "Camille, this is Barbara. Henry take this phone," Barb demanded.

"Hello," Henry said. By the sound of his voice, he had been woken from the dead, like Lazarus.

"Henry, this is Camille Young from Chimney Rock."

"Hello Camille! How have you been? Barb told me this was some kind of business call."

"I'm doing well and yes, I do have a business proposition for you," Camille said.

Henry placed her on speakerphone, so his wife could hear the conversation. Camille presented a convincing pitch, making sure to leave out the details to discuss with Henry privately, she knew Barb would tell the world, exposing her secret.

The next day when Camille saw Barb posting from work, she called Henry back, hashing out everything. Within three weeks, Joshua had his very own football coach.

When Mia first asked for help with the wedding, Camille awkwardly balked at the idea – *that takes a lot of time, are you sure you don't want a professional, I have to check my calendar,* witless excuses overlooked by an anxious bride. Hard to believe that Mia would ask Camille, especially after hearing the story of Jill's wedding cake fiasco. Cami only agreeing to help because Mia put her on the spot in front of God and everybody.

Like nails slowly clawing a chalkboard, Camille cringed at the notion. Maybe because she didn't know Mia all that well, or because she could think of a million other things she'd rather do. But the more likely motive for her resistance, a reason Camille denied even to herself, was her growing fondness for John.

This awkward request made two things glaringly obvious. For one, Mia trusted Camille implicitly. And secondly, Camille wanted John for herself. The more time she spent alone with him, the more the hurt memories of the relationship they had in college faded, the more she begrudged his bond with Mia. After a brief period of sulking, the whole planning your first love's wedding to another woman and all, Camille had a change of heart, in more ways than one. She decided to use the situation to her advantage.

The unraveling she plotted was akin to burying landmines in a crowded playground, someone was bound to get hurt. And if Mia was the woman John touted her to be, Camille knew it wouldn't be the children, but that was a chance she was willing to take to affect the desired outcome – John and Mia apart permanently.

Between work and the occasional date, Camille dedicated herself as planner extraordinaire – buying wedding magazines, doing internet searches, cake tastings, looking for the perfect invitation design, second Save-the-Dates, and even visiting different florists and reception venues.

She communicated with Mia, mostly through texts and pictures. Cake flavors – Almond? Red velvet? Chocolate? Colors – Champagne? Black? Platinum? A beach or church wedding? Reception ideas – Formal dinner? Finger foods? She asked all these questions and many more.

Expense was of little consequence. They had Huxtable money. And since Mia had done the traditional wedding thing before, she was open to different ideas. Regardless, Camille sold it – a short thirty minutes from Kittery, *The Knot* best of wedding hall of fame, the Kennedys, picturesque Kennebunkport, waterfront ceremony, a resort, only one date open.

She had Mia with *The Knot* reference, Mia's favorite wedding magazine. Not to mention, the significance of the only available date. It just happened to be Mia's deceased grandmother's birthday, a fact that Camille had no way of knowing, but was icing on the cake.

"Mia, all this planning, I neglected to ask about the kids."

"Thank you for asking, that's so sweet. They're just fine. Joshua has improved so much in football," Mia gloated, a mothers wishful thinking. "The coach you recommended is so good with kids. Thank you so much."

"I'm glad he's working out for you guys." Of course, she didn't really care, just probing for information. "How's that Shelly doing?"

"Grown as ever," Mia joked. "Between cheerleading and her boyfriend, I barely see that child."

Camille laughed, remembering how she was at that age, overhearing her mother tell someone the exact same thing.

"Yea, I'm not too hard on her," Mia said. "Weren't you a cheerleader?" Mia remembered.

"I was. I loved it so much that my mother would send me to cheerleading camp every summer," Camille said, although that wasn't the complete truth.

She liked cheerleading just about as much as she liked doing chores. It was a necessary evil, the activity her father resisted the least. Mr. Young had an argument for everything. When Camille wanted to be in the band and play the saxophone, he complained. *How much is that? We don't have money to spend on passing fads*, he would say.

Camille wanted to play softball and was quite good at it. But she had really bad allergies and had to miss two games. *All that gas driving back and forth, and she can't even play*, was what Mr. Young told his wife.

When Camille asked to be a candy striper because one of her friends was doing it, this too was met with resistance. *No child of mine gone be cooped up in some hospital, round all those sick people. Read a book or something if you're bored.*

Although annoying, his negativity didn't stop Camille from doing everything she could to spend as little time at home as possible. When she decided to try out for the cheerleading squad, she didn't tell anyone. Waiting until she made the team as an alternate to share the good news.

When she needed money for her uniform, she didn't ask her parents. Instead she used what she had saved from birthday gifts and allowances, the money she hid in her favorite pair of Minnie Mouse socks.

She didn't want to give her father any reason to veto, so she told her mother that she would ride to and from practice and the games with her friend who lived close by and that her friend Amanda's mom had no problem with the arrangement.

Amanda was a kid who stayed on the next block. Camille would point her out to her mom from time to time when they passed by her house. *Hey, that's Amanda, she's in my Spanish class, her mother doesn't work,* saying things of this nature to make believe they were friends. In fact, they were in the same Spanish class, but aside from the occasional block sightings, class was the only time she ever saw Amanda.

Amanda's brother, Charles, however, was a different story. He was always in Camille's face talking about whatever he could think of to just be around her. Camille didn't mind, Charles wasn't half bad to look at, but most importantly, he had his own car. And since he had been trying to get Camille in it, she didn't see why he couldn't be the one to bring her home from practice.

What harm would that be?

None would be the wiser if she'd ride with him to his house and walk the short distance home. When Charles asked why he couldn't drop her off at home, Camille told him that her dad didn't like boys, all Charles needed to hear to set the plans in stone.

Camille smiled as she recalled the cheerleading tale.

"Camp?" Mia questioned.

"Yes. I loved going to camp," Camille claimed, having never once stepped foot in a cheerleading camp. "Shelly hasn't mentioned it?"

"No, not a word about camp to me," Mia said.

"If she's serious about cheerleading she might want to look into it," Camille told the doting mother.

"Thanks again, I'll talk to her tonight."

It hadn't even been a month since the wedding venue was secured. And sure, the wedding was less than six months away, but Camille was still blindsided when she opened the mailbox. To her surprise, there it was, the invitation, plans she helped orchestrate. Camille opened it hurriedly. She couldn't stop herself from reading it over and over and over again, as if somehow reciting the words would make them null or change the inevitability of the ceremony taking place.

RSVPs were coming in daily, along with other good news. It just so happened that Shelly met the mailman at the box as she was getting off the school bus. The child was excited before she even laid eyes on the letter with her name on it.

"MOM, look what came in the mail!" Shelly said, ecstatically waving the envelope in the air as if she were on the side of the road, stranded, hailing for help.

"Calm down, child," Mia said and reached for the letter, inviting the excited child to release it.

"I GOT IN, MOM! I GOT IN!" Shelly shouted even more emphatically than before, jumping up and down on an imaginary pogo stick.

Mia's eyes scanned the letter. As she read, she thought about how ever since her daughter was three years old, all she ever wanted to do was cheer – cheering in local parades, at family birthday parties and holiday gatherings.

It was only when Joshua made fun of Shelly about how uncool cheering was, that she would want to stop. Cheerleading was the only thing that Shelly ever talked about, ever journaled about, or dreamt about, aside from Mason. And even he took a back seat to cheerleading.

Congratulations, Shelly!

...you have been accepted along with a select group of students from around the country to attend this year's cheerleading training camp...

The following pages outline our intensive three-week schedule...

"I'm so proud of you," Mia said just as she turned the page, the date blazoned as if in bold and highlighted by flashing neon lights – *Sunday June 22 - Saturday July 12*. Mia was horrified and tried her best not to let it show on her face. *I need to talk to John*, her first thought.

"Mom, I'll be the first person ever from my school to be accepted," Shelly said still jumping up and down with excitement. "I'll practically be guaranteed a cheerleading scholarship to any college I want."

"This is so wonderful, dear," Mia said, handing the letter back to Shelly, mustering an enthusiastic hug. "You know that's the...," Mia started, but was abruptly interrupted when her daughter's phone rang.

"Sorry, Mom, I have to take this, it's...," Shelly said, running away, like it was the most important person in the world. And to Shelly it was. She answered the phone with a scream. "I GOT IN, I GOT IN!"

Shelly must have repeated it a thousand times as she ran up the stairs leading to her bedroom. Immediately, Mia's face dropped, she called John but there was no answer.

"Call me ASAP!" She demanded on the voicemail. And then she called Camille who had been waiting for this exciting news to surface.

"Hello, Mia. How are you?" Camille said, lowering the volume on the TV.

Hurriedly, Mia returned the greeting and asked, "Is John around?"

"He's in New York again, I think. Did you try his phone?" Camille knew it was a dumb question but asked anyway.

"YES, YES!" Mia responded in anguish.

"Is there something wrong?" Camille questioned.

"Everything! Everything's all wrong!" Mia exclaimed. "It's the same day as the wedding!" An avalanche of tears cascaded down Mia's face, colliding on the kitchen counter.

"Mia…Mia…what are you talking about?"

"Shelly was accepted to this hard-to-get-into cheerleading camp, the first person ever from her school to be chosen. All she's ever wanted to do is cheer. It's been her whole life. After her dad died…and, and it was cheerleading that brought her through the sadness."

Mia rambled for what seemed like the entire Old Spice commercial causing Camille to miss the shirtless horseman once again. "That sounds like great news, Mia," Camille said.

"It's awful. No, no…it's great news but, it's awful timing!"

"Why do you say that?" Camille pretended.

"IT'S THE SAME TIME AS THE WEDDING!" Mia shouted just as Shelly returned.

Mia was big on fostering her children's independence. Partly because it was responsible parenting, but more than that, she was always pressed for time, the whole single parent/physician thing. If she had more time, had family been around to balance the burden, she would have helped her daughter with the application and noticed the conflict before the plans were set.

"Mom, what's wrong? What's the same time as the wedding?" When the child saw her mother's face, she looked down at the paper clutched in her hand. "NOOOOOO," Shelly shrieked, "IT'S THE SAME TIME AS THE WEDDING!"

This was exactly the way Camille planned it. Not the screaming and yelling part, that kind of made her feel bad, but the wedding coinciding with cheerleading camp was one of her craftiest schemes yet.

THIRTEEN

·····················

the reception

EVERYTHING can be so right, pure and true, faith-filled and well-intentioned, yet be so, so wrong. Sometimes, that's the problem with love.

John was a successful blossoming attorney, a loyal gentleman. Granted, he was a little messy at times, leaving the toilet seat up, socks lingering in odd places around the house, and a touch of unfettered flatulence. He loved sports, his therapy when he was free, which was rare lately. All things that could be worked out, no deal breakers to speak of.

And Mia was a respected physician at a new and thriving practice, a loving and devoted mother, a faithful and committed partner. Granted, she was not a perfect person, a fervent Internet shopper, owning more shoes than one person should be allowed, preferring takeout to cooking most days. She wasn't all that good at keeping house either, hiring help at times for maintenance, schedule just too busy. All things that could be worked out, no deal breakers to speak of either.

Joshua loved football, living in the heart of football country with a new coach helping him hone his skills, and showing signs of development. And Shelly, equally as passionate about cheerleading as Joshua was about football, if not more so, was recently accepted into a prestigious cheerleading camp, overlapping with the date of her mother's impending wedding.

All these things going so right and yet here they were. The children and John already bonded, the plan for Mia to relocate already in place, the wedding date set in stone, the vendors paid, the cake chosen, the vintage pale peach wedding dress hanging neatly in the closet. Yet all these things were not enough to be enough.

Not sure now who thought about it first, but somewhere between John's newly packed work schedule, the increased traffic at the clinic Mia worked for, Shelly's acceptance to cheerleading camp, and Joshua's improving football prowess, Mia and John knew.

They knew there was no getting back to the place they once had been before John moved to Kittery. They knew Mia couldn't leave Dallas any time soon. And they knew that a long-distance relationship was not an option for them any longer.

John hopped on a plane, traveling to Dallas to see Mia and say goodbye the proper way. They came to the decision together. There would be no wedding and they would remain friends. Maybe one day in the future when their lives settled down, they would be together again.

And since the money had already been spent, the wedding venue nonrefundable, Mia and John came together one more time, surrounded by family and friends, and had an old-fashioned shindig in celebration of their love. The spectacular event, an outcome orchestrated by an envious woman, punctuated something that was extraordinary. And for years to come, thinking back on their time together, Mia and John would both recall it with fondness.

John moved out of the brownstone not too long after he and Mia broke up, purchasing a condo in downtown Portsmouth, just outside of Kittery. He kept himself busy with work and the occasional date, just to have something to do, though he found his interest waning. Even the most attractive, successful woman couldn't compare to what he had with Mia, at least not until he accepted the fact that they were not getting back together.

After John left, he and Camille rarely saw one another – John despondent over the breakup with Mia, Camille guilt-ridden for the same reason.

Camille held on to regret for her part in the demise of their relationship, but there was no fixing things now, especially after the monsoon of mishaps she had set in place. And even though she didn't want John to move out, what could she say? The idea of getting back with him seemed too far-fetched, even for her.

Out of the blue, Camille received a message from an unknown number, 'I'm coming to town. I'd like to see you.' Camille didn't recognize the voice, but her curiosity got the best of her, so she returned the call. "This is Camille Young," she said when a lady answered.

"Why are you so formal?" the lady jokingly questioned. "This is Angie."

"Oh heeeyyyy," Camille said with fake enthusiasm, still unsure who she was talking to.

"Dodi," the lady said, dispirited.

"Doooooooodddddiiiiii!" Camille yelled. "How have you been?" she asked. She hadn't spoken to Dodi in years.

"Life is great…got my own baseball team," Angela said in jest. "Knucklehead gave me your number. I'm coming to visit him in a couple of weeks, leaving the fam home. Let's get together – hang out."

"Definitely," Camille said.

The women talked briefly until Angie's children one by one sabotaged the conversation with their constant bickering.

"Can't wait to see you," they said before hanging up.

Angie and Camille agreed to meet at a bar in Portsmouth, John dropping his sister off. When the ladies saw one another, they were more excited than a kid at F.A.O. Schwarz, hugging for what seemed like hours.

"What has been up?" Angie asked out the gate.

Camille told her all about the business, and all the places she had traveled, before being interrupted.

"Are you dating anyone?" Angie asked next.

"No one special," Camille responded.

"Then what's up with you and my brother?" Angie asked bluntly, classic Dodi.

Camille smiled, recognizing herself. "We're just friends," she told Dodi.

"Why are you guys just friends? He's single, you're single," Angie continued her inquisition.

"Umm…well, he dated one of my friends," Camille said exaggerating her relationship with Mia.

"Really? He didn't mention that. Who?" Angie asked.

"Mia," Camille said.

"Texas Mia?" Dodi asked, confused.

"Yea, Texas Mia," Camille told her, attempts at being convincing.

"Girl, stop the madness. That chick has moved on. Isn't she engaged again or something?" Angie questioned.

"I hadn't heard anything about that," Camille responded.

"Then she's not your friend, just someone you were friendly with. And that's not the same," Angie said. "Girl, you better jump on that man. My brother's a great catch, if I do say so myself. Besides, my whole family already loves you."

"Is that why you wanted to meet me?" Camille asked.

"No, but why not kill two birds?" Angie said, winking.

They both laughed, ordering their first round of drinks. The DJ played some honky-tonk square-dancing music, the ladies got up, egged on by a man at the bar and tried their hands at the two-step and the do-si-do.

Simply put, they were awful, but having the time of their lives. They challenged the DJ to play the *Cha Cha Slide*, the *Wobble* or something similar. And when they heard the first few bars of the *Cupid Shuffle*, they hollered with delight. Most of the dancing patrons now looking at them for instruction. They turned the dance floor out that night and made many new friends.

The ladies were well past buzzed, so they decided to share a Lyft home, John's place was closest, so that was the first stop. When they got there, Angie insisted that Camille stay the night, arguing it would be the best option, that John could take her to the car in the morning. The alcohol said yes before Camille had a chance to say no.

Wearing John's old t-shirts, the ladies sat on the rug in the middle of the living room talking and watching whatever was on Comedy Central. Angie bragged about her family, telling touching stories of each of them, including her husband. Camille, not having bragging rights in that respect, switched gears, instead reminiscing about their college days.

"Remember when I came to visit you in Florida?" she asked.

"Yes, I do. We had the most fun, hiding in the closet and scaring the crap out of my brothers," Angie recalled. "I remember walking in on you and John getting busy."

"What?" Camille questioned. "We've never had sex."

"You're grown as hell, you don't have to lie about that," Angie said.

"For real. I'm not kidding. We never made it that far. That must have been somebody else he brought home," Camille said.

"No, Camille, it was you because I remember you bought winter clothes and it was hot as hell that week. I had to let you borrow some of mine. You said it was snowing where you came from," Angie reminded her.

"I remember that, but John and I have never had sex, we must have been playing around or something."

"Then there's got to be some backed up tension between you guys! You should see, since you're here and tipsy," Angie was kidding but serious.

"You're so crazy, Angie," Camille said, but what she was really thinking was, *I wouldn't mind that.* Sitting around hashing up old memories has a way of making a girl want things she's never had.

The next morning Camille showered, put back on the clothes she had worn to the club and waited for John. It had been months since they were alone together. She took the opportunity to pick his brain, asking him had he heard from Mia, and how they were doing, trying to get a sense of where he was emotionally.

He told her everything he knew about them except for the engagement, only confirming its validity after she pressed him for an answer. Then she asked about his relationship status. He chuckled at the inquisition, telling her that he wasn't seriously dating anyone, which meant he was having sex with someone.

"Do I know her?" Camille asked, taking notes from Angie's playbook.

John laughed apprehensively. "Are you alright?" he questioned. "You real nosy!" he told her.

"Me?" she said, acting offended but continued anyway. "Have you ever thought about getting back together with me?"

John was surprised, curiously scoping her out before answering. "A long time ago, maybe. But you made it pretty clear that that ship had sailed," he told her.

"Can I be candid with you?" she asked.

John chuckled. "Sure, why not."

"Ever since you moved out, you've been on my mind, a lot!" she told him, the truth.

"Really?"

"Yes, in every way. Wondering why we never took it to the next level," she said, looking at him in the sultriest way.

"At the time, you said you weren't ready."

"That was then – in college. I was a silly little girl, not ready for that. I'm a full-grown woman now," she assured him, her dress pulled up slightly so he could see her thick glossy thighs.

Camille hadn't been with anyone in that way since before John moved out. He, on the other hand, had been sleeping his cares away, disguising his hurt with variety.

Hugging him before she got out the car, she kissed him on the cheek, rubbing herself up against him as suggestively as possible. "You should come by one evening and let me cook dinner for you," Camille suggested.

"That sounds like a plan," John agreed.

He watched her walk away, intrigued at the possibilities, though he didn't want a relationship, he still wasn't ready for that. They were on the same page as far as that was concerned. Camille's interest piquing as she recalled the words of John's pushy sister, reminding Camille what a catch John was.

It was a Friday night, one week after the dinner invitation. Angie had gone back home to her family, Camille telling her about the plans to get with John beforehand. And John was on his way over to Camille's. She had ordered something from a meal delivery service so the food would look gourmet. She timed things so she would just be finishing up when he arrived.

When John rang the bell, she opened the door in her robe telling him to have a seat, that she had to go slip on her clothes.

He recognized the intention in her eyes.

John sat on the couch, turned on the TV and waited. As she walked by him, toward the stairwell, the corner of her robe snagged the coffee table. And although she felt the tug of the garment pulling away from her body, she allowed the robe to slide off, exposing her thong clad bottom and braless breasts. She didn't flinch once, confident in what she wanted.

John smiled slyly, not wanting to appear overly excited. He thought about their college days, when all he wanted to do was have her, physically. Camille, on the other hand, was right here in the moment, knowing she wanted John more than she wanted anything else.

She eased past him. He admired her succulence. She could see his desire rising, the longing in his eyes penetrated her. But just then, when he thought she was his, Camille grabbed the robe as if she had just realized it no longer covered her body. She put it on, taunting his desires, a test to see if he wanted her as badly as she wanted him.

"We're having grilled steak lettuce wraps with spicy string beans," she said.

"Huh?" he exclaimed, confused. Dinner was the last thing on his mind right now. "Come here," he commanded, grabbing her hand.

She made a half-hearted attempt to pull away and he sensed it. She was still facing the stairs. He pulled her close enough to grab her waist, turning Camille around.

They were now standing face to face. His restraint failed. He pulled the robe from her body, unveiling her firm nipples. She was cool and indifferent while allowing him to have his way. John gently eased his hands behind her neck and slowly pressed his lips against hers. The passion of their kiss was fiery and full of yearning. Their eyes connected.

Slowly his lips moved from her ears, where he whispered sweet longings, to her neck. He lifted her up onto the table, the light of the candelabrum shadowed them. She caressed his neck with her gentle touch, and he laid her down, lightly coaxing her backwards with his kisses to her abdomen and thighs.

That night, more than a decade after they first dated and fell in love, Camille and John devoured one another for the first time. The food went untouched until they were done, six hours after his arrival. Thinking about them finally getting together, he wondered why they had waited so long. And she wondered why she ever let him get away.

They didn't talk about what happened that night or about him and Mia, but as days turned into weeks, as they spent more of their time together, Mia became a distant tender memory, and Camille and John unintentionally fell in love, again.

Several months after the breakup, Mia started dating a doctor she worked with. Two years later that doctor became her second husband, John and Camille in attendance at their wedding.

Eventually, Shelly did get a cheerleading scholarship to the University of Kentucky. Mia and her husband relocated to Katy after Shelly went off to college, the prime location to foster Joshua's football skills. With the help Henry offered and dedication, Joshua would go on to become a high school football star.

And four years to the day, on her grandmother's birthday, Mia and her husband welcomed twins, a girl and a boy, Camilla and Edward Jonathan, named after their good friends.

FOURTEEN

....

steven

IT'S funny how all those Mia and John memories seemed so, so long ago, yet like they only happened yesterday. The fondness and regret dancing in unison. Looking back now, as Camille waited at the terminal for her Singapore flight to board, there were many things that she would have done differently. Top of the list, interfering in John and Mia's relationship. But then again, if she hadn't, there would be no Sammy, and what would her life be without her baby girl?

While Camille waited, her time was preoccupied with countless memories, girly magazines, social media, emails, and people watching. The once empty terminal was now bubbling with commotion.

Camille tried fruitlessly not to stare at the lady sitting next to her, whose face publicized age. The lady's pale skin had clearly been overexposed to the sun, or nicotine, or stress. Maze-like indentations resembling those of a raisin covered every inch of her forehead, cheeks, and chin, even invading her neck.

When the lady's cane fell on the floor, Camille was nudged out of her staring marathon. As the woman bent over to pick the cane up, a little girl Sammy's age emerged out of nowhere, standing all alone in front of the old lady, taking her turn gawking. Camille chuckled in silence and took the child's hand in attempts to stop her from doing the very thing that seconds earlier she had done in secret.

The child's father abruptly grabbed his daughter's other hand and nodded thank you. He scooped the girl up in his arms giving her a kiss on the cheek, before chastising her for running off. Just as quickly as the girl and her father appeared, they faded into the growing crowd. Camille knew from watching the brief encounter between the father and daughter that there had been many loving kisses exchanged. Even with forced recollection she couldn't recall ever being held or kissed with such affection by her own dad.

Before sentiment took hold, all passengers for United Airline flight 2215 were summoned to gate 26. She gathered her belongings, which included her multi-colored crocheted lap blanket, that her favorite auntie made for her one Christmas, her pocketbook that some people considered an overnight bag because it was so big and was loaded down with everything from lipstick to notebooks, and her little suitcase that was made just small enough to fit under the airplane seat.

The line to board the plane was short. The agent scanning tickets commented on how sparse the flight would be. *Good*, Camille thought, *I might be able to get comfortable, even lie down.*

The announcer continued to call for passengers, all boarding in an unusually speedy pace. Camille found her seat. She placed her purse on the seat closest to the window as a pillow and was just about to relax when a man in a blue pinstriped suit and tie cleared his throat and asked if the seat was taken.

Camille gave him an 'are you freaking serious?' look, all the while clearing her belongings. The man placed what appeared to be a laptop in the overhead compartment just before sitting in the aisle seat.

"Steven Louis Bissette," he said, extending his right hand.

"Cami," she said. *Oh boy, and he smells good too*, she thought. 'And thank you,' she mouthed to the airline gods. "What are you wearing?" she asked. "You smell amazing."

"Thank you. It's Clive Christian," he told her.

She turned away slightly and puckered her lips as if to say, 'fancy, fancy.' Now her fantasy was complete – a fine, nicely dressed, good smelling man with great taste. *Stuffy though – the entire government name thing. Why not just Steven or Steve*, she wondered. *Steven Louis Bissette, eeewwwwww, so official.*

The male flight attendant made the usual safety announcements once all the passengers were seated – turn off your cell phones, fasten seat belts, oxygen masks, blah blah blah. After the captain made his brief announcement, the plane took off headed for Singapore.

"My friends call me Steve," he felt inclined to say.

"Where are you from, Steven?" Camille asked. "Are you traveling to Singapore on business?"

"Originally, I'm from Boston," he told her. "What makes you think I'm traveling on business?" he asked.

"For starters, you're a little uptight, Steven Louis Bissette," Camille said, pompously puckering her lips, mocking at his expense. Camille rarely bit her tongue. "…not to mention you're wearing a suit and tie on a sixteen-hour flight. Either that's a fluke or you're traveling on business," she pointed out.

"Well, you're half right," he explained.

"Am I?"

"I guess it's just habit – the telling my whole name thing. The suit – I was running late," he told her, feeling a need to explain.

"Nice meeting you, Mr. Bissette," she said.

"….so that's why I am wearing my suit on a sixteen-hour flight. I didn't have time to change," he continued to explain.

Steve turned to look at Camille, wondering what she would say next. She said nothing, just reached in her bag and pulled out a book and began reading. He pretended to be content with the silence, but something about Camille sparked his interest.

After about ten minutes she chuckled quietly. Her shoulders bobbed up and down causing her plump breasts to jiggle. Steve took notice, her eraser-sized nipples vigorously penetrated her thin white shoulder strapped shirt. He tried to focus on anything else. Turning from side to side, attempts to get comfortable, but he couldn't. He retrieved his computer from the overhead compartment, promptly opening it, he began typing.

"The meeting is set for 4:00 p.m. Is everything in place and ready for the presentation?" Steve typed, emailing his assistant back in New York. "Liza, please send me a copy of my updated schedule ASAP."

After about twenty minutes Camille turned her body in his direction. They hadn't long ago taken off, but she was already starting to get squeamish. She would have been sleep by now but found it difficult sleeping sitting up. She got tired of reading her novel, so she folded the corner of the page she had been reading and placed the book back in her bag. Then she stood up to go to the bathroom. Shuffling by Steven, their eyes connected. There was something between them, a silent spark.

When the flight attendant came by to ask if they wanted snacks, Camille was in the restroom. "I'm not really sure what she would like, maybe…a ginger ale and some crackers," Steve said, ordering for Camille. "…a vodka and cranberry juice for me, please."

The flight attendant wrote the order on a pad of paper then continued taking the orders of all the passengers who were seated behind them, which couldn't have been more than twenty. She then scurried to the back, disappearing behind an off-white and blue curtain.

Steve ended the email to his assistant just as the flight attendant returned with a cart of drinks and food. Row by row she divvied out the snacks and drinks. Steve pretended to be interested in what the other passengers ordered, when in reality he was wondering what was taking Camille so long to come back.

"Did you need anything else, Sir?" the flight attendant asked, the moment Camille returned.

"No, thank you," Steve said.

"Ooh, thanks," Camille said. "What did you get me?"

"…ginger ale and crackers. I didn't know."

"That's fine," she assured him.

Steve took a long gulp from his drink. Then he pulled the seat tray out and placed the half-full cup on it. His mind was busy. He was nervous about a new business venture, the reason for this trip. And although he was an astute businessman, a tinge of nervousness always accompanied the start of new projects. This time was no different.

He turned to Camille to strike up a conversation.

"What are you so anxious about?" she asked, picking up the cup he had placed on the tray, gulping it down.

He looked surprised at first but then smiled and gestured for the flight attendant to bring him another one. "The closer we get to Singapore the more excited I get," he told her.

"You act like you're going to bring home an adopted child, or something."

"In a way, I am," he admitted.

"What do you mean?"

"My company, BisCom, is opening a location in Singapore. I'm going to ensure that the launch is successful."

"BisCom? Isn't that the company that single-handedly put Micros out of business?" she asked without waiting for a response. "I read about you guys in Newsweekly."

"...not exactly, maybe one day. We did manage to win a substantial share of the computer software market, though," he explained.

"Who knew I was seated next to Mr. BisCom himself. Now I understand the Steven Louis Bissette thing. You should have just said that in the first place," Camille told him, in jest.

"Hi, I'm Steven Louis Bissette, CEO of BisCom. Who wants to start a conversation like that?"

"True. I guess that would be a bit off-putting," she joked. "...a lot worse than introducing yourself with all of your ten thousand names," she said, exaggerating.

"That really bothered you. Huh?"

"I wouldn't say it bothered me, but when a nice looking, great smelling man sits next to you on an all-day flight, it's kind of a killjoy for the conversation to start out all proper like. You're not really sure what to expect next, you know what I mean?"

"I guess I do, but I'm as down to earth as they come and thank you for the compliment."

"Qui savait, beau et intelligente! Mon jour de chance!" Camille muttered under her breath, turning to look out the window, hoping he didn't understand French.

"What did you say?" Steve asked.

"…nothing, just admiring the scenery, how gorgeous it is outside," she said, her sly suggestion.

"It is," Steve agreed, turning to look out the window before returning to the conversation. "So, tell me something about yourself."

"What do you want to know?"

"Why are you going to Singapore?"

"I'm traveling on business too, not Mrs. BisCom yet or anything of that sort, but I hold my own."

"What do you do?"

"I'm an interpreter."

"An interpreter?" he asked.

"My company seeks, or should I say, encourages companies to hire qualified people with disabilities and people whose second language is English, mostly the deaf and blind."

"That's admirable," Steve commented.

"I'm glad you think so," Camille said.

Steve wondered what she meant, but he let the comment go unchallenged.

"Not only do the companies get tax incentives for hiring the 'disabled', but they also receive great press, boosting their bottom line. A win-win for all."

Steve had many questions. As an astute businessman, he was always looking for ways to grow his businesses. He didn't know it, but Camille was already part of the Singapore expansion. Intrigued, he wanted to know everything about her business— what influenced her career choice, how she connects with clients and employers, everything.

Camille was surprisingly chatty, eager to fill his head with whatever came to mind. She told him lies about how as a child she traveled extensively with her family, her father reenlisting. In her make-believe life, her family had lived all over the world before she was in middle school.

"Not only do I get the 'disadvantaged' hired, I serve as a liaison until they're acclimated, on average about two years. Usually my services are required for non-English speaking clientele, however, my Singapore clients are deaf and need an ASL certified translator," she told him.

"Really, ASL?"

"Yes, American Sign Language."

"…you sign?" he asked.

She learned to sign from a childhood friend. "Yes. I also read and write in Braille for my blind clients," she told him.

Camille and Steve talked effortlessly for hours. The more she talked, the more enamored he became. She divulged tales of her clients, how she was fluent in several languages, even showing off her skills, speaking to him in Spanish.

"Creo que ya casi llegamos," Camille said, sarcastically suggesting that they were almost in Singapore, when in actuality they had more than eight hours to go.

"Su sido un vuelo suave," Steve countered, shocking Camille. He learned Spanish years ago on the advice of a business associate. And although he didn't speak it as effortlessly as she did, Camille was still impressed.

"Impresionante," Camille commented.

"Gracias," he said. "El tiempo vuela..."

"Cuando te estás divirtiendo," they said in unison, appreciating their mutual admiration.

Steve had so many questions but decided to wait until Camille finished talking to ask them. Intermittent turbulence made the plane bobble, causing Camille to pause each time, not fond of flying. To help calm her nerves, Camille ordered mimosas and other spirited cocktails. Steve, on the other hand, was relaxed, feeling the effects of his drinks, the flight attendant had already served them five times, at least.

As time passed, their conversation waned. Steve took a nap. It had been a day and a half since he last slept, the anticipation of the new venture left him restless. While he rested, Camille took some time to read a little bit more of her book. After she polished off another drink, she needed to go to the restroom, again. She stood up, but this time didn't face Steve, taking notice of the passengers in the surrounding seats.

"Excuse me," she said softly, not wanting to wake him. Groggy, he shifted his body to the one side to allow her to pass. Her leg inadvertently brushed against her bag exposing a brochure. Steve was nudged out of his sleep by the sighting.

Camille was oblivious, instead focusing her attention on the young man and woman seated two seats in front of them. It was evident when they got on the plane that they were strangers.

Upon boarding, the man immediately staked his claim to the seats they currently occupied. The woman, on the other hand, was decidedly unsure about where she wanted to sit, moving her carry on around several times from one overhead compartment to the next. There were many empty seats, so Camille wondered why the woman chose to sit next to the twenty-something year old, sleeved tattoo man.

The first time Camille excused herself to the restroom she noticed the two of them cozying up to one another. So, this time she wasn't shocked to see him busily fondling and kissing his seatmate on the neck. The sideshow ignited something inside Camille that the alcohol surely enhanced.

Before Camille completely made her way pass Steve, the plane hit a huge pocket of turbulence. The strength of the jolt forced Camille to fall backward into Steve's lap. Her bottom firmly pressed against him. He was pleasantly distracted by the commotion, she could tell. So much so that he forgot to investigate the brochure that was sticking out of her bag.

"Please take your seats and secure your seatbelts," the pilot announced. "We're experiencing heavy turbulence. Remain seated until the 'fasten your seat belt' sign is turned off."

Although the alcohol had diminished her reaction time, Camille wanted to make sure that Steve knew he was equally admired, so she delayed peeling herself off his lap. Behaving uncharacteristically, Steve hesitated to help her get up.

FIFTEEN

....

cakewalk

THE sudden turn of events surprised Camille, but she was far from being embarrassed. She had a knack for machinating her way out of situations that would humiliate most people.

Just out of college, one of Camille's good friends was getting married. Jill Parker and Camille met the summer after their freshman year while interning. The next school year they were hallmates in Everett dormitory.

Needing to cut costs and remembering Camille's baking prowess, Jill asked Camille if she would consider making her wedding cake. Camille's almond pound cake was a dorm favorite. It was her great-grandmother's recipe passed down through the generations. And although Camille had never made a wedding cake before she agreed to take on the task.

Jill wanted a three-tier cake with a strawberry cream cheese filling and cream cheese buttercream icing. She fancied edible pearls and scalloped ridging. Camille stayed up all night on the eve of the nuptials baking the cakes and preparing everything she needed to complete the order.

On the day of the wedding it was sizzling hot out, which wasn't unusual for this time of the year in Savannah. With a few hours to go before the ceremony, Camille was ready. She transported everything she needed to the reception site. After arriving, she took her time icing and stacking the tri-tiered square cakes. It looked so beautiful that even she was surprised.

Her first wedding cake, she had to take a picture. She got her phone from the car and snapped a quick photo of the cake and the decadently decorated reception hall. She sent the picture to Jill with the message, "Your beautiful cake has been delivered. No worries."

Camille left the cake on the venue's kitchen counter for the wedding planner to move to the reception hall, as prearranged. Rushing, she then returned to the Parker's home to get ready for the wedding. About an hour or so before the ceremony, Camille's phone rang. She started to ignore it, but it continued ringing nonstop. She reached in her purse for the phone and answered. It was Jill.

"Camille, the caterer called and said you need to come back and check on the cake!" Jill barked, panicking.

"Why, what's going on? It was fine when I left. Didn't you get my text?" Camille asked.

"Please go back and see what they are talking about," Jill said hysterically.

"Okay, I'll check on it right away," Camille agreed.

Camille immediately stopped putting on her makeup. She jumped back into her car and returned to the reception site. She wasn't prepared for what she saw. Her beautiful cake was all slumped to one side, looking droopy like a melted snowman.

Unfortunately, she had failed to completely shut the door to the kitchen when she left. The humidity filled the room and melted the buttercream, causing the cake to topple beyond repair. She didn't know what to do. The guests would be arriving shortly. Camille quickly got back into her car and drove to one of the local bakeries.

"May I help you, ma'am," the clerk said as Camille frantically rushed in the door.

"Yes, I hope so," Camille responded. "I am going to ask just in case," she said under her breath. She was beyond stressed, she was desperate. "Would you by chance have a three-tier cake, that can be ready in twenty minutes, with plain icing and filling?"

"Sure…," the clerk smirked acrimoniously. "No problem at all, this happens all the time."

Camille was not at all pleased with the clerk's off-hand comment. "Is the manager in?" she asked.

"She's not. I'm in charge at the moment."

Summoning Julia Roberts from *Pretty Woman*, "Well, you just made a big mistake! You obviously don't know who I am." As she spoke, she cunningly fabricated a tale beyond belief.

"Have you heard of the reality show, *Under Pressure*?" she asked the clerk.

"No," the clerk said, anxiety setting in.

"I don't have time to go into detail, but I am one of the contestants. I need a cake for a reception that is taking place in less than an hour."

"Ma'am, I don't have a three-tier cake that can be ready in twenty minutes. That's impossible!" the clerk emphasized.

Camille rubbed her head in anguish and looked out the bakery window. As she turned back around to face the clerk, she saw an off-white model cake sitting on the shelf behind the counter.

"Can I borrow that cake? You'll help me win this week's challenge," she asked the clerk in her most sincere voice.

"What?" the clerk asked, more perplexed than ever.

"If you let me borrow that cake, I am certain that I will win. Winning will mean publicity for your bakery," Camille said, trying to persuade the clerk in her favor. "Isn't there another bakery around the corner? Maybe they can help me."

The bakery needed the 'free publicity' Camille proposed. The clerk looked at Camille, then at the five-tier model cake, and then back at Camille. "Let me call the manager," she finally said, not knowing what to do.

"I'm sorry, but you have to make a decision now. I really don't have time to wait any longer. Here, I'll even give you a deposit. How much do you need?"

"I…I don't know," the clerk stuttered, puzzled.

"Here's $200.00," Camille said, pulling a wad of bills from her purse, which in reality was only about $67.00. Camille made her way behind the counter. The clerk watched, frozen and dumbfounded. Camille placed the money on the counter in front of the woman, thanked her for her help, although the woman never consented.

Camille picked the model cake up and proceeded to walk out the bakery. As she was leaving, she added one last cinching comment. "The grand prize is $250K. I've won every challenge thus far except this one and I know your generosity has just helped me clinch this victory."

Camille folded down her back seats and placed the cake back there wedged between her computer case and a couple shoe boxes. She shut the door and drove to the nearest grocery store. She ran in the store and purchased twelve pints of fresh strawberries. Then she returned to the reception site, where she took the fake cake out and placed it on the cake stand in the reception hall.

Around the stand she meticulously placed some of the lilies, roses, and other flowers that were scattered throughout the room. On the back side of the pedestal, where the couple would stand to slice the cake, she placed two small slices of the almond pound cake that she had made.

She rushed back into the kitchen where she washed and decoratively sliced the strawberries. She laid dessert plates out on the available counter tops and positioned two-inch slivers of the almond pound cake on each dish. Next, she adorned every plate with the strawberry slices. Her work was done.

When the wedding planner arrived, Camille informed her of the mishap. Unfortunately, because of the cake ordeal, Camille missed the ceremony, but thanks to her quick thinking the reception was grand and proceeded without a hitch or at least that's what the guests thought.

There were comments abound about how spectacular the cake looked and tasted. The number one query, aside from the dress and honeymoon plans, was where Jill got her cake.

"This is the best cake I've ever had," Moxie Turner told her boyfriend. She was seated at table number 5 just close enough for Camille, who was seated at table number 2, to hear her.

"I hear she got it from Artsy and Edible Bakery," Camille added.

"Really?" Moxie questioned.

"Really. I think it's downtown, not too far from the all girl's college," Camille added, trying to stay true to her word about the free advertising.

Camille had sat through the reception listening to Moxie babble on about everything from butterfly chrysalises to Oprah's new network and she knew Moxie would be the perfect mark to spread the word.

Moxie did not disappoint.

If she got through that wedding cake fiasco unscathed, this airplane slip-up would be a breeze. Her greatest gift, some would say, was her seemingly genuine naivety.

"Oh, my goodness!" Camille said. "I am so sorry."

She placed her hands-on Steve's legs and pushed herself up onto her feet. Still having to use the restroom, she sat back in her seat and fastened her seatbelt, following the instructions of the pilot.

"Are you okay?" she asked, turning to Steve, looking him dead in the eyes. She placed her hand on his leg and waited for a reaction.

"Most definitely," he said. "Boy, that was some turbulence," continuing, impishly referring to the awkward situation they found themselves in.

Steve was a strong and confident man. He spent the major portion of his adult life building profitable enterprises. He negotiated and won in the trickiest business endeavors. He even lost and regained his vast fortune twice. His achievements afforded him the opportunity to meet many beautiful, successful women. But all the education and accolades in the world could not prepare him for a woman of Camille's cunning.

He was taken by her beauty, her intellect. But it was her cool composure that fascinated him the most, her demure temperament intriguing him beyond his understanding. He forced himself to maintain eye contact with her. Sensing his struggle, she pounced on his apparent uneasiness.

"I agree. I've never felt anything like that before," she said, referring to his virility, not once shying away. "That's exactly why I don't like flying," she continued, intentionally being ambiguous to confuse and goad him. "Why are you looking at me like that?" she asked him.

Steve was inwardly pining. It had been some time since his last relationship. For the past year BisCom Singapore had been his only companion, aside from the occasional romp with his ex-girlfriend, Susan.

"How am I looking at you?" he asked.

"Like there is something you want to say," Camille teased. *Like a piece of meat, like you're famished,* was what she was thinking, but stopped short of saying that, not wanting him to be embarrassed.

"No," he said, pondering.

"There is something I'd love to ask you," she said.

"Oh really?" Steve questioned eagerly.

Camille didn't mind telling a man that she was into him. You know, the type of woman that spilled the beans and let her man know exactly what was on her mind at all times. The kind of woman that you sometimes just want to say, 'give me a break, please.' Well, that was not Camille at all.

In fact, she only told you what she wanted you to know. And if by some chance she appeared to slip and tell something that she didn't mean to, make no mistake about it, it was all a part of her plan.

Now, of course, Steve couldn't possibly know this about her. So, when she asked him if he was married, he had no possible way of knowing that she already knew the answer. And when Camille followed the 'are you married' question with an 'are you in a relationship?' this, too, he couldn't have imagined that she already knew.

Camille first got wind of BisCom and Steve when she went to the conference in Texas years earlier. When she saw Steve, heard his accomplishments, his goals, she made it her intention to get to know him, if for nothing else but friendship and networking. This was long before she and John got together, before Sammy.

Just so happened that one of the guys that Camille attended the conference with, had a backdoor ticket to Steve. Mike, her colleague, had gone to college with a guy that was Steve's business partner, and was the primary reason Shapleigh received the invite to the conference in the first place.

Camille used her connections with Mike to meet his friend and casually pitched her business to him. Mike, it turns outs, was the man she was having the affair with. The very same man that Sammy walked in on her having relations with, the man that prompted her exit from Kittery.

Mike's friend remembered Camille when the Singapore expansion inked and offered her the opportunity of a lifetime, as she saw it, to work with Steve. Camille had no idea that Steve would be on this flight, much less that he would sit right next to her. But it made her job, finagling an acquaintance with him, a cakewalk.

"Are you married or in a relationship?" Steve asked her.

"Not yet," she said, touching his forearm that was on the armrest between them.

Steve loved her confidence. "Not yet," he repeated, chuckling.

"I suspect that at any moment I'll meet the man that is perfect for me. Maybe even on a sixteen-hour flight to Singapore," she said, smiling.

"That would be nice, wouldn't it?" he said, returning the gesture.

"Yes, it would," she replied, her eyes still locked on his.

SIXTEEN

....

singapore

IT was almost midnight back in the States and United Airlines flight 2215 would soon be landing in Singapore. The 'fasten your seat belts' sign was on again. Everyone on board prepared themselves for the descent.

Between announcements both Steve and Camille tried to milk the conversation as much as they could. He was a breath of fresh air, a guy who was attracted to her but could keep his composure. And she was a rare gem too, educated, beautiful, and couldn't care less about his stature, or so he thought.

"It was really nice meeting you," Camille told Steve first.

"It was good meeting you, too," he said, returning the compliment.

"I hope everything goes well with your new business venture, as I know it will," she continued, last minute small talk as they prepped for landing.

"You'll be in Singapore for two years?" Steve asked.

"Yes, that's the usual acclimation period," she said, reciting her usual spill as she would any prospective employer.

"I don't know how long I will be in town, but…,'" just as Steve was about to tell her that he would love to see her again the pilot landed the plane and came over the intercom thanking everyone for their patronage.

Following the pilot's announcement, the flight attendant made the 'stay in your seats until…' announcement. It all went so fast. By the time Steve was ready to continue what he was saying, one of the male passengers came up the aisle from behind them, looking for Camille.

"Excuse me," the man said, pushing his way toward her. "…Camille," he called loudly from several rows back. "Excuse me. CAMILLE," the man called again, this time a little louder, trying to get her attention, finally pushing his way to the seats where she and Steve were. "Excuse me, sir," he said to Steve. "Camille, I thought you were coming back," he said. "I wanted to catch you before you got off the plane."

"I was, but Steve and I were having such a great conversation, I didn't get a chance to." She looked at Steve to gauge his reaction, totally shocked by the man's gall, storming up the aisle calling her name like that.

"I know you're not going to be in Singapore long. Right?" The man questioned. Camille looked at Steve, grinning impishly.

"Not quite sure how long yet," she said.

"Please give me a call. I would love to take you out and show you around Singapore. You're welcome to go to the wedding with me if you'd like," he said. He pulled out a business card and handed it to her. On the back he had written the name of his hotel with the words 'PLEASE CALL' underlined several times.

"I will," she told him, skeptically. *It's so unbecoming for a man to act this pressed*, she thought. He had stopped her on her first trip to the restroom. The heaviness of his glare was palpable, staring so hard that she had to say hello. He was a nice looking fellow, a tad obnoxious, though.

His name was Jason "J.R." Herring and he was from Chicago. His best friend from college grew up in Singapore. The best friend met a girl from the States, fell in love, and popped the question. So now Jason was in Singapore for the three-day fiesta.

Hello wasn't enough for Jason. As she was returning to her seat from the bathroom, he asked her if she would join him. *Oh, why not*, she thought, *we still have ten or more hours left on this flight*. So, she sat down next to him, and talked briefly.

It doesn't take long for people to put you in a category — 'just friends' or 'going to be mine.' Most often the category is based purely on attraction, before a word is uttered. Camille didn't waste time filing Jason in the 'just passing time on a long-ass flight' category and he earned it. Jason was full of compliments but not much of anything else.

Although Camille was used to men admiring her, she never showed an air of arrogance. This was another of the qualities that attracted people to her. In fact, she was more than accommodating even in circumstances where conceit might have served her best.

"I will call you. It was nice meeting you," Camille said again, dismissing Jason nicely. She wanted to settle things with Steve before departing the plane. J.R. didn't budge. He stood in the aisle and waited as Steve and Camille gathered their belongings.

"Oh, I'm sorry," Camille said. "Honey, this is J.R. Herring," she said to Steve, egging him to play along. "J.R., Steve. Jason is from Chicago, sweetie. I met him on the way to the lady's room earlier."

"Nice to meet you," Steve said, extending his hand to shake with J.R.

"Want to go to the wedding?" she asked, turning to Steve for a response.

"I don't see why not," Steve agreed, right in step.

"Jason, I will definitely be calling you," Camille continued.

Camille was first to depart, then Jason, with Steve following behind them. Jason gave her an unwanted escort through customs, reciting the day-by-day wedding itinerary. Steve waited briefly, sensing Jason wasn't letting her go.

"Nice meeting you, Camille," Steve said, excusing himself.

"Please, wait a moment," Camille pleaded. "Jason, I will call you. I have to go now," she insisted.

Camille didn't want to be rude, but Jason had obviously never done well with rejection. She accelerated her pace to catch up to Steve, leaving Jason standing alone. When she reached Steve's side, she motioned for him to speed up.

Speeding through terminal 3, they admired its spectacular architecture. The walls had to be fifty feet high and adorned by ornate greenery and a waterfall. The tropical feel was enhanced by the airport's lavish décor.

"Where are you staying?" Camille asked.

"Marina Bay Sands."

"Isn't that a coincidence? That's where I'm staying, too," she said falsely. Nothing that a quick trip to somebody's .com couldn't solve. As they walked to retrieve their luggage, Steve suggested that they ride over to the hotel together. She agreed.

"Give me a minute, Steve, I'll be right back." She pretended to go to the lady's room, again. Her sixth trip since they boarded the plane in New York, but Steve wasn't counting.

Lost among all the passengers headed to baggage claims, she slipped into the nearest gift shop. She pulled out her phone and made reservations. Afterwards, she sent a quick text to her mom, sister, and John, to let them know that she had landed safely. Camille navigated her way back to Steve just as her baggage was rounding the carousel.

"There are my bags now – the pink and blue ones," she told him, waiting for him to grab them.

"Are you ready?" he asked. "Here come my bags now too."

Camille followed him out of the terminal where outside they flagged the driver for the Marina Bay, who was parked near the terminal entrance. The middle-aged man pulled the van to the curb. He got out and welcomed them to Singapore.

"How do you do?" he greeted.

Carlo, his name badge specified, loaded their luggage into the rear of the van. Once the luggage was firmly secure in the back he came around and opened the doors for Camille and Steve to enter.

"…Marina Bay Sands?" a voice squawked from behind them, a tiny woman was rushing to the van. Her accent sounded British or Australian. It wasn't quite clear which one from the few words that she had spoken.

"Yes ma'am," Carlo said and helped her load her belongings.

The four of them settled in their seats for the short ten-minute ride to the hotel. They all exchanged pleasantries, initiated by Camille.

"Camille," she said, extending her hand to the lady who was now determined to be Australian.

"Megan," the lady said, shaking hands with Camille first, then Steve.

"Steven Louis Bissette," Steve said, smiling at Camille as he shook Megan's hand.

"Megan, this is Carlo," Camille offered, introducing the fashionably dressed lady to the driver.

"That was quite some flight," Megan continued. "I must have consumed way too much caffeine," she said. "…couldn't get a wink of sleep the whole flight."

It was as if she forgot anyone else was in the van because she went on talking nonstop. Talking about her family back in New York, telling them that she had moved to the States almost five years ago, relocating there with her husband and two young girls.

"Lisa, my baby, was born on Christmas day," she told them, pulling her phone out showing Camille and Steve the photo of her girls that she had saved as her wallpaper.

"Do you have children?" she asked.

Camille was staring out the window admiring the landscape. She appeared to be mesmerized, pretending not to hear the question.

"Camille," Steve called, "…I don't have children," he responded.

"Oh, don't bother the lady. She seems to be in deep thought," Megan said.

Recharged, Megan continued talking about her girls. Her eldest daughter was named Joslyn and had a head full of bright orange wavy hair just like her mother. Joslyn was seven years old and as Megan told it, adored her baby sister.

Megan had come to Singapore on a girl's getaway. Six of her closest friends planned the outing years ago. The friends were all traveling from different cities, that's why she was alone.

Megan was anxious to explore Singapore, having heard of its beauty. This was her first visit.

"Have you traveled here before?" she asked them.

"No," Camille said, reentering the conversation.

"Only once before," Steve replied.

Megan continued her ramble. She told them how her friend Samantha was an expert at finding great internet deals. Samantha had booked their all-inclusive one-week trip for the six of them for around $975.00 each.

Camille silently questioned this. For one, the Marina Bay Sands was one of Singapore's more exclusive hotels, and, two, she couldn't get a word in edgewise to debate the claim.

Megan told them that she was a stay-at-home mom and that she had never spent one night away from her girls. Her husband's mother, Amelia agreed to come all the way from Australia to attend to the girls while she took a much-needed break.

Take a breath, Camille mouthed to Steve, signaling with her hand that this woman talked way too much. By the time they reached the Sands, Camille and Steve knew what seemed like the complete life history of the Mallory family, volume one.

Megan's husband was the chief counsel for some prominent New York law firm. She said the name, Mc… something or other, but was talking so fast that it went right over their heads.

They found out that on Mondays and Wednesdays the nanny, Ms. Josephine came to help with the girls for five hours while Megan worked out and took care of some female refinement matters. And on Fridays, the maid service picked up what little was left after Megan cleaned house the whole week. She even spoke fondly of her chef, Buttons, who her husband Bobby hired to help with their weekday vegetarian diet.

They were eight miles into their ten-mile commute to the hotel. And although she had no need for it, Camille got the attention of the driver to inquire about a lavatory. Carlo told her that the hotel was just minutes away, news that was like music to her ears.

"Steve, you're awfully quiet," Megan commented.

You must be kidding, lady! Who could get a word in with the epic you just chronicled? Camille thought.

"Just enjoying the conversation," Steve answered. His grandmother had the same gregarious nature. And the truth was, he genuinely meant it and could have listened to her talk for hours.

Moments later the van pulled up in front of the hotel. Carlo rushed out of the driver's seat to assist the ladies before retrieving the baggage from the booth.

"Thank you for staying with us here at the Sands," the driver said.

"Thank you, Carlo," Steve said, handing him a tip.

They each took a moment to gaze at the ancient landscape outside which was dwarfed by the enormity of their hotel. On what appeared to be an ark garden in the sky, the surfboard-shaped roof sat atop the three towers of the hotel.

They could see people peering off into the distance from fifty-seven stories high. And although Megan deplored heights, she couldn't wait to get a look at Singapore from that viewpoint, if only briefly. What she wanted more than the view of Singapore's financial district, was to wade in the lavish infinity pool her friend Samantha touted.

At the lobby desk, two attendees aptly adorned with hotel garb greeted them. "May I help you," they said in unison.

Camille stepped up to the middle counter.

The three tourists were thoroughly impressed by the surroundings. And although she was accustomed to glamorous affairs and lavish venues, Megan was awestruck by the unrivaled architecture and artistic renderings.

"Bonjour?" Camille said to the clerk who had a French accent.

"Bonjour," the clerk replied.

Camille reached in her purse and pulled out her passport, handing it to the clerk. "This is a lovely place you have here," she said.

"Thank you, ma'am. I am glad it meets your approval."

"I have a reservation…Young," Camille told the clerk.

Megan was at the counter to Camille's right being helped by José. Camille could hear her carrying on about their ride from the airport. Megan told the clerk that she was meeting six of her best friends, even going into some of the plans that they had scheduled for the day. The clerk was shockingly participatory.

Steve patiently waited just steps away.

"Ms. Camille Young, I see you'll be staying with us for three weeks," the clerk said to Camille, who was still distracted by Megan and her jibber-jabber.

"Yes, that's sounds about right," Camille said dismissively, wanting the clerk to hurry along.

"Ah, you just made your reservations today," the clerk said.

"Ne, ne, ne, ne, ne!" Camille emphatically snapped, waiving her hands, signaling for the clerk to stop talking.

Did it really matter when I made my reservation, Camille wondered? She looked over her shoulder to see who was listening. Steve was standing close enough to hear what the clerk had said but was being drawn into the conversation between Megan and José.

"Right, Steve?" Megan turned and asked him. He shook his head in agreement.

"Parlez-vous français?" Camille asked the clerk, almost whispering.

"Oui," the clerk replied.

"Cet homme m'a suivi, pas plus de détails, veuillez," Camille spoke in French, telling the clerk that a man had been following her, implying that it might be Steve. She demanded the clerk withhold the details of her reservation.

Camille giggled as if she had said something funny. "Look again, Young is the name," offhandedly accusing the clerk of a mistake. Unfortunately for Camille, Megan was fluent in French and paused her conversation with José upon hearing the interaction.

"Who's been following you?" Megan quietly questioned, as she looked around, truly concerned.

Camille was dumbfounded. A reply didn't come easily. Steve had briefly turned his attention to his cell phone and didn't hear Megan's query. The clerk continued her search.

"Oui," the clerk said again as she typed the same information in the computer. "Sorry for the confusion, ma'am. I have your reservation."

"Je vous remercie," Camille said.

Seeing that Steve was distracted, she ignored Megan and concluded her business. "I'll point him out later," Camille said under her breath, walking away from the counter, motioning to Steve that it was his turn.

Camille waited for them to check-in. Megan, of course, took a little longer than anyone else. They all agreed to get together for dinner at a later date. Actually, Steve asked Camille to meet him for dinner. Megan, never the one to be left out, invited herself and her friends along.

After they exchanged room numbers, the ladies made plans to visit the hotel's casinos, theaters, museums, and vast culinary eateries before heading off to their respective rooms. Megan and Camille were on the sixteenth floor, while Steve was in room ten thirty-two.

The plush Feng Shui-inspired rooms were just as marvelous as the hotel's grand entrance. And they each settled into their accommodations comfortably.

Camille had to meet with clients later, so she rested long enough to call her mother, shower and change, while Steve and Megan toured the hotel's many attractions, separately.

SEVENTEEN

....

fun, fun and more fun

CAMILLE settled into her luxurious room. She spent the first couple of nights in Singapore relaxing out on the balcony, catching up on some reading and sipping on champagne.

Not only did she love her accommodations, her new assignment was going well too. Her clients, two men and four women, were steadily adjusting to their new environment, which was reflected in the training scores the company required for all their employees.

Camille had been in Singapore a little over a week and was ready to socialize after nights of a self-imposed seclusion. At 4:00 p.m. sharp, she rushed from the office, heading back to the hotel to ready herself for her dinner date with Steve and Megan.

She showered and gave herself a fresh shave – grooming usually reserved for dates were intimacy was the expected conclusion, but one never knew.

Time was limited, so her hair had to play second fiddle to the other primping regimens. She took the curling iron and made two huge whirls atop her head that quickly sprung up and down once released from the heat. Then she loosely gathered her hair, twisting it upward, starting in the lower middle back, placing a Japanese-style hairpiece vertically down the center of the twist to hold the hair in place.

She searched through her clothes and pulled a formfitting, off-the-shoulder, sleeveless black dress from the dresser drawer. Luckily for her it was wrinkle-free. The shoes she chose were black silk strap up wedges. When she tied them just right on her bare legs, they made her five-foot seven frame appear six feet tall.

Before getting dressed she placed a smidgen of perfume on her midriff, wrists, inner thighs, and behind her ears, 'just in case' dabs of Chanel Mademoiselle, her favorite. She loved silver jewelry but decided on the antique gold set she got for Christmas from a good friend. She was ready in no time at all. She checked herself in the mirror one last time before heading out.

They planned to meet at 8:00 p.m., it was 7:50 p.m. The restaurant was standing room only. Luckily, Megan's friend made reservations when she booked the rooms months ago.

When they checked in, Megan added five to the booking. They'd be dining at Cut, one of the hotel's ritzier establishments.

Megan was in the lobby waiting for one of her getaway friends. Camille alerted the hostess of her arrival and retreated to the bar area until it was time to be seated. Moments later, Megan, escorted by her friends, joined Camille, informing her that the others were on their way.

"Camille, this is Lavinder Toussant," Megan introduced her friend. "Lavi, this nice lady is Camille Young. We met on the ride from the airport," Megan slurred.

The strangers greeted one another, shaking hands.

Camille openly admired their outfits. Megan had on a shiny plum colored cocktail dress. Her shoes were perfectly matched as though they were custom made. Hints of gold dust were sprinkled about which made the shoes look like they had twinkling stars on them. The color of the dress complemented her orange hair to perfection. The golden necklace she wore was draped with jewels of orange, violet, plum, and red. Her bracelet and earrings were similar but smaller versions of the necklace. She smelled delightful too.

Something was different about Megan. She was unusually quiet. This pleased Camille immensely.

"Is everything okay?" Camille questioned.

"Yes," Lavinder responded. "Meg just had a little to drink," tipping her hand to her mouth in a drinking motion.

Camille was dying on the inside, laughing at Megan. For most people alcohol was like truth serum, coaxing inappropriate conversation. But not for Megan, Ms. Mouth herself got quiet, like she swallowed her voice right on down with her liquor. *How funny is that,* Camille thought, *liquor is Megan's kryptonite.*

Camille lived for times like these. She was good at studying people, learning what made them tick. It was a gift, of sorts. She knew that a person's imperfections could be used to her advantage. This present situation meant that she might actually have an enjoyable evening, not having to listen to Megan's constant jibber-jabber.

Megan's friend Lavinder was stunning too. At most she was five feet two inches tall and that was with her three-inch high heels on. Camille towered over her. Lavinder was way too busty for her small stature. Her dress was made of a tan crepe material. It was plastered to her chest and flared out from there giving the illusion of an hourglass figure. Her hair was adorned with a bright orange calla lily, which made its auburn pigment all the more brilliant. She had a dark olive complexion that glowed magnificently with the lighting.

Lavinder, Megan and Camille walked into the restaurant together. Steve and three of his male business acquaintances greeted them. The rest of Megan's getaway friends were seated at the bar awaiting their arrival. When they saw Lavinder and Megan they screamed, ran over to them, each person greeting the other with hugs and kisses, complimenting one another's appearances and playing catch up while they waited to be seated.

"Is everyone in your party here now, sir," the hostess asked one of Steve's colleagues, who was the first to arrive.

"I think so," Mark replied.

"Right this way," the hostess said.

The ladies led the way as the hostess escorted the party to their window table. Being the gentleman, Steve pulled out the chair as Camille was seated. "What gentlemen," the ladies commented as they received the same overture by the other men dining with them.

Megan sat next to Steve, who sat next to Camille and everyone else filled in wherever they could. Megan's kryptonite was losing its effect. Camille kindly offered rounds for everyone at the table under the pretense of enjoying the great company, though she really wanted to keep Megan quiet. Too bad for Camille, everyone except Tip declined.

The gentlemen refused to have a lady extend such a gesture but thanked her anyway. Instead, Steve ordered a couple of bottles of the best Cabernet Sauvignon to share with the table. The server returned with the bottles on ice and filled everyone's glasses.

"I love nuts," Samantha said to Camille, grabbing a hand full of nuts from one of the three dishes that the waiter placed on the table for them to enjoy. "I don't, really," Samantha admitted, "I'm just hungry as hell."

"I'm so hungry my stomach's touching my back," Camille countered.

The two women introduced themselves, engaging in the usual small talk – where are you from? what do you do? do you have a family?

"So, how's your stay been?" Samantha asked.

"Oh, I love this hotel. I don't really want to leave," Camille told her.

"You're leaving soon?" Samantha questioned.

"I plan on being in Singapore for a while, so I've been busy looking for an apartment or rental for the rest of my stay."

"Megan was telling me, you're quite the businesswoman."

"Thank you," Camille said. How's your stay been so far?" Camille asked, quickly diverting the conversation.

"Actually, it's been great. At first, I thought I had made a mistake."

"Really?" Camille questioned, surprised by Samantha's response.

"Checking in was a beast!" Samantha told her.

"What happened?" Camille was curious to know.

The clerk at the front counter was very busy on the afternoon of Samantha's arrival. It wasn't exactly clear why she was alone, but she was alone and multi-tasking was not the clerk's strong suit. Three guests waited patiently to be helped, Samantha was third.

The male customer who was first appeared to need a tour guide because he asked the poor clerk directions to all the more popular sights – from the Jurong Lookout Tower, with its panoramic views of Singapore, to Haw Par Villa, where tourists experience brilliant depictions of Chinese culture and mythology.

Fifteen minutes later, even after the clerk told the growing line several times that she was sorry for their wait, that she would be with them shortly, the tourist suddenly realized, as if jolted out of a coma, that there were other people behind him, excusing himself from the line. Samantha was a patient lady, but this was far beyond tolerable.

When it was finally Samantha's turn, the clerk, in her haste, gave Samantha the wrong room key, which was not discovered until her luggage had been hauled up to the twelfth floor. Understandably, Samantha was pissed when she returned to the front desk to correct the problem. It didn't help that the little irritating tourist man had begun his second inquisition.

"Pardon me," Samantha said to the man. "Miss, this key doesn't work, and I am extremely tired. Could you give me the proper key, please?"

"Go ahead," the man said, allowing Samantha to interrupt. "I'm just getting directions."

"I'm sorry, ma'am. Room twelve-fourteen," the clerk said as she handed Samantha the new room key, another mistake. Samantha wheeled her luggage up to the twelfth floor, again, this time to room twelve-fourteen.

She placed the card key into the designated slot and to her delight the door opened. She sighed in relief until she saw someone's dark blue luggage sitting neatly by the desk. From out of nowhere, a man barely five feet tall appeared in his birthday suit, coming from the bathroom. The two patrons stared at each other in shock. Samantha, who was normally not easily moved, let out a piercing scream. The very last thing an exhausted woman wants to see is a naked stranger with a napoleon complex.

Needless to say, Samantha's accommodations were on the house, and had she not been so doggone tired she would have played the drama to the hilt and gotten much more out of the ridiculous debacle.

As the rest of the people at the table engaged in polite conversation, Samantha finished telling Camille about her ordeal. After a long and heated interaction with hotel management Samantha finally settled comfortably into her room, fourteen-twelve. The clerk was obviously dyslexic.

"You have got to be joking!" Camille said, quietly chuckling. That was the funniest thing she had heard in a long time.

"I wish I were, but no, it actually happened," Samantha said. "Here's his card."

"You got his number?" Camille asked, excitedly.

"Well, of course!" she said, looking at Camille like she had two heads. "He was short, but not everything on him was. Besides, he has great taste," Samantha said. "And honey, the competition is way too fierce to be persnickety, if you get what I mean."

Camille slapped Samantha on the leg, laughing uncontrollably. "Girl, you are crazy!"

"Am I wrong, though?"

"No, not at all. You sound like my friend Maria," Camille commented.

By this time everyone's glasses were filled with wine. Megan was well on her way back to drunk. Steven and some of his colleagues were engrossed in a heated debate over the best wine to pair with filet mignon.

"Let's make a toast," Tash Saunders said. Tash was another one of the getaway girls. She recently moved to Cupertino with her husband and twins, Mika and Park.

Tash's skin was a dazzling raven tone. Her slender body was draped with a mint three-quarter arm length coatdress that came to her knees. It was beautifully accessorized with a wide belt of similar color that accentuated her ample derrière superbly. Her skin tone made her simple gold jewelry and iridescent bangles more brilliant. Tash's ensemble was completed with platform pumps that were a lovely shade of creamy tan.

It was rumored that Tash's husband was the richest of all the friend's mates. And if the size of the diamond on her finger was indicative of her husband's worth, it screamed, 'WE'RE RICH, BITCHES!'

"Sounds like a great idea," the table agreed.

"Cheers to great friendships," Tauni Oliver said first.

"Cheers to new business ventures," Steve's VP of Operations Singapore, Curtis Enlo said, holding his glass towards the middle of the table.

"Here, here," Steve chimed in.

Megan began to slowly sip her glass of wine as she talked. While the others toasted, she exchanged stories with one of her friends. Megan's exhaustive banter was understandable, being that it had been six years or more since all the getaway girls had been in the same place at once.

Megan recounted the story of her family. The very same story she had told Steve and Camille in the van on the way from the airport earlier that week. By the end of the story Megan had finished her third glass of wine.

"I have a toast, too," Megan slurred, jumping in like she had been paying attention the whole time.

"Go ahead," Samantha said, chuckling at her friend's noticeable intoxication.

"Cheers to Botox, collagen, breast lifts and tight asses," Megan said, putting her hands under her breasts and juggling them a couple of times before pointing across the table at Leslie's newly minted C cup cleavage.

"That's enough wine for you, Megan," Tauni said, moving Megan's glass out of her reach.

"Amen," Camille chimed in, finding joy in this spectacle.

"Do you have any photos, Megan?" Leslie from Phoenix asked trying to get the attention off of her breasts.

Lo and behold Megan pulled some photos out of the little bag that Lavinder was carrying and began passing them around to everyone at the table. All the women were captivated by the pictures except for Camille, of course, who wanted to gag.

And although the people gathered at the table that night were from all over the world, Camille would soon discover what a small, small world it really was. As Megan passed her pictures around, Camille recognized a familiar face in one of them.

"This is my husband, Bobby….," Megan said, passing the picture in Camille's direction.

Camille struggled to gain her composure.

How did this woman from New York via Australia have a picture of him? Of all the people in all the world, Camille ended up dining with a woman whose mouth ran five thousand miles a minute, who also just so happened to be married to the man in the picture who was shaking hands with the one man in the whole entire world that Camille had ever loved.

"…with one of the partners in his firm." Megan continued, trying not to sound drunk. "He's a single dad of the cutest little girl," she continued. Megan looked at Camille with the weirdest expression, and then said, "…as a matter of fact, Camille."

Camille almost choked on the peanuts that she had been eating, she knew what was coming next. Before Megan could utter another word the honey roasteds miraculously ended up spread across the restaurant floor.

"Oh, my goodness," Camille said, appearing flabbergasted by the peanut caper.

Megan was compulsively neat and just a tad inebriated. She couldn't fathom a floor full of peanuts. She hopped out of her seat, got on her knees in the plum cocktail dress and began to gather the nuts one by one, completely forgetting what she was about to say.

With the commotion, Camille skillfully placed the photo of the two gentlemen under her leg while the table's other guests busied themselves trying to get Megan off of the floor. Camille arranged the remaining pictures and took over the conversation, leaving Megan no room to pick up where she had left off. In no time at all, every single nut, including Megan, had been scooped up off the floor and returned to their rightful places.

The food that night was superb and all the people at the table had a wonderful time. They ate and drank until the restaurant closed, at which point most of the getaway girls, Camille, Steve and two of his colleagues scurried their separate ways, until only two people from their party remained. Megan and Curtis couldn't be pried away from each other.

No one noticed the black clutch that was left on the floor nicely tucked away under Megan's chair. It was displaced when the nuts did their tango with the floor.

As Megan and Curtis were poised to leave the restaurant they were stopped by the hostess. "Ma'am. Sir," she called, trying to get their attention. "Ma'am," she called again. "…you left some things." The hostess was practically at their heels when Megan finally turned around. "Ma'am, you left these?" the attendant said, trying to hand her the clutch and pictures.

"Oh, that's not my clutch, but the photos are mine," Megan said, reclaiming the pictures.

"I found them at your table, under the chair where you were seated," the hostess said.

Megan took the clutch the hostess offered and opened it, trying to identify its owner. Inside there was a tube of pale pink colored lipstick, some green and white mints in plastic wrappers, a small silver container housing the owner's business cards, a cell phone, a tiny mirror, and a photo of a little girl, held in the clear pocket of a leather credit card receptacle, along with some cash and one credit card. Megan smiled when she saw the photo. She didn't need to look any further.

"This is my friend's," Megan said to the hostess. "I'll take care of it."

"Thank you, ma'am," the hostess said. "Goodnight."

"No, thank you! I'm sure she'll be happy you found it," Megan assured her. She was delighted. Now she'd have a little fun at Camille's expense.

EIGHTEEN

....

the hookup

CAMILLE asked Steven to come to her room. And although she and Steve had spoken several times since the flight, this would be the first real time they had spent alone. As they walked, Camille paused midway down the corridor. She leaned toward him and whispered softly in his ear, "I want to kiss you."

He was carrying a bottle of wine from the restaurant. He gripped it tightly anticipating what was to come. He placed his left hand behind her head, coaxing her closer. She wrapped both her arms around his neck. Slowly, their lips were drawn together. She closed her eyes and kissed him gently.

Then without warning or reason, she took off running in the direction of her room. With his lips still puckered in kiss mode, he followed with enthusiasm, rushing behind her. They made their way to room sixteen forty-six simultaneously. She faced the door, attempting to unlock it, she didn't have her room key. Where was it? In her purse?

He leaned over and lightly tickled the back of her neck with his soft lips, pressing her gently against the door. She twitched with glory.

"Open the door," he commanded with his kisses.

Not wanting him to stop, but unable to go further, she stuttered, "I…I…I must…must have left my p…p…purse at the rest…aurant. My…my key."

His mind bounced around like a pinball having just been discharged. *Let's go to my room then. No, I'll go get your purse. No, then you'll be standing here in the hallway all alone. No, let's go to my room.* "Let's go back and get your purse," he whispered in her ear, grazing her lightly with sensual words. He turned her around and pressed her against the door. "Come here lady. Let's finish this first," he said, kissing her again more lustfully than before.

Under similar circumstances Camille would be the model of control, but it had been a while since she entertained activities of this nature and she was ready to see what Steve was talking about, the kind of talking where you didn't need words to communicate.

As they stood in the hallway fondling and kissing each other Camille heard footsteps heading in their direction. She didn't attempt to pry herself away from the zealousness of his lips, her poise was nonexistent.

"We have to get the key," she whispered in his ear.

"You're right, but somehow I don't think it's going anywhere. The restaurant was closing when we left. We can go to my room or the front desk," he offered.

Reluctantly, they stopped kissing and retraced their steps, walking back toward the elevator. "You hear that voice? It sounds like Megan," Camille whispered.

"…and Curtis too," Steve added.

"Curtis?" Camille questioned.

As she said his name, Megan and Curtis came around the corner laughing and hugging each other. Megan held the black clutch in her right hand. When Camille saw Megan, she struggled to understand what was going on. *Isn't she happily married, all those stories about her husband, her family*, Camille thought? Her shocked expression spoke before she could. "Goodnight?" Camille mustered.

"Goodnight," Megan said, answering for the both of them. It was Megan's intention to deliver the clutch to its rightful owner before returning to her room, just as she had promised the hostess. As the couples passed one another, Megan hesitated slightly. "Excuse me one minute," Megan motioned to Curtis with her left hand.

He continued to walk toward her room. Steve and Camille stopped. Backtracking slightly, Megan handed the clutch to Camille.

"I think this is yours," she said.

Steve was relieved, grateful that they could pick things up where they had left off sooner than he had thought.

"Thank you. Where did you find it?" Camille asked.

"The hostess found it, said it was under my chair," Megan told her.

Camille took the clutch, opening it to inspect its contents. The first thing she saw as she unlatched the silver button that held it shut, was the picture of Sammy.

Sam was wearing a blue shirtdress with white stripes. The blue leggings Sam wore had little bells around the ankle. For a moment, standing in the hotel hallway, Camille was taken back to the time not too long ago when it was just the two of them waiting for John to come home.

Camille could hear Sam's little voice as if she were there in front of her. "Mommy, where me at?" Sam said to her mother, beckoning Camille to play along.

Camille smiled then as she did now.

The bells on the little girl's leggings led Camille to the child's exact hiding spot, though she pretended not to see Sammy behind the plush cushioned chair in the bedroom she shared with John.

"Sammy," she called. "Where are you?"

Sam's little toes were sticking out from behind the chair as she tried her best to be quiet, a hard task for a toddler, though. The little girl struggled her hardest, trying to be still, but the bells that surrounded her pant legs jingled as she squirmed around.

Camille turned away from the chair as if she were going to leave the room. When she did, Sam got up and ran. Camille turned back around and grabbed Sammy tightly in her arms, covering the little girl's face and neck with soft wet kisses.

"Got ya!" Camille said, squeezing her baby as close as possible. Sam giggled infectiously.

It's funny how in a flash a picture can take you back to places you've tried futilely to forget. This precious memory thwarted by the quandary of a secret revealed. Camille looked up at Megan to gage her motivation, then thanked her again.

"It's amazing that I was able to shove all this stuff in this tiny little clutch," Camille sheepishly commented.

Megan leaned in close enough to Camille to mutter a reply. "That's not at all what I was thinking," she said, "…women are good at that…tucking things away. Aren't we?" Then with a wily smirk, she said goodnight, scurrying off to join Curtis, who was well down the hallway by now.

Camille wasn't prepared for this, she was inwardly undone. Upon entering the room, she fought to regain the lecherous spirit that she had just moments ago, before Megan and the clutch. She began speculating Megan's intentions. *Maybe all she meant was keep my secrets, I'll keep yours.* Camille didn't know Megan well enough to know for sure and didn't want some talk-a-lot busybody ruining her fun.

"Is everything okay?" Steve asked. "…are you having second thoughts?"

"NO…of course not," she assured, straddling him on the leather couch that was positioned in the center of the room. He kissed her neck again, but her thoughts were elsewhere. "Excuse me for a moment," she said. She smiled and kissed him as passionately as she could muster. Both of them were still feeling the effects of the wine from dinner. "I'm going to get comfortable," she said, retreating to the bedroom to pull herself together.

Once she was behind the security of the closed restroom door, Camille continued to unravel. The companion she had so willfully invited to join her didn't even enter her mind. She paced the coffee-colored stone tiled floors, contemplating her next move. Rarely was she so unprepared.

She cracked the door to the bathroom to see what Steve was doing. To her delight, he dozed in and out of sleep on the couch. Not wanting to arouse suspicion, she wanted to wait as long as she could before going back into the living area, calling out to Steve, "I'm coming, babe."

"Take your time," he mumbled.

Camille ran the water, pretending to wash up. Remembering the bottle of wine Steve brought back from the restaurant that was sitting on the table in the living room, she hatched an outrageous plan. She just needed access to the floor surveillance cameras, *easy enough*, she thought.

She opened the dresser drawer, retrieving a terrycloth housecoat, which was neatly folded next to the lavender silk negligée she would have normally adorned for male companions. Still in her dinner clothes, she tightly strapped the housecoat over her black dress. The fuzzy, lounge-around-the-house-alone slippers soothed her aching feet.

Steve, still drifting in and out of sleep, patiently waited for Camille to return. Her attempts at 'not tonight honey, I have a headache' went unnoticed. Steve wasn't dissuaded in the slightest by the robe or the slippers. He had already undressed her a thousand times in his mind since the turbulence stumble on the plane.

The wine was where she remembered. "I'd like some more wine," she told him.

"Let me open it for you," he offered.

"I need some ice first, though," she schemed.

"I should have put it in the fridge," he said. "I'll go get ice."

"Relax, baby," she said, subtly persuading him back into his seat with her gentle touch. "I got this." She grabbed the ice bucket and headed out the door in her housecoat and slippers. "…be right back."

Megan and Curtis had long ago settled in. Megan hadn't given a second thought to their hallway exchange. In fact, she and Curtis were deeply engaged in the pleasures of the night. Camille, on the other hand, allowed herself to be consumed for fear her secret would come to light.

Camille was so delighted to find the surveillance cameras, that she completely forgot about ice. So, when she came back into the room several minutes after leaving with an empty ice bucket, Steve was perplexed, but said nothing. Besides, she had an excuse ready, telling him she couldn't find the ice machine.

He was tired but wanted to please her. Without asking, he took the bucket and ventured out to find ice. Right outside the room, on the opposite wall, there was a sign that pointed to the vending area, which struck Steve as strange, but he let it pass, his mind on more pressing things.

Back in the room Camille hurriedly disrobed, putting on a teddy and retiring to the bed. When Steve returned with the ice, she pretended to be asleep. Steve joined her, pulling back the cover and kissing her on the lips. The taste of her cherry-flavored lip gloss enticed him to do more. She didn't resist.

His lips kissed her neglected thighs, sending shivers over her entire body. She guided his head gently, he didn't oppose. When he was done, she was done too. Then they proceeded to do what two slightly tipsy, extremely tired, sexually charged, consenting adults do in a lavish hotel room in the middle of the night, they fell asleep.

When Camille woke up it was not yet morning. She had calmed down, thinking she knew how she would get dirt on her Australian friend. There was just one small obstacle standing in her way, accessing the hotel's surveillance tapes.

Quiet as a thief, she slipped out of bed, put her clothes on and left the room without waking Steve, who slept soundly. She took her phone and the handheld USB storage device that she kept in her computer case. She made her way to the hotel lobby, where two clerks tended the front desk.

"Good evening ma'am," the tall woman on the left said. "How may we help you?"

"Good evening," Camille said. "I was just wondering if the hotel had surveillance cameras on all the floors?" she asked.

"Yes, ma'am, we do. There are several on each floor," the gentleman that was also at the counter picked up where his co-worker left off. "Is there a problem, ma'am?"

"Well, I'm not sure," she said, a look of concern clouded her face. "When I checked in, I told the lady who helped me that I thought someone was following me." Both clerks nodded, acknowledging her concern. "I think I saw him following me again tonight," she said, fabricating a tale as she spoke, pausing occasionally to think her way through, pretending to be distressed.

"Inside the hotel?" one of them asked.

"Is there anything that can be done about this?" Camille asked.

"We do have hotel security to assist with matters of this nature," the man named Sungi told her, then asked, "Do you know who the man is?"

"I'm not sure," Camille told him.

"If he is following you inside the hotel, we have it on camera," Sungi assured her.

"Is there any way I could look at the surveillance from the sixteenth floor?" Camille asked. "...around eleven o'clock tonight."

"Ma'am, I'm not sure about that, we have to get security involved," Sungi told her.

"Is that really necessary?" she asked. "I prefer not to have that type of attention, especially if I'm mistaken. If you just allow me to look, I can make sure."

Another customer approached the counter as she was talking. The tall lady stepped away to attend to the waiting patron. Camille's impromptu plan wasn't going well. She plopped her head down, resting it on the counter, in pretend torment.

"Are you okay, ma'am?" the man asked, followed by the tall clerk who noticed her leaning down, followed by the customer who the clerk was trying to help.

"This is what I was talking about," Camille said. "I don't want all this attention. Okay, okay, call security please," she relented. "I just need to sit down," she said and walked behind the counter, slumping down in a chair that was in the small room behind the front desk.

Sungi picked up the phone and dialed the extension for hotel security and in no time at all, an average height man with security attire on arrived. His name was Wu. Sungi and Wu bantered back and forth about the situation, giving Camille all the time, she needed to come up with an even better plan.

She overheard the conversation between the tall lady clerk and the customer, and knew that this had to be the clerk Samantha told her about at dinner. There was no way that such a posh establishment would hire two incompetent people to work their front counter. *She must be related to someone important*, Camille thought.

While the two gentlemen tried to figure out how they could help Camille, she told the lady clerk, who was now free, that she had forgotten her room key.

"I'm sorry about that, ma'am. You're just having the worst night ever," the clerk said, snorting an awkward giggle.

Had this been a real crisis, Camille would have been incensed at the inappropriate response, but she was certain that the lady was making her best attempt to help.

"I'm in room sixteen-seventy. Megan Mallory," Camille said. "Remember, you helped my friend Samantha Bogart when she checked in."

Camille went on to describe Samantha, reminding the clerk of the fiasco. And without further hesitation from the panicky clerk, Camille had in her possession the key to Megan's room.

The two gentlemen turned their attention back to Camille. "Ma'am, this is Wu, the head of hotel security here at the Sands. He'll be glad to assist you," Sungi said.

"Good evening, ma'am. Sungi was just telling me about your concerns. I'll be glad to help you," Wu said.

Camille, no longer needing them, shook the men's hands, thanked them for their help, and thanked the tall lady clerk too. She placed her hand on her forehead, in phony anguish and told them that she was just too distraught over the whole matter to deal with it any longer tonight, that she needed to return to her room to get some rest.

She asked if she could meet with Wu at a later time. Wu offered to escort her, but she declined. Instead she agreed to phone him once she was safe in her room. Camille turned toward the elevator in retreat. Once back in her room she put

Megan's key in the side pocket of her luggage for safe keeping. She got in the bed beside Steve and fell comfortably asleep.

When daylight broke, Steve awoke to a room smelling of freshly baked muffins, eggs, bacon and a table filled with strawberries, blueberries, yogurt, water and coffee. On the counter, next to the tray of cooked foods, Camille purposely placed her wallet, openly displaying the photo of Sammy.

Steve stepped out of the bedroom, after brushing his teeth and gargling a capful of the mouthwash he found in the restroom. He was greeted by Camille who stood behind the kitchenette counter wearing nothing but earrings.

His hands caressed her entire body eagerly, rubbing her legs first, moving upward to her hips, her stomach and then her breasts. He gently fondled her nipples causing them to stand erect. His lips traced the steps that his hand had taken as she turned around to face him. Their eyes connected only briefly before he continued his lip dance on her body.

His head was positioned in her gap once again. She slid her finger into his mouth, wanting to feel his tongue that had yet to make an appearance. The heat and moisture awakened nerves that needed attention. She helped guide his head, while he propped one of her legs on his shoulder. The counter was her brace. Feverishly, he devoured her.

The tension Steve felt had grown in intensity since they met. Between breaths, he asked if she liked his performance. She uttered no words, only moans that in a matter of moments turned into shaking and sighs of uncontrolled ecstasy.

She tried to return the gesture, but he stopped her, opting for something better. She jumped on the counter with his help. They kissed passionately as they became one. A duet of pleasure poured from them both as she grabbed him firmly, his thrusting, sending her into a tailspin. Explosions of pent-up frustrations were released within minutes, as they both exhaled.

Her pleasure, aside from his prowess, came from the certainty that he was now hers. She retreated to the restroom to tidy up before returning to the table to eat breakfast. While she was away, Steve warmed up the food, noticing the perfectly placed photo she intended for him to see.

"Camille," he called from the kitchenette. The running water prevented her from hearing him. The semblance was so striking that he carried her wallet into the bathroom. "Camille," he said again.

As she stepped out the shower she responded, "Yes."

"Who is this little girl? She looks so much like you."

"…that's because she's my daughter," she told him.

Shocked and confused, he questioned, "I thought you said you didn't have children?"

"It's not exactly something I talk about," she responded.

"Okay, now I'm really confused," he said.

"Let me explain."

Shame made itself at home, cloaking her with sadness long before the fabricated words formed in her mouth. Camille had rehearsed what she would say to him many times during the night. She began with the truth.

"Her name is Sammy. She lives in New York with her father," embellishing as she proceeded. "Her father is my best friend. He asked me if I would be his surrogate, having exhausted all other avenues. It didn't exactly help his chances being single, black, gay, and a man. Adoption agencies wouldn't even return his calls."

Steven's stance softened.

"It was nearly impossible for him," she pleaded. "So, I agreed to have his baby."

Sensing his stunned acceptance, Camille keenly directed the discussion away from her daughter, speaking on more newsworthy topics, conversation sure to impress him.

NINETEEN

....

out on a limb

SINGAPORE is hot and humid year-round, which is perfect for margaritas by the pool and air conditioning, but not so good for stakeouts or women whose hair danced wildly at the slightest hint of moisture.

It's hot as hell on this balcony. What was I thinking? I'm getting outta here, but I can't leave. I have to get something on Megan. No one threatens me without consequences, all thoughts of a desperate woman.

It was approaching eighty degrees, and forecasts called for it to get even hotter. The temperature wasn't the worst part, though. The humidity made the otherwise amazing view from the balcony, unbearable and caused Camille's hair to frizz like a frightened blowfish. This made her all the more irritated and determined.

She hadn't completely thought this one through, though. Her only comfort was the cushioned patio furniture that she sat on, waiting. As morning dragged into afternoon, beads of sweat danced on her back like drunken concertgoers bobbing to their favorite songs.

From sixteen stories up you could see for miles on a clear day. She tried to concentrate on the scenery around her and the crowds that gathered on the streets below.

What was the plan? To wait on Megan, for the uncertain possibility that Curtis might come back to the room with her, today. And maybe they would cuddle or more. *I could snap a picture from my position on the balcony. But what if they come out here*, she thought. She and Steve had made love on the balcony, and from what she had come to know about Megan, the balcony was a real possibility. What would she do then?

Was it the heat or was one of the women she saw at the fabric market from sixteen stories up Megan? It had to be. No one she had ever met before had that same blazing red hair. Camille had to make up her mind, especially if the woman she saw was Megan. *What if I wait under the bed*, she thought? *That would be uncomfortable*. But she was far from comfortable now, out on the balcony.

She thought about calling Tania. But the time difference meant Tania was probably sleep. Besides, she couldn't really tell her what she was doing. It would mean having to tell her about Sammy. Something she was unwilling to do. She knew no one would support her, even knowing the full story.

She could hear Maria's voice, *girrrrl, get off that damn balcony!* *Have you completely lost your damn mind?* Camille laughed at herself, at the sweat streaming all over her body, at her hair that was flat when she left her room this morning but could now pass for Roseanne Roseannadanna's. Surely, she smelled a lot worse than she looked.

As she pulled the sliding-glass door open to surrender her balcony stakeout, there was a knock on the door. Camille stumbled. *Megan wouldn't knock on her own door*, she reasoned.

"Housekeeping," a voice called out from the hallway, then another knock. "House...oh Miss, I was just about to clean your room," Camille heard the housekeeper say.

"OH SHIT!" Camille said, under her breath.

But she had just seen Megan at the market. Camille ran to the door that connected Megan's room to the adjoining room. She quietly opened the first door, then tried the other. It was locked. It's possible that she started sweating more now than she had been out on the balcony. She could hear a faint reply but not enough to make out anything, the other voice mumbling something undecipherable.

"Yes ma'am, extra towels?" the housekeeper said.

Camille looked out at the balcony doors but decided against going back out there. She gathered herself and quickly elbow-inched her way under the king-sized bed. When the door opened Camille stopped breathing. She could hear footsteps traipsing across the floor. She didn't move. The water came on in the bathroom. Camille took a breath. Moments later the room was quiet again except for the footsteps. She heard a door open and then another one right away.

"Got it," the other voice said, off in the distance.

"Good, Miss," the housekeeper said. "I'll clean your room now and leave you some extra towels."

"Thank you," the other voice said.

Camille could hear a door close but nothing else. She took short quick breaths. Slowly she crawled from under the bed and peeped to see what was going on. Nobody was in the room with her. She heard the housekeeper singing in the adjacent bedroom, which allowed for her escape.

As she was leaving, she noticed Megan's clothes hanging in the closet near the entrance. She took the sleeves of the lightest colored silk shirt she could find and thoroughly wiped as much sweat as she could from her body. With that, Camille gave up the idea that she would ever get revenge.

Later, when Megan would find the stains, she would blame them on her kids.

Fall turned into spring and life was going well for Camille. Before he left, she wound up hanging out with J.R., the hound from the plane. No true southern girl would ever pass up a chance to go to a free destination wedding, especially one that was three days long.

Once J.R. relaxed, she actually found him interesting, thanking him in her own southern way and promising to keep in touch with him when she returned to the states. In fact, Jason helped her find a rental. The quaint two-bedroom home she moved into belonged to the bride's aunt. At a bargain price, it was the perfect size and location, just blocks from work.

She and Steve spent as much time together as they could. When she finally told him that he was her boss they thought it best to keep their relationship private, going as far as just greeting one another if by chance their paths crossed at work.

Steve knew that he had found his wife. Camille, however, was not on the same page. One thing plagued her. Since that night in the hotel when she told Steve that she was Sammy's surrogate, she had been riddled with guilt. It was rare for her to feel this way, but every time she felt overwhelmed with emotion for him, it would immediately be followed by anguish and shame at how easily she denied the one person she loved more than anything in the world.

That's how she knew they could never be together. That one reason alone. She could never tell him she had lied about her baby girl. And even if she could have gathered the courage to out herself, he would have never looked at her the same way again, and that was something she simply couldn't bear.

Sammy's birthday was on Saturday and Camille wasn't sure when John would call. She told Steve that she couldn't see him, that she had to catch up with work. He joked about being the boss, that he could extend her deadlines. He laughed, but she was not amused by his humor.

"What's going on, Camille?" he asked, sensing something was wrong, that something was different.

"Nothing, bae." She never called him that. She hated the word.

"Now I know something's wrong!" he laughed.

"Steve, everything is fine," she assured, before hanging up the phone.

When Saturday came, Steve had made it up in his mind that they were going to see each other. It had almost been a week. Camille needed a break from the roller coaster of emotions that happened every time she was around him. The ecstasy. The guilt. Euphoria. Guilt. Bliss. Guilt. Every single time.

Camille decided to veg out around the house all day, reading and catching up on Netflix until she heard from John. When Steve texted her at noon, she ignored him, which made him more anxious.

"Hello!" he texted again.

She ignored him. Then her phone rang. She thought it was John. But it was Steve. She couldn't believe he was sweating her like this. She ignored him again. When he called back again, she answered.

"What is going on?" she said, annoyed.

"Hello to you, too," he said.

"What's up, Steve?"

"I want to see you, baby."

"That's so sweet, Steve," she said and really meant it. She sighed and paused briefly before continuing, "Look, I'm not trying to be funny, but I already told you that I had work to catch up on and that I couldn't see you."

"What's wrong with you?" he probed.

"No, what is wrong with you? You act like you can't hear me or aren't listening, or worse, ignoring me. You're not acting like…"

"Like what?"

"Like a CEO."

"What are you trying to say?"

"I said it," she told him matter-of-factly. "I've been running around here working, cooking, sexing, conferencing, emailing, every-womaning it for a solid six months. I ask for one day to my freaking self and you act like it's the end of the world!"

"Wow! Really?"

"Really! I'll call you tomorrow," she said and hung up. Soon as she hung up her phone rang again. She was disgusted until she saw it was her sister. "Hey, baby girl," Camille said.

Tania was not cheerful at all. "Hi, Camille."

"Ok, what's the bad mood all about?"

Tania sighed deeply. "I really hate to be doing this over the phone, but…"

"Doing this over the phone – is Mom okay?"

"Mom is fine, considering."

"What's wrong with Mom? What do you mean considering?"

"MOM IS FINE! It's Dad."

"Oh girl, you scared me. Dad will be fine."

"Camille…" Tania's voice cracked trying to hold back tears.

"Are you crying? What's going on, Tania?"

"Camille, you need to come home!"

Mr. Young had been sick for a long time and hadn't told a soul. He was even able to keep it from his wife, who knew him better than anyone else in the world. When she questioned him, he always dismissed her as being foolish or overly protective or paranoid.

He couldn't dismiss her anymore. He was in the hospital and this time he would not be going home. He was the typical man, too proud to go to the doctor to get his prostate checked. So, when he started going to the bathroom frequently at night, and then could barely urinate when he did go, he knew something was wrong, but just thought it was his sugar. He didn't even go to the VA when he saw blood in his urine.

The funny thing, if there can be anything funny about this, is the reason he was persuaded to go to the doctor was because he started having painful ejaculations. Isn't that just typical? By this time, his cancer was in its final stages, nothing could be done.

He was prescribed pain medication which caused him to sleep a lot more than usual. He slowed down some, taking longer to do normal stuff, but he still told his wife he was fine, *just getting old*, he would tell her.

He didn't ever ask the doctor how long he had. *How the hell would he know anyway*, is how Mr. Young felt about it. Besides he didn't care. He made up in his mind that he would make the most of the time he had left, however long that might be.

He spent his days contacting old friends that he hadn't spoken to in ages. He even called his cousin Earl, who owed him ten thousand dollars from a business deal that went south thirty years ago.

He thought about all the women he had been with, and all his cheating, lying ways. He thought about his wife and how he was the luckiest man in the world to have been loved by her.

His parents had died many years ago, but he was from good stock – seamstress mother and mechanic father. All he knew was how to work hard and provide for his family, so that's what he did.

He prayed for the first time since his mother's death. He didn't know if he even believed in God or not, but he asked for Him to watch over his family anyway, when he was gone. He asked for forgiveness for the people he had hurt, mostly, his daughter Camille.

He never understood why he treated her the way he did, and not until this very moment, had he ever thought to apologize. An apology required accepting blame, and blame wasn't something he was willing to accept before now.

One day it was like his heart just opened up and he was able to see things clearer than ever before. All this time he thought his wife had known who he was, about his cheating and all. He thought for sure Camille had told her, especially when his wife stopped leaving the child home with him. He was certain that Mrs. Young was just overlooking his behavior. If she had known, she never let on.

All this time and nothing ever changed between them. Lynn hadn't said anything or acted differently, or maybe he had been too selfish to notice or care. When the light came on inside, he saw his wife. He really saw her and saw things as they really were, for the first time in his life. And he knew instantly, in that moment, that her soul had never been touched by knowing what he had done.

What he felt was real, tangible, though he couldn't have explained any of it, if he had to. Like how he was changed when he found out that his wife, then fiancé, had been with another man while he was away in the military. Like when he found out she was pregnant, and it wasn't his child. But he loved her so much that he married her anyway, even though he could never erase or change what had happened, his soul had been altered forever.

Lynn always told him that he was different somehow when he came back home. She blamed it on the military. He didn't know then what she meant. He just thought she was being emotional.

All this time, Lynn hadn't known. Camille never said a word. He began to cry. He cried for his family, but more than that, he cried for his baby girl, for all the things he had put her through, the things a little girl's eyes should never have seen.

For the first time as a grown man, he cried. He cried so much that he almost cried the life right on out of him. It was a soul cry. One that went right down in the pit of his stomach and pulled all his guts, and animosity, and hate, and regret right out.

He fell down on his knees right where he stood and stretched his hands in the air and yelled with the power of all that stuff that came up from down in him.

"THANK YOU, LORD!" he cried. This was the moment, the first time he knew that God was real.

That day Lynn rushed home. For some reason she just had to get to the house. When she got there, he was laid out on the floor in their bedroom, smiling. She hadn't seen him smile like that since before they were married. She whispered in his ear after calling the ambulance, "God's been in this place." And she was right.

Every day Richard felt life leaving him, though he was more alive than ever before. He was waiting to see Camille. Struggling, he asked Lynn, "When will Camille get here?"

Lynn looked to Tania for an answer.

"I spoke to her Tuesday. She said she would be home as soon as she could," Tania told her mother.

"Chile, it's Thursday. Nothing since Tuesday?" Lynn admonished.

"She texted me and said she had to tie up some loose ends before she could leave, she's waiting until someone can replace her, you know, help her clients and all that stuff."

As Mr. Young drifted in and out of consciousness, Lynn pulled their youngest daughter out into the hallway. Quietly she asked, "Did you tell her? Does she know he's dying?"

"Mom, I told her she needed to hurry home."

"Did you tell her why, child?"

"I told her Dad was very sick."

"When I tried to call her, she didn't answer, just texted me her flight arrangements. That was Monday night," Lynn said.

"She should be here soon?" Tania said, trying to comfort her mother.

"I hope so," her mother said, holding back tears.

They returned to the room where Mr. Young appeared to be resting peacefully. Mrs. Young opened her bible and started reading John 3:16 aloud. She must have read it ten times at least. When Mr. Young came to, the first words he murmured were, "...so loved the world." Then he passed back out again.

TWENTY

....

abrupt endings

YOU know that anxious feeling when something is wrong, and no one is telling you exactly what's going on? When you can't really think straight and don't know your left from your right? Camille didn't feel that after speaking to her sister that night, but she should have.

For one, she didn't have time. She knew her mother and sister needed her to be strong for them, like she'd always been. Plus, she had to schedule an emergency meeting with her clients and find someone to take over. As soon as she got off the phone with Tania, she called Jill.

She had never been in this situation before – needing a backup – so she hadn't planned for it. But she knew that Jill knew everybody. And Jill's everybody might know somebody that could do what Camille did and drop everything to come to Singapore.

As she was telling Jill about her family situation and describing what was required of the potential replacement, the doorbell rang. She knew it was Steve and was so glad she hadn't given him a key. She waited until she finished her conversation with Jill before she answered the door. He didn't call first, and with all that was going on, Camille was furious.

Jill offered words of comfort for Camille regarding her father and vowed to find someone. As soon as they got off the phone Jill called fifteen people, but no luck. Her husband just so happened to walk in on the tail end of her sixteenth call and told her that he might know someone who could help.

Camille unlocked the door for Steve without even a hello. She still hadn't spoken to her baby girl yet on her birthday and when it crossed her mind, it made her even more pissed at Steve for being so inconsiderate.

He walked through the open door, not quite sure what to say. He hadn't met this Camille before. "Did I do something wrong?" he asked, speaking to her back as she walked from the front door into the living room.

"Steve, I really don't have the time or energy to deal with this right now."

"Deal with what?" he questioned.

"You, too," she said. "You just disregarded everything I said."

"I'm sorry. I just thought…"

She interrupted, "That was your mistake."

"I love you, Camille. I just wanted to see you."

"Steve, that is the most controlling thing I've ever heard," she told him. "I'm not one of your acquisitions. When I say I can't see you, I mean it!" she exclaimed, with her back still to him. "So, goodbye!"

"...are you saying you don't love me?" he asked.

"Huh? No! I don't love you," she said coldly. "Not like that. I never told you that." She was telling the truth. In fact, neither one of them had ever said 'I love you' before.

"What did you think we were doing? I told you that you were the first woman I ever thought about as wife material. You said the same thing to me."

That was also true. She had said it, but they obviously didn't mean the same thing. He meant it literally. She was speaking figuratively, an on-paper husband.

"I didn't mean it how you took it," she told him.

"How else could it be taken?" he wondered aloud.

He stood at the door confused and hurt. She took a deep breath. The stress had gotten to her. She turned to him for the first time that night, as she walked back toward the door and told him everything that was going on with her father. She apologized for her glib behavior and assured him that they would talk in person before she left.

He felt foolish now and couldn't stop apologizing. They hugged one another, kissing before he left. All she could think of, even as he held her, was her baby girl and how she wished she were there in her arms. She started to cry, prodding him tenderly out the door. She shut and secured the door, deciding she wasn't going to wait for John to call her. The phone rang several times without an answer. She waited briefly before calling back. After the fifth call, a groggy John finally answered.

"Hello, Camille. Is everything okay?"

"No," she stuttered. "I need to talk to Sammy." John knew Camille and didn't bother asking her what was going on before waking their daughter from her nap.

"Mommy's on the phone," he said, as he shook the sleeping child. "Wake up, Mommy is on the phone," he repeated.

"Mommy," she squealed, half sleep. "I lub you, Mommy!"

"I love you more. Happy Birthday, baby girl! I miss you so much!" Camille said, trying to not let the child hear her crying. "Did you get your presents?" she forced out through the tears.

"Yes, mommy. My bear is right here. Can you see her, Mommy?" They weren't on video, but John took the phone from the child and told Camille that he would call her right back.

"Hi, Mommy. See Mommy. Her name is Free."

"Free? Why did you name her Free, Sammy?"

"Well, Daddy said that I was free to growed up and be whatever I want to be. She can too, Mommy."

"That's right, baby. That's right."

Just in that moment Camille thought about the lie she told Steve, crying like her lie had been uncovered. She told John and Sammy that she was losing her signal before hanging up, but not before telling her child how much she loved her, again.

When Camille regained her composure, she called John back and told him that she had met someone she really liked. He kept silent while she spoke. Then she told him that she didn't think it could work. He asked why.

Ashamed, she confessed that she had lied to Steve about her relationship to Sammy. John was deeply saddened by her candor. Nonetheless, he listened to his friend as she shared her truth. And although he didn't understand, he didn't chastise or belittle her, not once. He just listened, exactly what she needed.

"Camille, you won't know until you tell him the truth," John told her. "Look baby, I know it's not easy, but you have to tell him the truth. You have nothing if you don't have truth."

"He'll never look at me the same," she said. That was something she needed, the look she never got from her daddy.

"Maybe not, but you'll never look at yourself the same if you don't tell him."

She agreed. Even so she didn't know how she would do it. They sat on the phone, their daughter's fourth birthday, Camille in Singapore, John in the States, and they prayed for each other and for their child. After they hung up, he continued to pray for his daughter's mother, the woman he loved, still. That's all he knew to do.

Camille's tears helped her fall asleep. She cried because she missed her baby, and for John and what she had done to him. She cried for her mother and sister, what they were going through. She cried for herself and the heaviness of the guilt that weighed on her like a monkey on her back. She had forgotten to tell John about her father. And unconsciously she hoped that her father would be all right, which made her cry some more.

The next morning, she woke up early. Her mind drifted from one thing to another. The pressure was an uncomfortable companion.

"Steve, call me when you wake up," she texted him first.

Then she cooked breakfast and booked her flight home three days out. Her clients were responding to her site posts throughout the night. She was just waiting to see if she'd hear from Jill so she could tie up her business obligations.

As luck would have it, Jill's cousin-in-law-ish Alice Dooger offered the help Camille needed. Alice's stepson was deaf, and she could sign with the best of them. She spoke fluent Spanish but couldn't read a lick of braille if her life counted on it.

Alice had been a housewife for ten years and recently divorced her husband Frank, who decided he wanted to be Francis now. Alice didn't even wait to hear the offer before screaming 'YES' to Singapore.

When they spoke, Camille meticulously detailed what was required, offering to make herself as available as possible, considering the circumstances. Alice understood she would be needed for a minimum of twelve months and was comfortable with that. The deal included the prorated salary, perks and even the house that Camille was renting which was paid up for two years. Alice was on a flight that evening which gave Camille time before she departed to show Alice the ropes and to introduce her to the clients and the employer.

Camille had been up for at least two hours when Steve called. They arranged to meet for lunch at a café close to where she stayed. As she dressed, she rehearsed her lines. *Steve, I lied to you and I need to confess. No, that's too harsh. Steve, I have to clear some things up before I leave. That's not good either. Steve, I'm sorry.* This was a good starting place, but she knew he would ask what she was sorry about.

He would tell her it was all his fault and just like that she would be back to where they started, Camille trying to figure out what to say and where to begin. She was still rehearsing when he walked up behind her in the restaurant.

"Hi baby," he said, kissing her.

"Hi handsome," she replied.

"You look delicious," he told her.

He knew how to make her smile. *If only they had met under different circumstances*, she thought. A common sentiment for someone intent on ending things.

They talked and ate, and it all seemed like things were back to normal. Her body craved his touch. A wanting that he also shared. And even though she was alone in the knowledge that this would be their last indulgence, she relented to their common desire.

When they made it back to her rental, he kissed the entirety of her body like he had unearthed an heirloom, starting at her toes, suckling them like they were his favorite flavored lollipops, ending with nibbles on her earlobes. She breathed deeply, trying to join herself to this moment for eternity, wanting to slap the person who coined the phrase 'all good things must come to an end.'

Her lips wanted to feel him. His body was strong and smooth, the perfect specimen. A kiss on the neck drove him crazy, so that's where she began.

The floor next to the couch is as far as they could make it, but who was taking notes. Her hand touched him first and he was ready. She moved slowly down to where her hand was and began to mimic with her lips, the same motion that her hand was making, until he could no longer hold on. He stopped her, gently assisting her body on top of his, standing up, holding her tightly, skin to skin.

The wall near the bathroom became their home. They moved in unison with like pleasure. He forced himself to wait on her. Her quivering body was his signal to let go. Weak with pleasure they fell to the floor, right there, next to the bathroom. They held each other and drifted off to sleep.

It was still light outside when they awoke.

"I really missed you," he spoke softly before kissing her on the cheek.

"I know it doesn't seem like it, but I missed you too," she told him.

She returned his kiss and hugged him tightly. After tidying themselves, Camille pulled Steve to the couch and told him that they needed to talk. Men hate it when women say this. Steve was no different, but you couldn't tell.

"There's something I really need to tell you…things I need to clear up, that I wasn't exactly truthful about." She took a deep breath and thought about what John said. She knew he was right. But somehow when she started to talk, what came out her mouth wasn't what they had discussed.

"I kind of planned…," and she paused.

"Planned what?" Steve questioned.

"Let me start over," she said.

"No problem."

"I knew who you were before we met on the plane, about your company and the Singapore launch," she announced before she lost the courage.

He looked confused, and for the first time since their flight, he recalled the brochure that he saw hanging from her bag. "How?" he asked her.

"It's my job to know."

"I thought you were a translator."

"I am, but there's more to it than just translating," she admitted.

"Stalking?" he said. His face, now displaying the very look she wanted to avoid, and she knew telling him about Sammy was out of the question.

"Really? Is that what you think?" she asked, hurt by his response.

"What would you think, Camille?"

He doesn't really want to know, I'm trying to spare your feelings, she thought. *Or, I didn't have to tell you a damn thing.* She got mad at

John. Then mad at herself. Then she decided to come up with a different lie, one to make herself seem less crazy.

She told him that she read about him and his company in a business journal, which was true. And that BisCom was a company she wanted on her résumé. That a mutual friend introduced her to one of his executives, and everything else that happened was just opportunity and luck. That's how she retold the story, which put him at ease. He apologized for doubting her, but it was too late. Unfortunately, she would use his comments against him.

"This can't work. We can't work," she told him.

"WHAT?" Steve didn't understand what he had done, why Camille was acting this way. He just wanted to see her, to be with her. Before this weekend he knew she felt the same way. But now, he was sure she hated him.

"You doubt my intentions?" she told him.

"Did I say that?"

"Yes. In so many words," she replied.

"What words?" he questioned.

"You called me a stalker. And then that look."

"What? What look?"

"The way you looked at me."

"I'm sorry. I misunderstood. But you explained it," he said.

"I shouldn't have had to explain anything!" she told him.

"I can't believe you're acting like this," he said.

"You can't believe me!" she exclaimed. "I can't believe you!"

"Are you serious? Are you being serious right now?" he questioned.

"Now you take me as a joke!" she exclaimed.

"No, that's not...you're getting me all wrong," he said, trying to make her understand, but it wouldn't have mattered if he had done and said all the right things, nothing would have been right in her eyes. It couldn't be, not with him, not now, not ever.

"Steve, I just have so much going on, and then this on top of all the other stuff. It's too much!" she told him coldly.

"What are you saying, Camille?"

"I can't handle my dad, the mistrust, the distance. I don't know when I'll be back or if I'm ever coming back," she said trying to let him down easy.

"Wait...are you breaking up with me?" he asked.

He was disgusted and confused. She decided it would be best for him to leave. He hesitantly conceded, retreating in defeat.

And that was how their relationship ended – punctuated and abrupt.

Steve tried to contact Camille numerous times afterwards, checking on her father and wanting to see how she was doing. She never answered his calls, only texting with the basic, 'everything is fine' or 'hope you are well' brush-offs.

After several months, Steve gave up.

TWENTY-ONE

....

farewell singapore

THERE'S a certain confidence accompanying youth that flounders with age – falsely thinking we know everything, that we're invincible.

Camille was young.

If she could have seen her father, she would have believed he was dying. Instead, she thought he would be fine, like all the other times he had gone into the hospital, like all the previous texts and calls from Tania and her mother.

Or maybe she was thinking about her clients, about Steve, that's why she was reluctant to leave Singapore. Because although she had found someone to fill in in her absence, she thought it was bad business to abandon her clients, especially since she had just dumped one of the company founders for no reason at all.

The flight she told her sister she had booked, left Singapore yesterday without her. Back home her dad pleaded with God for more time. He wanted to see his baby girl, to tell her how much he loved her, to apologize for his short comings.

"I missed my flight," she texted John.

"You what? That's not like you. Call me if you can," he texted back.

"I didn't think you would be up. Okay give me a minute," she texted, freshening up a little just in case he wanted to video chat. He answered the phone on the first ring. "Why are you up?" she asked him. "How's Sammy?"

"I have a big case I'm prepping for," he told her. "She's sound asleep and growing leaps and bounds."

"I miss y'all," she said, something she neglected to say days earlier.

He snickered. "Y'all...haven't heard you say that since college."

"Oh be quiet," Camille said, and laughed at herself. He was right. "I'm sorry to disturb you. It's not important. We can talk later."

"You only say 'y'all' when something is wrong. I needed to take a break, anyway. Besides, I wanted to know why you missed your flight. What's going on, Camille?"

"I hate to come all the way back to the States for nothing."

"Has your sister ever sounded this worried before?" he asked.

"No…yes…no. I don't know," she said, unsure.

"That's why you have to go, because you don't know. Whatever it is, whatever happened between you and your father, aside from abuse, you have to put it behind you, if only until he gets out of the hospital, if he gets out. He has to meet Sammy."

"What?"

"She's never met anyone in your family, just Maria."

"I don't think this is a good time," Camille told him.

"There's never a good time," he told her. "Stop through and pick up Sammy. My case should conclude tomorrow, else I'd offer to tag along. You really should take her to meet her grandpa," John insisted. "I'm getting ready to book your flights now."

"John, you don't have to do that."

"I know I don't have to, I want to," he insisted.

Camille was fraught. Of course she couldn't tell John that her family didn't know about Sammy. He had no idea, couldn't fathom that a woman of her achievement and intellect could be so overwhelmed by the fear of disappointing her family. So before hanging up she agreed to his urging.

"We'll see you tomorrow," he said.

"Okay, I'll see y'all tomorrow. Thank you, John."

"Sammy is going to love spending time with you and your family," he said before hanging up.

Restless, Camille stared at the ceiling. It was 4:00 a.m. She was waiting for the alarm to sound. As her eyes traced a small crack, she plotted how she would avoid taking Sammy with her. Scanning the room, she spotted a cobweb that swung from the far wall to the light gray accent wall, the spider long gone, dust collecting along the web's straggly droop.

Troubled, she looked at the dresser that sat between the only windows in the room. The top drawer left open just so. She thought of John, how he never quite pushed the drawers completely shut. She smiled.

No use going back to sleep now, her flight was at 9:00 a.m. The phone on the nightstand commanded her attention. She had twenty-five unread emails and three texts. She clicked the emails first, but didn't bother reading any of the new ones, instead clicking on the one that Samantha sent her last week, the one she skimmed over at work, pictures of their outings.

This time she looked more closely, thinking about her relationship – Steven throwing her in the pool, the girls posing in front of the theater, the hotel, the squid that looked alive that she ate on a dare, the waves slamming against the beach.

And then there it was, the picture she had missed the first time, the picture of her and Steve walking in the marketplace, she in her canary yellow halter-dress and espadrilles, he in his linen shorts and top. They were as happy as the sun, pure bliss.

She didn't know it, but that was the day Steve knew he wanted to be with her forever. Anyone looking could see that he adored her, how his eyes smiled without smiling, his hand embracing hers, taut and secure. As for her part, she knew that he made her giddy, like a child. And she had only felt that with one other man, John. The more she looked at the picture the more she was flooded with regret.

Her eyes widened as disappointment quickly turned into jubilation, jogged out of her Steve trance by a chance snap of the camera. As she stared, she enlarged the picture with her fingers. The shot worth a thousand words – Megan and Curtis walking directly behind her and Steve, locked in a lover's embrace, lips plastered, one to the other, his hand cupping her butt.

Camille jumped from the bed, as if startled by a bug, looking at the photo again, ensuring she had seen what she thought she saw. *I've got her now*, she thought, *I've got her now.*

The excitement of the discovery took her mind off the trip home. She showered, double checked the house for all her belongings, booked an Uber and departed for the airport. It was 6:00 a.m.

She fumbled through more emails, responding only to the urgent ones. Then she read her texts. One was from Maria, who she had texted to see if she could keep Sammy. Maria responding, "I'm on the other side of the world and won't be available," which meant she was booed up.

The second one was from her sister, Tania, who wanted an update as to when she would be arriving. Camille replying, "Saturday afternoon, and I have a big surprise… :-)."

The third text was from John. He texted to let her know about their dinner plans Friday night. "I know you will be tired, but one of the partners is having a surprise party for his wife. I committed weeks ago."

Camille was always down for a good dinner party. And John had influential friends, the networking would be a bonus.

The twenty-hour flight from Singapore to New York was uneventful. Camille texted John as soon as the plane landed. "I'm already here," he responded. In fact, he had parked and made his way to baggage claims, where he waited.

When he saw her from behind, hair pulled in a ponytail on the top of her head, torn & rolled up stonewashed jeans, a white t-shirt that read 'don't even think about it' in bold black letters on her back, and a pair of pink high-top converse tennis shoes, he knew it was her, her contour etched in his mind. An unconscious shimmer invaded his face as he called out to her, eager and wistful. They hadn't seen each other since Kittery, well over a year ago now.

Grabbing her bags as they rounded the carousel, she turned to face him. He was as handsome as she remembered, smooth dark chocolate.

She quietly admired the way his jeans adorned his frame, touching his chestnut Wallabees without creasing. A lightweight cardigan opened to expose a long sleeve polo that hung untucked, slightly longer than his sweater. Although it was chilly, the sun was bright which explained the shades. His hair was cut close all over, which was a new look, but she liked it.

As they embraced, a million unspoken thoughts bombarded the both of them. *I missed her. Why did you leave? Why did I leave? I'm such a coward. Does my cologne still smell good? You smell delicious! Steve who.*

She was surprised by the influx of emotions, just as happy to see him as he was to see her. When they finally released one another she asked abruptly, "Where's Sammy?" Her heart pounding with anxious anticipation.

"Good to see you too," John said sarcastically. "She was sleep. Ms. Monroe is at the house with her. Here, take my sweater," he offered. "It's cold outside," he said draping the sweater over her shoulders.

"Oh, please, get over yourself," she said in her Joan Rivers voice, and they laughed as he loaded her bags in the trunk.

"Camille Young," he said, opening her door.

"Why do you insist on calling me by my full government name?" she asked in jest.

They laughed again but she was telling the truth. Every time they went a while without speaking or if they were arguing or if things were awkward or if he was trying to get his point across, he would always call her full name.

"It's just good to see you," he said, beaming. "Just really good to see you again."

She could feel the tension mounting, so she started talking about any and everything except the one thing that was on his mind. And although she missed him too, the life they had built, the family they had, she didn't want to think about all that in this moment. Those memories were of little consequence to the life she had now.

"I wish you could go with us," she told him, fibbing. She didn't want either one of them going with her, it would be too emotional, too much to explain.

"I do too," he said. As they drove, John flooded her with talk of Sammy. "She's so smart, Camille. Her best friend is a little guy down the hall named Adam. We already know he's going to be gay, but that's alright. We read a book every week and sometimes two. She has three favorite colors. You'll know what they are as soon as you see her. She likes to wear flip flops all the time just like you, but I don't let her. I didn't tell her you were coming. She would've been so excited that I wouldn't have gotten anything done. She goes to one of the best schools, you'd love her teachers."

His excitement was palpable. Camille loved how much John loved their daughter, a feeling Camille never felt from her own father.

"John," she called his name, and placed her hand on his leg. He turned to look at her, their eyes meeting for the first time since Kittery. "Thank you," she told him.

"She's my baby girl, Camille."

She thanked him for all the things said and unsaid, all the secrets that remained. She thanked him for being a real man, when she was still acting on circumstances created before she was ever born. She thanked him for never turning their daughter against her. And to break the tension, she thanked him for smelling so damn good.

"Do you mind pulling over?" she asked him.

"Right now?" he questioned.

"Yes, please."

He found the safest spot and exited. While the vehicle slowly rolled to a stop, Camille climbed to her knees and reached her hand between his legs, her eyes focused dead on his. His chivalry, the way he smelled, his kindness, his forgiveness, all excited her.

His hands reunited with her skin, his lips to her neck. They unzipped each other's pants. Reaching his hand between her legs, he felt her warmth, her wetness, and knew she was still his. She wanted everything he had to give but gently persuaded him back onto his seat. His eyes were full of wonder, his body stiff and excited. Their lips mingled with passion as she 'thanked' him once again.

TWENTY-TWO

....

sammy

JOHN pulled into a parking space, the garage in the high-rise was nearing capacity, only because most people used the subway or walked wherever they went. As he removed the keys from the ignition, Camille faintly heard him announce their arrival.

She took a deep breath, too nervous to say anything. She reached in her oversized purse and pulled out a small box covered in Elmo wrapping paper, Sammy's favorite character the last time she saw her daughter. Enclosed in the package was a handmade cloth doll that she found at the marketplace in Singapore. Its hair, shoulder length and wavy, just like Sammy's.

The doll had on a chef's apron, white paint splattered on its face and hair, resembling flour. Camille bought it because she remembered how Sammy loved to watch her cook, even helping when allowed. One time when Camille had run to the restroom, leaving Sammy in the kitchen, she returned to a child and floor covered in flour. Camille could do nothing but laugh.

Sitting in the car, frozen, Camille looked to John for comfort. Always the gentleman, he opened the door for her to get out before retrieving the luggage from the trunk. He gave her a hug, sensing her anxiety.

She disguised her remorseful tears in his chest, holding him tight, wishing she could have a do-over, a chance to right the mistakes made in foolish contemplation, to make a different choice. But, of course, all she had was now. She only hoped that she hadn't done irrevocable harm to her daughter. Before letting go of John she offered her apologies. Recognizing a sincere heart, he accepted with a nod.

Camille followed John to the front door at a sluggard's pace, mind racing, heart pounding.

"It'll be fine," he assured her.

He opened the door and it felt like she walked smack dab into the home they shared in Kittery – the couch, the Ghanaian afghan, the pictures scattered about of them as a family – and she was comforted. Ms. Monroe sat reading a book at the dining table.

"Ms. Camille," she said and got up to give Camille a hug. "It's so good to meet you in person."

"Same to you, Ms. Monroe. Thank you so much for taking care of my baby," Camille said.

"The pleasure's all mine. She's the sweetest child."

John stood back and watched the two ladies gabble. It was still early. "Is Sammy sleep?" he asked.

"Yes, but she woke up. She had a dream and was calling for you Ms. Camille. Almost like she knew you were coming."

"Oh Lord!" Camille cried out in agony. "Where is she?"

John took Camille by the hand and led her down the hallway, Sammy's bedroom door cracked just enough, the night light still on. They pushed the door open together, Camille darting to the bed, sitting on the edge, right beside her daughter. She slept on her side, facing the lemon-yellow wall. It was painted with pink and sky-blue balloons that reached over on to the ceiling.

"Mommmmmmmy! I knowd you wuz coming," Sammy woke up, whimpering when Camille leaned over to give her a kiss on the cheek. "I knowd you wuz coming. I told Mama Roe I seent you."

Her parents looked at one another, amazed.

"Hi baby," Camille said, picking up her daughter, embracing her in her arms, kissing her all over. Each kiss came with assurances. Camille's heart was whole once again, and nothing, not fear, not lack of self-control, nor self-inflicted shame for doing things out of order, would make her abandon this precious child ever again.

As Sammy giggled and squirmed in her mother's arms, John looked on. Not jealous, but grateful for their reunion. All the pain and hurt that accompanied Camille's absence was instantly erased. There was so much that he wanted for his daughter, so much that he knew she needed, things that only a mother could give a daughter. Regardless if he and Camille mended their relationship or not, he knew with certainty that they would work together for the sake of their child.

Camille handed Sammy the Elmo-wrapped gift. Once opened, Sammy's smile lit up the entire room.

"John, she looks like you now!" Camille said excitedly, holding Sammy at arm's length, staring into her big grayish brown eyes, relieved at the discovery. John smiled, unaware that there had ever been any question.

Eventually, Camille and John would talk face to face about everything. She would answer all his questions, ease his angst. He would know her fears, her shame, and be sympathetic. But she would omit the affair, now sure that Sammy was his child. No need to indict herself over a meaningless tryst. Knowing that in matters of the heart, men are much less forgiving of indiscretions, never trusting, never fully committing again.

It was still early, the sun hiding beyond the horizon. Everyone was tired. Camille unable to sleep during the flight, John working ahead to have time for his family, and Sammy excited, sure she would see her mama.

They all napped in John's bed, Sammy sandwiched between her parents, safe and happy, clinging to her mother like a security blanket fresh from the dryer. And just before closing his eyes, John told them both he loved them, Camille returning the emotion with a nod of her head and misty eyes, but it was love all the same.

They slept well past noon. Camille awaking to find John at his desk typing away on the computer, Sammy snuggled at her mother's bosom. She stroked her daughter's hair as if she was touching rare silk.

"What time do I need to be ready," she asked from across the room.

"He wants everyone there by 6:00 p.m.," John responded. "He's hiring a shuttle to transport guests from the Starbucks, so his wife won't see the cars outside the house."

"That's a great idea," Camille commented. John dusted his knuckles on his chest, indicating it was his idea. She smiled. "Is this someone you work with?"

Camille, too preoccupied with the photos Samantha sent, had skimmed through John's text before leaving Singapore. All she remembered was dinner and party and was all in.

John reminded her, showing her the invite on his phone. And like the shock of discovering that you're having triplets, Camille was blown away. Splattered in front of her in full color was the invitation, a photoshopped picture Camille was sure, welcoming guests to surprise Megan Mallory as she turns thirty again.

First seeing Sammy and now this. *God is surely smiling down on me*, she thought. She wrapped her arms around John's neck and locked lips with him until he needed to catch his breath. She was drunk with excitement. John, thinking it was him.

The enthusiasm that Camille felt when she saw the invitation, her chance to get even with Megan, faded as the day progressed, but she didn't know why. *Megan tried to mess things up with Steve and me*, she thought. That was the lie she told herself. *Megan threatened me*, she thought. That too was a lie.

In reality, when Megan returned Camille's clutch with the look-a-like picture of Sammy and whispered in her ear, it was an unspoken agreement, *if you don't say anything, I won't*, at least that's what Megan thought.

Camille, on the other hand, wasted frivolous time and energy, intent on getting even, when what she felt was guilt. Guilt because she lied to Steve, guilt for not telling her parents or sister about Sammy. Megan just happened to be the catalyst, bringing those guilty feelings to the surface. And for that, Camille sought retribution for the lie and the secret that, at inception, could not survive.

I'll just bring my phone and pass it around, fake bragging about our vacation, she thought. *Or wait until people ask how I know Megan, then I'll bring out the picture. Ummm…no. Maybe I'll scare Megan by showing her the picture when we are alone. No, that's no good either. We'll still be the only ones in the room that know what happened in Singapore*, Camille thought.

"What's on your mind?" John asked, tapping Camille on the shoulder, "Don't you hear Sammy calling you?"

Startled back to reality, she found Sammy playing with the chef doll in the kitchen. Sammy had climbed on the four-step stool and gotten in the sugar canister, scooping a tiny handful on the counter, the doll's face down in the crystals. When Camille walked in the kitchen, Sammy was about to open the flour canister.

"Wait a minute, Sammy," she told her daughter. "What are we making?" she asked, pushing the flour container out of reach.

"Piper wants cookies, Mommy."

"Sammy, is Piper eating the sugar?"

"Noooo, Mommy," she said, smacking her lips, as if that was a stupid question. "Piper mak'n cookies."

Camille chuckled to herself, the silly things she missed. Then she smiled remembering how Sammy used to bring her diaper to them when she needed to be changed. She was only two then, too grown. That's how they knew it was time to start potty-training.

"We have to get some chocolate chips to make the cookies really good for Piper."

"Choco chips, yes, Mommy."

Sammy twisted the doll around in the sugar before Camille could stop her, it scattered all over the floor. Camille carried Sammy out of the kitchen to her bedroom to put on her shoes, so they could dart to the store. She wanted to make cookies before the party. There would be no time in the morning before their flight.

Out of the blue Sammy said, "I mess you, Mommy."

"You mess me?" Camille questioned, not sure what her daughter was saying.

"You wuz not here, Mommy. I mess you," she told her mother emphatically. "I…wuz…sad."

Camille was heartbroken. She wrapped her baby in her arms and told her she had been working, that's why she was gone so long. "I'll take you with me next time. Would you like to go with me?"

"Daddy too?" Sammy asked.

"Sometimes, maybe Daddy too," Camille said.

"I wan Daddy too," Sammy whimpered.

Camille was at a loss for words, not sure whether to agree, and make her daughter feel better or tell her the truth, not exactly knowing what the truth was. She hadn't thought beyond this moment, as far as she and John were concerned. All she was certain of was that she would never abandon her daughter again.

"Daddy too," John said joining them, wrapping his arms around them both, gently kissing his daughter's forehead. Sammy reached out for her father. He lifted her up, head resting on his shoulder, her eyes struggling to stay open.

"Mommy, I don' like werk'n," Sammy muttered just before drifting off to sleep, forgetting all about the cookies.

They would have laughed at the remark under different circumstances, it would have been cute. Instead, they looked at each other, speechless and numb. Camille softly rubbing her daughter's hair, John, intuitively doing the same to Camille, as dollops of tears formed, mascara blackening Camille's eyes and cheeks. Her eyes connecting with his, Camille mouthed, "I'm so sorry!"

TWENTY-THREE

....

megan's party

THREE fifteen-seat shuttles awaited the party guests in the Starbucks parking lot. When Camille and John arrived one of the shuttles was already leaving for Megan's house. Shortly after 6:00 p.m. the remaining two shuttles followed. Everyone was a stranger to Camille, so she introduced herself to some of the passengers as they traveled the short five miles from the rendezvous point to Megan's party.

The Mallory home was surrounded by immaculately manicured shrubbery and trees, only the red-brick chimney could be seen from the street. Two stone-paved pathways allowed passage through the greenery.

The shuttles parked in the circular driveway directly in front of the house, allowing the passengers to exit. As they disembarked to enter the house, they were greeted at the door by a familiar face. Megan's friend, Samantha smiled as she collected phones, watches, wallets, and purses, a condition for entry.

Each guest was given a Tyvek type bag and sharpie, with which they could write their names and place their belongings in. The bags were then alphabetized and locked in a closet for safe keeping, attached to the bag was a snapshot of its owner. John was quite familiar with this protocol, having attended Mallory parties before.

Had Camille not been set on vengeance, she would have seen that all this was outlined on the invitation John showed her, along with a number for guests with children to give caregivers in case of emergency. Defeat dampened Camille's usually peppy persona. So much so, that although she recognized Samantha, she was too in her feelings, flinching when Samantha tried to give her a hug.

"Remember me – Samantha?" Camille faintly heard, snapping out of her disappointed-induced gaze.

"Oh hey, girl," Camille said, a bit too loud, causing Samantha and John to stare at her curiously.

Camille returned the hug and apologized for her reaction, excusing her actions as having something on her mind. There were people waiting behind Camille and John, so the ladies agreed to catch up later when everything settled down, though they never found the time.

The guests entered the home's opulent open foyer, framed by matching stairwells that led to the upstairs living quarters. Following the other guests, everyone gathered in the main living area, which must have been the size of a small gymnasium, with walls that approached thirty feet high or more.

There was a large dark grey concrete island that separated the living room from the kitchen. Seven colorful handblown glass lights of different sizes and shapes hung evenly interspersed along the length of the island.

The room was alive. Bright paintings of nothing in particular were dispersed about the dwelling. A large concaved couch with oversized pillows was centered in front of the fireplace. Two pooches seemed to greet every guest by name. The stools pushed under the island were all different. And at least eight petite serving tables were spaced throughout the room, each with hors d'oeuvres the other didn't have.

Massive windows on one side of the room were unadorned, allowing views of the glossy green courtyard. If you dared, just outside, a brick walkway forged a path to the hidden entertainment area, which included a modest-sized pool and covered kitchenette with a bar. A casually dressed woman attended the delightfully fragrant pineapple grill that infused a sweetness that filtered throughout the air. There were two open bars, Camille's first stop after the cheese and cracker table.

By 7:30 p.m., a five-member band would begin playing, the guests later learning that the songs were all by Australian artists. *Nice touch*, Camille thought.

Almost everyone relocated outside near the pool, the lounge tables were comfortable out there. John remained inside, suspended in a heated debate over who was the all-time greatest – Jordan or James. Someone even tossed Curry out as a possibility, his unanimous MVP nomination, and 2016 season, an argument met with laughter.

"...but they lost," John barked.

Samantha called everyone into the living room after Bobby texted that they were on the way. In less than ten minutes Megan and her husband made their entrance and everyone yelled 'SURPRISE!' in unison.

Megan turned and jumped into her husband's arms, kissing him, undistracted by the onlookers. The guests, including Camille, were in hysterics. Megan's thong showing beneath her mini-mini. She was oblivious but wouldn't have cared had she been sober. Her hubby seemed to not give a damn either.

Referring to Megan's drunken state, one guest yelled out, "We've got some catching up to do!" The crowd roaring even louder afterward.

"Before we go any further," Samantha said, turning to face her friend, "...MEGAN MALLORY, THIS IS YOUR LIFE!" Like clockwork, the lights dimmed as pictures of Megan began flashing on the wall above the fireplace.

"I remember that," one voice said from the crowd.

"... our trip to London," someone else said, excitedly.

"Megan and her siblings," Samantha announced, when the next photo flashed.

Frame by frame, Megan's life was on display for everyone to see. Joyous echoes erupted around the room, each photo telling Megan's story, her life in pictures.

"This is awesome," Camille whispered to the stranger standing beside her.

"Where was that taken?" a voice called out.

"That's in Singapore," Samantha responded.

Camille was still conversing with the stranger. Megan and Bobby clinging to one another like teenagers.

"Who's your boyfriend, Megan?" someone shouted from the crowd, the guests bursting into laughter again.

Camille quickly turned her attention to the screen. Her yellow dress played second fiddle to the kiss and ass grab that were plastered right there on the wall above the fireplace. Camille's mouth fell wide open, elated that she wouldn't have to do a thing. The picture that would exact her revenge was in full view for everyone to see. Their reactions, though, not quite what Camille expected they would be. It seems she was the only one stunned, more shocked by her own lack of participation in exposing Megan's exploits, than the actual photo itself. And when she saw Bobby's reaction, smacking Megan's ass, not in anger, but with a playful tap, followed by a kiss on the neck, Camille felt bamboozled and confused.

What the f**k is going on here, Camille thought. She searched for John in the crowd as the slideshow neared its end. By the time she found him, Samantha was shouting, "LET THE FUN BEGIN!"

The band took their positions and started their serenade with Olivia Newton John's, *Physical*. Camille laughed uncontrollably, not in the hee-hee, this is hilarious kind of way, but in the joke is on me, way.

"Okay, what's going on?" she whispered in John's ear. She was freaking out. John found it amusing. Before telling her that Bobby and Megan have a 'what goes on in Vegas, stays in Vegas' relationship, he gave her a great big hug. "But that was Singapore," Camille said, still confused.

"Do I need to spell it out for you?" he asked her.

"YES!" she exclaimed.

"They have an open relationship."

"And you were going to tell me this when?" she questioned.

To her, happy-go-lucky open relationships like this were fictional mumbo jumbo made up for TV. The closest thing she ever came to this were her parents, her father, having the open relationship that her mother knew nothing about.

She couldn't fathom a woman buying into this, much less a man okay with the whole world, well the people willing to sign the nondisclosure bit, seeing his wife slung happily all over another man. Camille's occasional philandering wasn't the same thing in her eyes, though anyone judging her situation would beg to differ.

"I didn't think it would ever come up," he told her, "…remember the nondisclosure agreement, taking the phones, and belongings? What did you think all that was about?"

"…just thought it was anal lawyer stuff," Camille said, making her way to the bar. She downed two greyhounds in minutes before Megan saw her from across the pool.

"CAMILLE!" Megan yelled. "That's my friend, Camille," she told whomever was listening, stumbling her way across the yard.

Camille, still rattled by the open relationship news, smiled. As they hugged, Megan further annoyed Camille. "Girl, did you see them hands? Oohhhh he was soooo good!" the lush slurred, attempting to whisper, unsuccessfully.

I was literally there, fool, Camille thought, and stared at the drunken birthday girl, knowing she meant every word. Megan was too far gone to hold any kind of meaningful conversation, and as soon as she saw another long-lost friend, she staggered her way over to them, kissing Camille on the cheek before leaving, mumbling, "I love you, girl."

Camille heard herself return the expression, one she'd uttered innumerable times before, like breathing. Each previous time, the words dissipated, replaced by the next thought – *what's for dinner? I want a piece of chocolate cake. Have I paid this bill or that? I wonder what Mom's doing.* This time was different. This 'I love you' dwelled, like blooming hydrangeas, pungent and sweet, the words lingering in the air like the smell of fresh cut flowers.

I love you, Camille repeated over and over in her head. She looked around and maybe it was the alcohol, but things moved in slow motion. She noticed the 'GRAB ONE' table, full of party favors for the guests, the table full of gifts for Megan furnished by the partygoers, the band still playing, by now moving on to top forty music, John engrossed in another too-deep-for-a-party conversation, the bars both pouring constant round after round, and Bobby eating bacon wrapped maple scallops.

She felt it, love was all around her. *These are my people, the kind I want to hang around, but I call B.S on the open relationship crap*, she thought. What she felt was tangible, just like when she saw her daughter again. Camille raised her glass, toasting the air, and gulped the rest of her martini. Overcome with emotion and liquor, she started going up to complete strangers, one by one, hugging them and telling them, 'I love you.'

This was nothing for Megan's friends, they had seen far worse antics. The 'classic,' as dubbed by the attendees, was Megan's actual thirtieth birthday party when she jumped in the pool butt naked. The funny part, if that's not funny enough, was sixteen others felt compelled to do the same. Suffice it to say, Camille's gesture of love, was normal to this bunch. And later when John would bring up this night, she was grateful no one had their phones.

When John saw Camille from across the yard darting from one person to the next, he thought she might need rescuing. "Hey, are you okay?" he asked, knowing the answer already. "We probably should be heading out…"

She interrupted, shouting over the band. "NO, THIS IS WAY TOO MUCH FUN!"

"Ssshhh," he said, looking around, "…remember you have to leave out in the morning."

"It's still early," she slurred. It was after midnight, and neither of them wanted to leave but it was best. "I just have to find Megan to tell her goodnight."

John ushered Camille around until they found Megan and Bobby coming out of the bathroom.

"Was it good?" spilled from Camille like loose bowels.

"We're heading out," John said to the hosts, embarrassed.

Bobby reached out to shake John's hand. Camille gasped in a drunken repulsion.

"Ewwww, did you wash your hands?" she blurted, trying to knock John's hand away.

As she did, she slipped, falling into the arms of the birthday girl. The two drunkards snorted with laughter. They gathered composure enough to give one another a hug, a bit too tight for Camille, causing a silent uncontrolled poot to be unleashed. No one heard a thing, but seconds later they all recoiled in disdain for the foul infraction, unplanned, but the sweetest revenge.

"She just shit on herself," Camille told John, a vain attempt at whispering, not even realizing she was the one who had passed gas.

"Let's go," John said, he and Bobby laughing out loud.

TWENTY-FOUR

....

home again

ITS always a little colder in the mountains than anywhere else, at least that's how Camille felt. Nevertheless, she was home again. This time she wasn't alone, she had her baby girl with her. There was no turning back now, everything she had been trying to hide would soon be exposed, a forced unveiling.

The flight landed on time, but Camille hesitated before calling for someone to pick them up, wanting to but not able to wiggle her way out of this. She and Sammy sat in baggage claim, the other passengers on her flight, all retrieving their bags, the terminal slowly clearing out. Sammy was asleep, slumped over her mother's shoulder.

"We made it," her text to John. He didn't respond, planning his own surprise.

The world could have imploded around her, she was distracted, looking for the words she would use to explain her actions to her mother, her sister, and most of all to the one whose disapproval she feared the most. Not realizing she was wasting her time worrying about the latter.

Mr. Young, who pleaded with God to see his eldest child one last time, was tiptoeing closer and closer to death. It wouldn't be long now, his organs, one by one, surrendering to the inevitable.

Tania texted Camille, "Have you landed yet?"

Camille felt the phone vibrate in her pocket. There was a missed text from John too. "I've landed," he typed. She was confused. While responding to her sister, her phone rang, it was John.

"Hello, John. Where are you?" she asked.

He walked up behind her, tapping her on the shoulder. "Right here," he said.

"What the…!" she paused, "…what are you doing here?"

"I'm here for you," he responded.

Camille was livid, Sammy still sleeping peacefully. He hadn't told her a thing. His important case, the scheduling conflict, settled. He made his reservation as soon as he found out but couldn't book the same flight.

He didn't tell her because he knew she would have every possible excuse, reasons for Sammy not to go with her – *she's too young, don't want her to see her grandfather like this, I have to take care of my mother*. All the reasons why he kept things to himself.

"I don't need this! Not now," she said, trying not to wake Sammy.

"Need what – someone to support you?" he asked. "What if something's really wrong with your father? You're not going to be able to take care of Sammy and take care of your family too."

"John, we're not together, not like that."

"What? Who said anything about us being together?"

"Why would you just pop up like this?"

He was getting mad. He was not usually one to say whatever he was thinking, but Camille needed a dose of her own medicine. "To be honest, I didn't think you could handle this by yourself," he told her.

"Handle what? My daughter?"

"Yea… Sammy. And your dad, too."

"Then why the fuck did you force this on me?"

"Force it on you? Force your child on you? WOW!"

"You knew my dad was sick when you made our reservations."

"I told you the only reason I couldn't come was because of this case. You said that you wanted me to come. Remember?"

"That's just something people say," she admitted.

John threw his hands up in disgust, he couldn't believe what he was hearing. Sammy woke up, most likely because of the commotion between her parents. But then, just as Camille was about to go full verbal Floyd Mayweather on John for popping up, for making that comment, she decided to use his presence to her advantage. Besides, although she would never admit it, he was right, it was too much for her to handle, too much to explain.

Tania was texting, "Can't leave Dad, grab a cab. HURRY!!! Room 417."

Camille had to rush but didn't want Sammy's first introduction to the family to be at the hospital.

"Look, I'm sorry. I didn't mean any of that," she lied. "Can you take Sammy? I have to run to the hospital, Tania is frantic."

"Of course," he said, reaching for Sammy.

"I'll email you the hotel reservations," she told him and walked out the terminal, jumping into a waiting taxi.

Life often forces you to do things you don't want to do. It was one of those times for Camille. Subconsciously, she hoped this was another false alarm, her father had been sick many times before, but this time Tania and her mom were so convincing, certain that the patriarch was dying. Sure, she expected her parents to die before she or her sister did, but not this soon. It was too soon, she was only thirty-two, still hankering for a relationship that would never be.

As the elevator accelerated toward the fourth floor, surrounded by five other people, probably visiting sick relatives too, Camille's mind raced. She thought about a lot of things, but mostly how empty she felt, void of any emotion, a place she had learned to live long before this moment. She couldn't pinpoint exactly when she started feeling this way, but there were many reasons for her to be here.

Aside from the many women her dad kept running in and out of the house, there was the constant doting and attention he gave only to Tania, the daddy-daughter dances he missed, the many broken promises, always something more important. There was a coldness, an invisible obstacle between him and Camille, that only recently, since his diagnosis, narrowed.

Throughout the years, she would do things to try and please him, like taking out the trash before her mom yelled at him to do it or cooking his favorite dinner when her mother was late or too tired or ironing his work clothes. Nothing was enough, so she stopped begging for his love, silently grimacing when her baby sister would get unconditionally all the things Camille jumped through hoops for.

The elevator door opened on the fourth floor, she stood motionless. The door closed with three occupants inside, one of them Camille. She rode the elevator to the top floor and back down again, twice, before getting off.

As she trudged towards her father's hospital room, legs like anchors, Pastor C.W. Johnson was coming out. Pastor Johnson had been the pastor of First Chapel Baptist Camille's entire life. On the occasion when they did go to church – not every waking moment like her grandmother, and her grandmother's mother – Pastor Johnson always called her by name, like a neighbor. For some reason, this made her feel special, like she mattered.

"Camille," he said, "…it's so good to see you again."

"Pastor Johnson."

"How are you doing today? "he asked.

No one had ever asked her how she was doing like this before. Sure, 'how are you doing' was a common question, but the 'today' part, unusual. And for some reason this lifted her spirits. 'How are you doings' always made her want to smack the person asking, *how the hell do you think I'm doing on the worse day of my life?* But now, Pastor Johnson's inquiry made her think that things wouldn't always be like this, that there was opportunity to feel better, tomorrow maybe, or the next day, or the day after that. And better is always better.

"It's so good seeing you, Pastor. You know...."

He reached out to give her a hug. The words she searched for were stuck deep down in a place that couldn't be reached right now, and he sensed it, another thing she admired him for.

"You'll find comfort in God's unchanging hand," he assured her.

"Yes, Pastor," she said, not really knowing what the heck that meant.

"Will we see you in service on Sunday?" he asked, smiling as he released her. "I have a word for you," he told her.

"We'll see how things go," she told him, her way of saying no.

"God bless you, Camille," he said.

Thankful, her eyes followed him as he disappeared onto the elevator. As she walked down the corridor, she smiled at the people sitting behind the nurse's station. Room 417 glared at her, the only room number she saw. She knocked on the door before entering. More of a gesture really, walking in without waiting for a response.

"Camille!" Tania's enthusiastic greeting, a quiet yell.

"Hi baby," her mother said, comforting her daughter with softly spoken words.

Tania, Mrs. Young, Uncle Art, Cousin Jonah, and Ms. Loretta were gathered around the bed staring at her father, praying for a miracle. Mr. Young laid still on the cot, unbeknownst to Camille, he was actively dying, a prognosis given by the doctor hours earlier.

A nurse ran water at the sink. The blinds, slightly open, enough to see the sun, still rising over the mountains. The TV was on but muted.

The family motioned for Camille to join them. She spoke to each one of them with a forced smile. Easing her way in between her mother and sister, each one wrapping their arms around the other's waist.

Ms. Loretta, the self-proclaimed prayer warrior, rubbed her dry cracked hands together, making a dreadful noise, one loud enough to wake the dead. Then she hovered her palms over the patient's groin and started an undecipherable prayer.

Camille lost it. She was angry and sad all at once.

"That's not helping! That has never helped anybody! You need to know that!" Camille snapped.

"CAMILLE!" Mrs. Young said in shock.

"I'm sorry, Momma, somebody needed to tell her," Camille said. "…and that chocolate cake, it's just awful. Please don't make that for my mom ever again, makes her sick every time."

Ms. Loretta gasped, flummoxed by the rudeness. "I'm sorry. I'm so sorry," Ms. Loretta repeated while she gathered her belongings from the chair near the sink.

The nurse, now cleaning the surroundings, snickered to herself. Everything was moving so fast. Tania turned away so that no one could see her laughter. Art and Jonah stood silent, unaware that they were nodding in agreement.

"Bonnie, don't leave," Lynn said.

And out of the blue, a rustic murmur escaped from the patient, weak attempts at laughter. Everyone turned to face him, surprised. He had been lifeless for days now. His left eye strained to open, only slightly but enough to see her. He was ready now, his one last prayer answered. Mr. Young smiled at Camille, just a sliver. She smiled back, happy that he was grinning at her and her alone.

They stood around the bed, ecstatic to see life in him again. The forced murmurs continued, everybody joining in, even the nurse, laughing out loud, one last time together. They were all thinking that there might be something to Ms. Loretta's prayer warrior claim after all, now.

Hours crept by like molasses, Mr. Young was lifeless again, his laughter long gone. Tania fell asleep in the reclining chair, while Mrs. Young and Ms. Loretta ate turkey sandwiches in the cafeteria, reminiscing about the good times. Art and Jonah went home, there was nothing else for them to do. And Camille sat in the chair beside her father's bed, contently holding his hand, like she had longed to do as a child. Periodically she checked on Sammy, but right now, in this moment, she was the little girl, finally.

At 5:38 p.m. Saturday evening, the sun was retreating, the chill in the air outside required a light jacket, shifts were nearing an end or a beginning, depending on the perspective, Darcel Grimes reported the news in silence, tears flowed from family and friends, and Richard Joseph Young, veteran, husband, father, brother, son, and not least of all, a Christian, took his last breath.

During his life, he had done the best he knew how to do.

TWENTY-FIVE

....

sammy meets the family

JOHN and Sammy were not in the room when Camille got there. She was relieved by the aloneness. Unfamiliar with her feelings, the intermittent onslaughts of pain were like menopausal hot flashes. She just needed something or someone to explain what she was going through.

When she left her mother and sister, they both seemed okay, like they had already come to terms with her father's death. Granted, they had time, knowing the definite outcome in advance long ago. But Camille, who had clung to denial, was haphazardly coasting through tonight's events, at best.

Her clothes weighed her down like bricks and she yanked them from her body as if they were on fire. The thickness in the air choked her and she just needed to breathe. She walked out onto the balcony, naked, gulping for air. *We held hands*, she thought, *he held my hand*, a complicated simplicity. She had wanted this all her life, for him to hold her hand. He never did until tonight, his last, and now, as she pondered on it, loving and hating the moment all at once, she wished that she could go back and erase it.

It was easier to hold on to the distance between them, emotionlessly expecting nothing. Before, she was sure of where they stood, allies only in their love for her mother and sister. But now, with that one fleeting gesture, there was a remote likelihood that there could have been another story, different than the one she had come to believe. And she was frightened by how easily and willingly she tossed the decades old story aside, for that of the wishful child, long ago locked away, a prisoner in a dungeon.

She watched as folks, unaware of her presence, walked by on the streets below. Couples hand-in-hand, some kissing, some cuddling, laughing, still living. She wondered why the world hadn't stopped. Didn't they know her father had died? If they knew, it sure didn't seem like anyone cared. She wanted to scream at them all, but instead the chilly mountain air forced her inside off the balcony.

She always found comfort in a hot shower, but tonight the warmth of the bath didn't wash away her sorrows as it normally did. She removed her shower cap and stood directly under the pulsating stream. Her honey-dyed roots expanded like a water-soaked sponge with each bead that flowed, rounding her forehead, down to her eyelids, where they joined her tears, together forming a brigade that steadily marched down her wet body, disappearing into the drain. She sluggishly dried her damp skin, her mind battling memories she never discussed with anyone.

When she was ten or so, she stood in the hallway and peeped from behind the screen door, her parents sitting on the porch swing, holding hands and laughing like they had just met. Hours earlier Camille had chased one of her father's many lovers away by calling the police, claiming that she had been hit by this stranger. Her father furious at the time, clearly had recovered.

Then, there was her thirteenth birthday, her father, at her mother's request, preparing the pullout couch for the sleepover. The more she remembered, the more she saw that despite his many faults, he would do just about anything to please her mother. And in this newly discovered revelation, Camille found some solace.

She had witnessed love from both sides and wondered if this was what it looked like, flawed and deceptive. And then she thought about John and how that's exactly what it was, her love for him, flawed and deceptive, habits she'd unknowingly adopted from her parents, like speech.

She found one of John's shirts, his scent still lingering on it. She put it on and nuzzled herself in the king-sized bed, underneath the plush feathered comforter, where she waited for her family. John, moments earlier having texted to say that he and Sammy were in the lobby grabbing a bite to eat.

When Camille awoke John was already up and dressed. Sammy was in the bed beside her, room service having delivered breakfast, placing it near the edge of the bed.

"Didn't want to wake you," John said. "You seemed to be sleeping so peacefully."

She sat up in the bed rubbing Sammy's hair. "John…," she said, but couldn't bring herself to say the rest. It was as if everything that she held inside wanted to come out all at once, a rare moment, she was unraveling.

"How's your dad?" he asked.

"Not good," a long sigh. "He passed."

"Oh, Camille, I'm so sorry."

He wanted to fuss at her for not calling to let him know but chose not to. Instead he coaxed her from the bed, snuggling her in his arms. As he kissed her forehead she started shaking, tears streaming from her eyes like waterfalls.

"John," she muttered, "thank you for coming."

He held her even closer. She was clearly struggling. "I love you, Camille," he told her. But that wasn't what she wanted to hear. She pushed him away, confused. "I love you," he said again.

"SHUT UP!" she screamed, waking the baby. "Why does it always have to be about you?"

He grabbed her arm and tenderly pulled her as close as she would allow. "I love you," he said again. She tried to get away, but she couldn't, her body trembling. Sammy, still groggy, looked at her parents.

"Shut up!" Camille cried. "I don't want to hear that!"

"I love you," he repeated again, covering her with kisses, her fight gone. "I'm so sorry about your dad."

He forced her face upward with his hands until she looked him in the eyes, and he told her again that he loved her. Her pain exited her body in the form of fist pounds on his chest. And although she was hitting John, it was her father she was fighting. Understanding, he let Camille explode until Sammy started to cry.

"It's okay, Sammy," he told their baby girl. "Mommy is okay," he said, comforting their daughter with his words.

John cradled Camille in his arms like a baby. Sitting on the bed next to Sammy, he rocked her back and forth like her mother used to do when she was a child. Sammy stood on the bed behind them, stroking her mother's hair.

"It otay, Mama. It otay," Sammy said.

With tears still staining her face, Camille's sadness was shattered by her daughter's sweet words and she erupted into an uncontrolled laughter, John joining in. And that's how it would be for years to come, Sammy always comforting and cute, bringing joy and happiness to her parents.

Camille, John, and Sammy entered the Young home. The smell of collard greens, black-eyed peas, ham, fried chicken, potato salad, chitterlings, apple pie, carrot cake and more briefly tricked them into forgetfulness.

Ms. Loretta and Mrs. Scott from the church, manned the food table. People skated in and out offering their condolences. There were chairs lined up against the living room walls, sparsely filled with people exchanging stories about Mr. Young.

There was no sign of the living room furniture that once shared the space, except for the grooves left behind on the carpet. In the background, music was playing at a whisper, The Temptations, Mr. Young's favorite group, now on rotation along with other artists from the 70s.

Camille spoke to everyone, hugging Ms. Loretta as an apology of sorts. Mrs. Young and Tania were outside on the back porch, they needed some fresh air. John, carrying Sammy, followed Camille to the back. When she opened the screen, her mother was handing Tania an envelope from their father. There was one for Camille too.

"Hey y'all, we're here," Camille announced.

Her mother and sister stood up to greet them.

"Hi, baby," Mrs. Young said.

"Y'all remember John? …and this is Sammy," Camille said.

Lynn gave them both a big hug.

"Sorry for your loss," John said.

"Thank you," they both responded.

Sammy reached out for Mrs. Young, although she had never met her grandmother before today, she recognized her from the pictures that Camille shared with her since she was a baby. Lynn smiled and took Sammy into her arms.

"Mom, Tania, this is my baby girl, Sammy," Camille said.

"I know. I know. You're my baby. I know," Mrs. Young said with sureness.

Tania, on the other hand was floored. She had to pick her mouth up off the concrete. "WHAT?" she protested.

"SamSam, say hello to your Auntie Tania," Camille said.

"Hi," Sammy said shyly.

"Camille, what are you talking about?" Tania questioned.

John looked on, wondering.

"This is my baby. Samantha is four," Camille told them.

"You adopted a baby?" Tania asked.

"Tania, stop. We'll talk about this later. We have company," Mrs. Young said. "Now is not the time." Lynn put Sammy down and handed the remaining letter to Camille, telling her that it was from her father. "Let's go inside," Lynn directed.

Sammy, holding hands with her grandmother, grabbed her Auntie's hand too. And although Tania was furious and outwardly hurt by the blatant omission, she held Sammy's hand as they all walked in the house.

While everyone else was in the living room, Mrs. Young retreated to the master bedroom, locking the door. The family's pillar of strength, she fell to her knees beside her bed, raised her hands in surrender, and called out to God.

First, she was thankful for her many blessings, even her husband's peaceful passage. Then she prayed for strength, she prayed for understanding, and she prayed for the right words to say to her children.

She knew Camille better than anyone else but found it difficult to understand why and how this was the first time she had heard about or met her granddaughter. *There must be a reason beyond my understanding*, her appeal to God. She remained on the floor until a peace overtook her, maybe it was the presence of God she felt, maybe it was the spirit of her husband, or maybe just her aching knees forcing her off the floor.

There was something that confirmed her goodness, telling her that she had been the best mother she could have been under the circumstances, and that Camille's decision to withhold this from their family was no reflection on her mothering. In that moment, Lynn was clear and free of the guilt she harbored and was able to accept things as they were.

John took Sammy back to the hotel to give the ladies a chance to talk. Camille and Tania sat in the living room, looking, listening, and talking to all the people who came to pay their respects. Skeeter Robinson stopped by. He was overheard telling Juanita Bishops that Mr. Young had paid his mother's mortgage for six months when she got sick and never asked for a dime of that money back.

The room roared when someone said how much Mr. Young loved Paul Sabastian, all remembering how they could smell him coming before they saw him.

Velma Brown told Tania how her father had a friend of his come over to fix her car when she was down on her luck.

Marcus Tucker talked about how they drank and played poker on Saturday nights for years. Then there was Reverend Thomas, who told the girls how their father came by the church on a weekly basis for the morning prayer group and how he helped build the playground for the church daycare.

Story after story Camille and Tania learned things about their father that neither of them had known. By 6:00 p.m., the food ran out and everyone was tired. Tania and Mrs. Young decided to stay at the rental, they needed some time alone. Camille decided to stay with them.

As they drove, Tania brought up the elephant in the room. "Is that John from freshman year?"

"Nooo, that can't be John. Well, he's a mannnn now!" Mrs. Young announced.

They all laughed.

"Yes, that's John from freshman year," Camille told them. "Can we get some wine or some smoke?" She needed something to help her relax before they talked.

"CAMILLE!" Mrs. Young exclaimed.

"I have a feeling this is going to be a long night," Camille said.

Tania pulled into the grocery store parking lot. Camille got out the back seat. After she entered the store Lynn told her daughter to take it easy on Camille.

"Mom, what do you mean? Don't you wanna know why she hid this from us?" Tania asked her mother.

"I don't need to know. It won't change a single thing," Lynn explained.

"You're right, it won't but I'm feeling some type of way about it," Tania said.

"Her actions had nothing to do with you, Tania."

"How do you know that, Mom?"

"Baby, you can't take this personally. Besides, I'm certain that whatever she says won't be good enough to take away the hurt you're feeling about it."

"You're probably right," Tania agreed.

And with that Camille got back in the car. While she was in the store, she pondered on the easiest way to talk about Sammy. She decided the best way was to just tell the truth. So that's what she did.

"I was ashamed," Camille stuttered as soon as the car began to move again. "I was ashamed and didn't know what to do," she repeated, tears forming in her eyes.

Her mother turned around in her seat and clasped one of her daughter's hands in solidarity. Tania said nothing, just continued driving past their exit and on to the highway.

Camille told them everything she had kept hidden all these years. How Mr. Young would always say to them, *don't bring no bastard babies to my house*. Tania mouthing the words of his mantra as Camille spoke them, nodding in affirmation.

Camille told them how she wanted to get an abortion but couldn't bring herself to follow through with it. Tania cried at this revelation. She had been pregnant before, never telling her family. The only difference between her and Camille was that she had terminated her pregnancy.

And then finally Camille told them what she couldn't tell John, about the affair that caused her to leave Sammy and John and how Sammy walked in on her having sex with another man, and how she didn't think she could stop, so she left.

By now they were all crying, about Camille, about shame, about secrets, about mistakes, about their father and husband who would never know his grandchild. Tania continued driving until Camille had said everything she needed to say, until they could cry no more.

When they got to the rental, they sat around the dining room table drinking goblets of champagne, talking about the stories they had learned earlier that night, laughing, crying, reminiscing, and planning their loved one's funeral.

TWENTY-SIX

....

the funeral

OFTEN what someone knows is only accurate within the confines of the limited knowledge they have at the time. And out of nowhere, new facts are revealed, nuggets of information that shine a light on what was believed before, forcing new opinions, new beliefs.

Five days after the patriarch of the Young family passed away, he was laid to rest. Everyone stood as the family entered the church. Walking down the center aisle, they were surrounded by people, young and old, whose lives Richard Young had affected in some way.

Approaching the casket, Mrs. Young was first. She stood before her husband, praying silently. She had loved this man for more than half of her life. Even after his diagnosis, she never imagined existing without him. And now their time as husband and wife was punctuated by this, their final moments together. His stiff, cold body openly displayed, barely resembling the man she had known. The tears gathering up in her eyes struggled to stay in place. She wanted to be strong for her daughters.

Camille followed her mother. As she walked down the long line of church pews, she secretly maneuvered the unopened letter from her father out of her purse. She waited until she was alone at the casket, peering at the man she lived with for sixteen years, up until she left for college. Camille stared blankly at her father who was now stiff and harmless. *He didn't love me*, she thought. *Why didn't he love me?* All she ever wanted was for him to love her and no matter what the letter said, it couldn't change the past.

As she stood there, she thought about the stories told earlier that week by Skeeter Robinson, Velma Brown, and Reverend Thomas. She wondered how this person that they spoke so fondly of could be the same person who ran women in and out her mother's home. How such kindness and such foolishness inhabited the same body simultaneously and how these people would never experience the side of her father that she had known. How they probably would doubt her tales if she spoke them aloud, and how she hated him and loved him, absolutely unable to control either emotion.

She fought back tears, caused by the momentary holding of hands, leaned over as if to hug her father one last time, and tucked the letter between his rigid left arm and the fluffy white puckered paneling that lined the sides of his coffin. She thought, *there was no use now for his words, good or bad, and that death would have the final say in their story.*

Tania paced behind Camille and saw everything. Instead of relishing her last moments with her father, she sneakily collected the letter her sister wanted to bury, slipped it into her own pocket, and sat down next to her mother.

Pastor Johnson officiated over the service. Reading the eulogy, condensed and sweet, composed by the sisters. After which, friends and family made statements of praise for Mr. Young's many acts of kindness. Things his family knew little about. Even Lynn was surprised by some of the things she heard.

By these testimonies, Camille hadn't really known her father at all. The man she knew was stern, distant, withdrawn, and often downright cruel. *Maybe people are just being nice, to comfort us,* she thought. But there were far too many stories of appreciation for them all to just be consolatory. When they closed the casket, draping it with the American flag, sniffling could be heard throughout the church.

"This ain't no sad time!" cousin Alfred stood up and shouted. "This man here, by all accounts, lived a good life and now he is in the hands of our Savior. Ain't no cryin' 'round here! We oughtta be shout'n and celebrate'n!" he continued, breaking out in song. The church, one by one joining in as they formed a procession behind the coffin.

At the gravesite, a smaller congregation looked on as Pastor Johnson delivered the last rights. A uniformed bugler played *Taps* on cue. This was a military send-off rivaling that of the most decorated officer, guns blasting in salute, three jets soaring overhead in formation, a hero's sendoff.

John had to head back to New York for work, but Sammy stayed behind with her mother. The ladies all met up at Tania's, no one wanting to be alone. This would be the first real time the Young women would spend with Sammy.

Tania, still hurt that Camille kept Sammy from them, set aside her feelings to enjoy this time with her niece. Children have a way of bringing peace to any situation – their innocence, and curiosity. Tania and Lynn fought for the baby's attention, reverting to kids themselves, singing jingles from cartoons, and making funny voices to entertain the child, until Sammy fell asleep in her grandmother's arms.

Mrs. Young took the child to the spare bedroom, peacefully tucking her under the cover like she used to do with her own girls. Then she joined her daughters at the dining room table. They drank wine, played cards, and watched girly movies. Anything to keep their minds occupied.

"Camille," Tania asked, "…what did Daddy write you?"

"I don't know," she told her sister.

"You haven't read it yet?" her mother asked.

"No," Camille responded. "What did yours say?" Camille asked her sister.

"You know Daddy. He tried to sound smart, telling me what I should do with my life…stuff like that."

"He was smart," Mrs. Young insisted.

"Can I read it?" Tania asked Camille.

"You're so nosy," Mrs. Young answered for Camille. "No, you can't read it. It's for Cami, from her father. Nobody wants to read yours."

One week earlier, Lynn sat alongside her husband in the hospital, reading, alternating between her bible and the tabloids she purchased in the hospital gift shop.

"I'm ready," her husband muttered.

"Don't say that," Lynn said, she wasn't ready for him to die.

He smiled at his wife, this time clarifying himself. "I'm ready to tell the truth."

"Tell the truth. About what?" Lynn questioned.

"Camille," Richard told his wife.

"She's not here, Richard," Lynn said, thinking he might be hallucinating.

"I'm fine," he assured her. "I know she's not here." He paused. "I don't wanna take this to my grave, Lynn."

"Ooooh…Richard," she sighed, shaking her head, rubbing it with her hand, "…you said you'd never want her to know."

Together, they'd kept a secret from their eldest child, Lynn hesitantly bowing to Richard's demand. Now, he wanted to clear his conscience before death came calling.

When she initially agreed, three decades earlier, it was a different time. Long before the independent women's movement when girls still dreamt of 2.5 kids and white picket fences. When having children outside of marriage was still taboo.

Richard was fragile, and Lynn wanted nothing more than to comfort him and help with his peaceful transition. Though she was torn, *tell the truth, the right thing to do thirty years ago*, she thought, *up front, but not now*, having committed to the story they made up together, having lived it for decades, it had become their reality. Not to mention, she would be the one left to deal with the repercussions of the admission, him dying with a clean slate.

Who knows, had they decided differently, Richard, may still have been a consummate womanizer, Lynn might have still overcompensated for her mommy guilt, Camille might have still abandoned her daughter and hid Sammy's existence, and Tania, the baby of the family, probably would have still been spoiled rotten. All these outcomes still possibilities had they played the cards as they were dealt, but there was no second-guessing, not now.

So that night, before Richard went to sleep, Lynn massaged his feet, combed his hair, read the Bible to him, and agreed to record letters to both of their daughters that she would deliver upon his death.

TWENTY-SEVEN

....

the confession

AS Richard and Lynn sat in his hospital room talking about old times, their children, and his final wishes, music from her phone played 70s R&B softly in the background. This was one of his few good days, so she gathered her notepad and pen, preparing to write letters to their girls.

As he thought about his past and his many mistakes, dollops of tears trickled down the sides of his face into his ears. Lynn rubbed her husband's arm for relief and assured him that everything would be alright, even though she didn't really believe it.

They were dedicated to one another, his constant philandering notwithstanding, that when it came to mind, saddened him all the more. Only recently wondering how this might have scarred his children, especially Camille.

The only thing that the girls knew about their parent's relationship was that they were high school sweethearts. It wasn't a topic of discussion in the Young household like in other families. Now that their relationship was nearing its end, it was important to Mr. Young that his daughters knew their love story. Important only because he didn't want them to make the same mistakes that he had made.

"What do you want to say?" Lynn asked her husband, preparing to write the letter to Tania first.

"I'm not going to tell Tania about Camille," he said. "That's up to Camille to do. Don't you agree?"

"I think so too," she said.

Mr. Young was proud of his daughters. He asked Lynn to let them know this first, so that's where she began, writing to Tania for him.

Aside from your birth, the day you graduated from college was one of the proudest days of my life.

She expressed to their youngest daughter how good it made Richard feel knowing that she loved his shrimp and grits more than anything and asked him to cook this meal at least once a week. How at Christmas time, with presents piled under the tree, the family waking at dawn to the fragrant cider simmering on the stove, Tania insisted her father open his present from her first. A bag of grits every year.

Lynn wrote about how when Tania was three and sick with a cold, her father was the only one that could coax her to sleep by singing his silly version of the Sesame Street song, *Sunny Days*, and how on the day she was born, Richard held Tania tightly in his arms, and cried like a baby, omitting the fact that this was something he noticeably didn't do at Camille's birth.

Richard wanted his daughter to know all the things he neglected to talk about before, about his childhood, people who had been kind along the way, about the importance of saving money, about finances and credit, about charity and giving back, about cars and the best people in town to go to if she needed something fixed or repaired, and the places she should travel to, his instruction book for life.

He praised his wife's devotion, her strength and wisdom, verses Lynn wrote reluctantly before concluding his letter with sweet, heartfelt words telling his youngest how joyous she had made his life. Only adding a P.S. to interrupt the burden of the letter's finality.

P.S. – If the man you date doesn't make shrimp and grits as good as mine, he's just not that into you, baby girl!

Lynn saw a rare glimpse into her husband's soul. She noticed how he tortured, in this brief prose, to recount stories and anecdotes that he hoped would best serve their daughter, giving some insight into how precious she had been to him. Lynn added her own little touches, too, only words a mother would think of, words a daughter needed to hear from her father.

"Let's take a break," Lynn told her husband. "It's time for the nurse."

"That's fine," he agreed.

"Do you remember when Greyson came by the house?" she asked.

"Yes, I do. The kids were toddlers."

"Yes, they were."

"I'm sorry, Lynn. I've been a jealous fool."

She wanted to say more but his surprise apology stopped her cold. Besides, the nurse had entered the room to check his vitals. As they sat in silence waiting for her to leave, they both thought about just how honest they were willing to get – she about Greyson, and he, his cheating. *What purpose would it serve her to know now*, he wondered, but then again, she was the one scribing the letter, she would have to know if he truly wanted to make amends with Camille.

Once the nurse left, he began. "I was a terrible person, Lynn. I did some awful things." He couldn't look her in the face, so she knew it must have been bad, but he continued anyway. "In order to apologize to Camille, I'm going to have to be real with you first." He was weak but audible.

"Richard, what in the world?" she exclaimed. "You're not a serial killer, are you?" For some odd reason this was her first thought, way too much Netflix and chilling.

"No, but I do need to ask for your forgiveness," he told her.

"Forgiveness? For what?" she asked.

He closed his eyes and took a deep breath. His lips moved but no words escaped. He was praying, asking God for the right words to say, but what he heard back was, there are no right words. With that, he turned to face his wife, her brows scrunched in dismay, his throat clogged from fear, and he began, slowly revealing his indiscretions one by one, naming the names he remembered.

Stunned, she listened intently, wondering when he had the time to do all this. Then he dropped the second bomb, telling her that all the women had been in their home, paraded in front of their daughter. Had he not been on his deathbed, she would have hauled off and smacked him with all her might. Instead, she screamed so loudly, a shriek from the depths of her soul, causing the nurse to run back into the room.

"Is everything okay in here?" the nurse asked.

"HELL NO!" Lynn yelled.

And before she could gather her composure, Lynn blurted out everything her husband had just told her. The nurse, not knowing what to say, stood still and quiet, just as shocked as Lynn was.

"Lynn," Richard called out.

"Don't you say another word, you sick son of a bitch!" she shouted, "NOT…ONE…MORE…WORD!"

"I'm going to leave now," the nurse announced, adding, "Is everything going to be okay?"

"I'm leaving with you," Lynn declared, looking at the nurse. She gathered her belongings, her head shaking in disbelief, and followed the nurse out of the room without saying another word to Richard.

Just outside in the hallway, the nurse gave Lynn a hug so tight, as the tears of thirty years of deception rained down on the nurse's shoulder. A soul tsunami.

Lynn gathered herself just long enough to make her way to the car, where she cried some more. An hour or more passed until she was incapable of crying another tear. A sudden peace came over her, the understanding of hindsight, all the things she had questioned before were suddenly verified by his disclosure.

She wondered why her daughter was always trying to be anywhere else but home with her father, why Richard and Camille's relationship was always so contentious.

One time, out of concern, Lynn even asked Camille if Richard had ever touched her in an inappropriate way. When Camille laughed at the question, Lynn gently grabbed her daughter's face, so she understood the seriousness of the inquiry, and told Camille, '*if anyone ever touches you in any way that makes you uncomfortable, including your father, tell me immediately, no matter how scared you might be.*' Still holding her daughter's face, Lynn assured Camille, '*I'll always believe you.*'

Lynn thought about the time she found Camille hiding in the backyard, her daughter pretending to have fallen asleep under the trees. Then there were the repeated awkward stares from strange women in church or at the market, the memories now crashing down on her like waves.

Lynn remembered the time three hundred dollars came up missing from their account, when she questioned Richard about it, he said he gave it to his brother. At the time she thought, *why didn't you just tell me, like you did when he needed money before*, but she took him at his word, now thinking he must have given it to one of his whores.

She immediately felt sorry for Camille and what she had gone through. How could she have not known? The list of women seemed endless, she stopped him after eight or so, but it appeared that he would have gone on 'til his last breath. She decided to call her daughter, still in Singapore at the time.

"Camille," Lynn called out in sorrow and sympathy.

"Is that a question, Mom?" Camille joked.

"When are you coming home?" Lynn questioned.

"As soon as I can, Mom," Camille said.

Lynn ached to let Camille know that she was blameless in her husband's extramarital affairs. To clear her name and comfort her daughter but instead she paused, keeping her feelings to herself, the distance between them, the only deterrent. When Lynn felt herself about to cry again, she rushed off the phone.

Her mind bounced around like a ping-pong ball, going over the minute details of their marriage, now feeling like it was all a charade. She felt so stupid and wanted to do to all his stuff what

Angela Bassett did in *Waiting to Exhale* but thinking the point moot. He wouldn't be coming home to protest the spectacle.

Hopelessly, she wanted to go back to yesterday, back to the life she believed they had. Go back to last year, before his illness, but she couldn't, and from now on there would be this stain on their lives. Like the permanence of the stretch marks that accompany pregnancy, the skin never quite as taut or flawless again.

Lynn got a goblet from the cabinet and poured it full, a glass of merlot. She drank the first glass like she had been lost in a desert for days, and immediately poured another full glass, this time retreating to the couch.

Camille still weighed heavily on her heart. The regret from her decision to betray her daughter was now an open wound that she had bandaged years ago. With each passing day, the farce had become easier to live with, easier to forget.

TWENTY-EIGHT

....

the letter

NOW more than ever Lynn knew she had to tell Camille the secret. But she also knew that she wouldn't be returning to the hospital for her husband to dictate his version.

At this moment, her anger with Richard and her sadness for the life she mourned, Lynn doubted she'd ever see her husband alive again. And had it not been for their children, she wouldn't have. As she sat on the couch, sipping her wine, lights dimmed, Shirley Caesar playing in the background, she removed the notepad and pen from her purse and started writing.

Just as in Tania's letter, she started with Camille how proud they were of her accomplishments and of the woman she had become. She also included some of the same ideas Richard wrote to their younger daughter, telling Camille about her father's childhood, and the people who had been kind to him along the way. Lynn wrote about the importance of saving money, about finances and credit, about charity and giving back, about cars and the best people in town to go to if she needed something repaired, and the best places to travel. Her husband's instruction book for life.

When Camille's letter reflected the same sentiment that Richard had expressed in his letter to Tania, Lynn, with hesitation, preceded to jot down all the things she had so feverishly fought to protect Camille from, the truth of her paternity.

> *...there are no excuses for what we did except that we were young, stupid and in love.*
>
> *Your father and I started dating in high school, he was a junior, I was a sophomore. We were inseparable from day one. Your father walked me to and from school every single day. First loves are so pure and sweet, untainted by life, the world revolving around just two.*

Lynn was astonished at how easily she was able to recall her feelings from three decades ago, how easily just remembering the younger version of their love released some of the sting of her husband's confession.

> *College wasn't an option for your father. No one in his family had ever gone before. When he graduated high school, he enlisted in the Army, initially for only twenty-four month.*

The day he left for Korea we had been together nearly two years. I remember so vividly…it was so cold and rainy. He told me not to come see him off, but I was too bullheaded to listen. I walked two miles to the bus depot, stood there in the pouring rain, my hair rolled in a bun on the top of my head. I had on my school uniform, a blue prep skirt, white oxford shirt and blue sweater. Your father in his Khakis. My black loafers and white ankle socks soaked up the water like the roots of a plant. The umbrella I brought to shield myself proved useless.

Lynn couldn't stop thinking about the day Richard left for the Army. As the bus pulled from the terminal on time, Richard looked out the window and could see Lynn's tears through the pouring rain. Moments like this stay etched in your memory for an eternity, the 'what-ifs' tap dancing a solo on your soul.

Richard always wondered to himself how they're lives might have been different if he had been a little smarter, a little richer, a little wiser. If only he had waited to enlist or came back sooner. But in the end, it all turns out the same – what is, is, and there's nothing at all to do about it.

Unbeknownst to them at the time, the day he left for the Army was the day that indelibly changed the course of their existence. Although they loved each other, something faded, the splendor their young love once enjoyed, never returned.

Thinking back on it now, the day your dad left for the Army was the day our lives changed. That's what I'm coming to understand now. I stood at the terminal and watched the bus pull away.

A boy from the neighborhood, Greyson Timmons, just happened to be at the station that day. He saw me crying and offered to help me. I refused his offer, but he stood there with me, concerned, saying nothing, until I walked away.

Our friendship blossomed from that day, but I remained totally devoted to your father, writing him long letters every chance I got, each one sealed with a kiss.

In our letters we spoke of marriage, and much of our time apart I spent daydreaming about him and planning our impending wedding.

Your dad came home on leave as often as he could, which wasn't much. Most of the time when he was here visiting, he would tell me all about his military buddies and Korea. I was young and poor and never stepped foot out of the North Carolina, much less dreamed about another country, so I was mesmerized looking at life through your father's new eyes.

His first tour was nearing its end and I anxiously waited for him to come back home, though he had different intentions. On one of his furloughs, he informed me that he was reenlisting. Telling me that it was the best decision for us, telling me about the benefits it would afford us, and the opportunities it gave him to make more money. I was numb, and heartbroken, not wanting to hear any of that.

It felt like life without him was moving in slow motion, but, while he was away, I graduated high school and applied to the local teacher's college. We should have gotten married then. I could have gone with him to Korea, but things didn't happen that way.

Greyson was there for me the whole time, listening to all my Richard woes. And gradually over time an unintentional distance developed between your father and me. Our conversations and letter writing dwindled.

I'm sure now that my bitterness attributed to the growing space between us. Most likely because he made the decision to reenlist without taking my feelings into account, he didn't even ask my opinion.

One night while with Greyson, I started crying about your father, I hadn't heard from him in over a month. Greyson comforted me and when he held me in his arms, it felt good. It felt right. Like he would be there for me forever, something I needed to feel. One thing led to another. Kissing turned into intimacy – my very first time with a man. It felt pure and innocent and right. That was our only time together, the night you were conceived.

Had Richard told me he was coming home, maybe I could have held on, I don't know, just second-guessing now. But one week to the day after Greyson and I made love, your father surprised me, coming home for good.

I was honest with him, telling him everything about Greyson. I'll never forget the look in his eyes, he was devastated and so was I. It changed him. He started drinking, he became mean as hell, but he wanted to stay with me. And I still loved him more than life itself.

When we found out I was pregnant we made the foolish decision to keep your paternity a secret – your father protecting his ego, me concealing my shame.

Greyson Timmons is your biological father's name. He lives here in town. He's a good man. He didn't want to, but out of his love for me and for you, he agreed to keep his distance.

Every year on your birthday and Christmas, he would send you presents by mail. Over the years I would send him pictures of you. He wrote you a lot and sent pictures as well. I kept everything. It's all stored in the attic.

When you turned eighteen, Greyson sent a statement for an account he had set up for you on the day you were born. He left it up to your father and me as to when and how to tell you about it.

Lynn recounted things that she had long forgotten. The flashbacks came clear and swift. When the girls were small, sometimes Richard would go into a drunken rage, Lynn would hold the girls tightly in her arms and tell them how much their father loved them, despite what he said or did. Each time, it seemed to ease their fears, if only a little. She made valiant efforts to praise her husband in front of the girls. This helped stroke Richard's broken ego.

One cold and rainy night their father ran into 'that man,' as Mr. Young called him, at the corner market. Richard walked home, umbrella unopened. When he arrived at the house, wet and cold, it wasn't long before he went into one of his tirades. He didn't even need a drink to get him started this time. Camille was in the living room playing with her doll. She smiled when she saw her daddy walk through the door.

"What are you smiling at?" he went at her. "You're dirty! Dirty, I tell you. Get out of my face!" he yelled. "I don't even want to look at you."

Lynn was horrified, and Camille burst into tears. Lynn was a meek woman by all accounts until you messed with her kids, and then she turned into a bull. Lynn never disrespected her husband before. But on this night, she bolted toward him like a charging stag, stood between their oldest child and her six-foot-three husband, fiercely looking at him eye-to-eye, a woman neither the girls nor her husband had ever seen before.

She pointed her finger in his face and viciously yelled, "DON'T YOU EVER, AS LONG AS YOU WALK THE FACE OF THIS EARTH, TALK TO MY CHILD LIKE THAT AGAIN!" Her face was red as fire, the veins protruding on her forehead. "If you even breathe another hateful word towards this child again, I will pack our bags so fast and we will be gone out of your life forever! YOU made the choice to stay. Don't take this out on my girls." From that day to this, he never spoke another unkind word to Camille in Lynn's presence.

Returning to the letter, she concluded with an apology. But before ending, Lynn added more about how this noticeably changed Richard, telling Camille that it wasn't her fault. And how, at the time, Lynn believed that their love could conquer the hurt. She told her daughter that when she was born, she looked just like Greyson – omitting that this made Richard resent Camille. A fact that had her young self in love known she couldn't change with all the love in the world, she would have left Richard for the sake of her child.

Richard hated Greyson. Not because Greyson was a bad man, not because he heard or knew anything reprehensible about him, not because Greyson infected their lives, but because the innocence that his relationship with Lynn once had was destroyed forever, and every time Richard looked at Camille, he was reminded of this. Camille represented a loss of purity, a loss of virtue.

That night Richard slept in his hospital bed, a medically induced rest. He cleared his conscience with Lynn. It didn't offer the relief he desired, and most likely irrevocably damaged what was left of their marriage. But he had to tell her the truth about his indiscretions, hoping she could help his daughter understand why he behaved so viciously.

Richard hoped that Camille could find it in her heart to forgive him for the isolation and the distance he kept between them. He couldn't help the way he felt, why his eyes never lit up for Camille like they did for Tania. But he hoped that if Camille knew their story it would offer some semblance of restitution. Every breath he had left held on to the hope that it would.

Lynn laid on the couch, trying to sleep. She couldn't. Without knowing it she was feeling the same thing, the same betrayal, the same hurt that Richard felt all those years ago when he found out about Greyson.

All of a sudden fear snuck up on her like a thief, she got scared, scared to tell their truth. She took out another piece of paper from the notepad and began writing a second letter to Camille. A letter much easier to stomach, one that mimicked, almost word for word, the letter she had written to Tania, adding sweet touches she remembered that only applied to Camille and ending with a simple, 'we love you.'

She signed her and Richard's names on both letters, folding them into different envelopes, and placing them in her purse for safekeeping. Only deciding on the day of her husband's death which letter to give Camille.

The letters now complete, she fulfilled her commitment to her husband. Exhausted by the purging of a shrouded past and persuaded by the effects of wine, Lynn fell asleep on the couch.

TWENTY-NINE

....

no more lies

SAMMY was sleeping peacefully beside her grandmother. Lynn soaking up everything she could about the child – the sweetness of her smell, her tiny fingers, her yellow Sponge Bob pajamas, her sandy blonde twists. Lynn gently stroked the baby's soft skin, and thought about her own girls, wondering if she could have done things better, wondering about all the things she had missed out on, the signs.

A secret, like cancer, is innocuous at its inception, before it's allowed to fester and proliferate. Before it spreads, seeping into its surroundings, before it takes on a life of its own. This family's secret was lethal in ways no one could have imagined, inconspicuously poisoning all of them.

Lynn didn't want one more day to go by with this cloud hanging over their family, not one more day living this lie. Being there beside her granddaughter she knew she had to put it all on the table, no more secrets would linger over her head. She looked at her phone, it was 5:30 a.m. Slipping out of bed, she went into the living room where Camille was asleep on the couch.

"Are you sleep?" Lynn asked, nudging her daughter on the shoulder.

Groggy, Camille answered, "No, ma'am, I'm just resting my eyes."

"Get up. I need to talk to you."

"What time is it, Mom?"

"I don't know, early o'clock," Lynn said.

They laughed.

"Mom, what's so important?" Camille asked.

Lynn sat beside her daughter on the couch and gave her a hug, snug and firm.

"There's something I have to get off my chest."

Camille thought her mom was about to give her a dissertation on Sammy, one she wasn't ready to hear or talk about. "I'm sorry, Mom," she said, trying to thwart the uncomfortable conversation.

"Sorry about what, child?" Lynn asked, not ready for another confession.

"Sammy," Camille said.

"I'm sorry, too," Lynn said. "I'm sorry too. But that's not what I'm talking about. I'll save that for later, for when you're ready. I have a feeling what I have to say might make it a little easier for you."

"What are you talking about, Mom?" Camille was curious.

The light was on in the kitchen, she could see clearly into her daughter's eyes. Lynn grabbed Camille's hands into her own, first asking where the letter from her father was and when she planned to read it. Camille confessed that she had no intention of reading it. With some prodding, Camille revealed that she had buried the letter in her father's casket. Lynn was floored.

Unbeknownst to Lynn and Camille, Tania had woken up and was attempting to eavesdrop on their conversation from the hall, the guilt of her theft made her tremble. The letter Tania had taken was still folded, unread, in her coat pocket. Tania stood motionless.

"Oh baby," Lynn said to Camille.

"I didn't need to know...nothing I could do about it now," Camille said, shrugging her shoulders.

"Your dad told me only last week," Lynn said.

Camille's eyes widened. She was clueless as to what her mom was talking about. "Told you what?"

Lynn, with tears gathering, told Camille that she had just learned about her husband's affairs days earlier, that only then had she found out about the things Camille had witnessed. Lynn pleaded for forgiveness, for herself, although she was blameless in the affairs, and for her husband.

Camille tried to assure her mother that she was okay, that she had long ago recovered from the things she'd seen, from the way her father repeatedly neglected her, but everything about her except for her words said otherwise. Her body stiffened, her face flush, the veins in her head protruding in grief, her thumbs twirling, one around the other.

Tania, not knowing these things had happened to her sister, bolted from her hiding place to Camille's side. She said nothing, words were of little use now. The women, all enveloped in sorrow held one another, crying quietly so as not to wake the baby.

"I took the letter," Tania blurted out.

"What? What did you do?" Lynn demanded.

"I took the letter from the casket," Tania repeated.

"Where is it?" Lynn shouted.

Tania jumped up, trotted to her bedroom, and returned with the letter. "Here it is," she said, extending it to Camille.

"I didn't want it!" Camille yelled, "You're so damn nosy!"

"I'm sorry, I couldn't help it," Tania pleaded.

Lynn took the letter from Tania, placed it on the couch beside her, and held Camille in her arms. She wanted to lay all the cards on the table, to clear the air, but now she wasn't sure that her daughter could handle learning the truth, learning that the man they had just buried, the man who had treated her so despondently her whole life wasn't her biological father.

"There is a reason he confessed, Camille," Lynn revealed, her voice stuttering, everyone in tears.

Camille looked at her mother, knowing it wouldn't be good news. With Tania seated on the floor in front of them, Lynn told her girls not to hate their father. She told them how he was trying to make things right. She told them that the secret they both agreed to keep had been a slow poison, contaminating their lives. Something she had been unaware of before her husband's confession. Only then realizing that the one was not separate from the other, and that the poison had spread.

Camille asked her mother for the letter. Instead of opening it herself, she handed it to her sister. "I want you to read it," she told Tania. "Read it out loud."

Tania took the letter reluctantly, guardedly opening it, she began. The three women held hands, now all seated on the couch, Camille slouching in the middle, staring blankly at a divot she noticed on the floor. With each word beckoning the next, Tania paused when her eyes saw, 'that night you were conceived.'

"Read it, Tania!" Camille demanded.

"…and that night you were conceived," Tania stuttered.

Camille was dazed.

"…and that night you were conceived," Camille repeated. "What?" She couldn't comprehend.

"Let her continue, Camille," Lynn insisted.

"Dad's not my dad?" Camille questioned.

"No, baby. He's not, not biologically," Lynn told her.

Camille slumped over even more, feeling bamboozled, but she stayed in place, listening.

"Go ahead," she told her sister, stammering.

Tania, struggling through, read on for what seemed like hours. As she read, Camille recounted events she experienced as a child, and though she was sad for herself, she pitied her father more, how tortured he must have been. She looked at the sadness in her mother's eyes, and only now recognized how her mother had always been juggling, overcompensating for her part in this circus.

"I was ashamed," Camille called out, interrupting Tania before she could finish. Everything Camille needed to know had been spoken. Lynn and Tania snapped to look at Camille. "I was so ashamed," she repeated. "That's why I didn't tell y'all about Sammy. That's why I abandoned my baby," she said in agony.

Camille had told them all this before, but the words sifted with renewed understanding. This time she was saying it for herself, each repetition igniting a clarity and enlightenment she hadn't known before.

"Oh, baby," Lynn cried out.

"I'm so sorry, Camille," Tania followed.

"I didn't want for her….," Camille stumbled, "…what I had gone through," she said, stoically.

The ladies stood up together, embracing one another as tightly as they could, all weeping, all quivering.

"I didn't want to stop, I didn't know how to, so I left," Camille repeated, an ocean of tears streaming down her face. "…and came home, so my baby….," she sputtered, her words failing, the weight of her actions, the revelation.

As they stood locked arm-in-arm, one comforting the other, Lynn felt a tap on her leg. "I won na hug too," Sammy called out, having awoken from her sleep.

The sun was above the horizon now.

THIRTY

....

endings are beginnings

CAMILLE and Sammy stayed with Lynn for months after Richard's death, John visiting them every now and then. When he couldn't take being away from his baby girl any longer, he told Camille he needed them to come back to New York. At first, she resisted, but when she saw them together, him showering Sammy with love, his eyes illuminating in Sammy's presence, Camille thought, *I'm not getting in the way of that.*

What she realized long after her daughter had grown up, was that somehow watching Sammy and John together, seeing how much he loved their daughter, seeing how Sammy trusted John, did more for Camille than it ever did for either one of them.

She knew her little girl would never have the same daddy issues that plagued her own childhood, her adulthood for that matter. And that somehow being around them, moment by moment, Camille was healing that seven-year-old little girl inside the grown and accomplished, broken woman.

Camille loved being back in New York, though technically they lived in New Jersey. She befriended Megan Mallory and started doing volunteer work with ASL. She worked part-time from home tutoring death and blind children, spending as much time with Sammy as she could, having missed almost a year and a half of her daughter's life.

Every Tuesday she frequented a local café not too far from their home – to read magazines, the newspaper, books. It was her 'me' time.

On this particular Tuesday, the café was unusually busy, her favorite seat was occupied, so she sat outside on the patio. Often the staff would bring her order to the table, but today they didn't.

"Camille," the young girl behind the counter called. Camille got up to retrieve her order just as the young girl was about to call her name again.

"Camille," someone else called, a man's voice this time.

When Camille turned around, there he was standing behind her, tall and buff, smelling amazing, looking as good as she remembered, it was none other than Steven Louis Bissette.

"Steve," she said, surprised. "How are you?"

Before he answered he gave her a great big hug. They hadn't seen each other or spoken since she left Singapore.

"I'm doing well," he replied. "How are you?"

"I'm doing well, too."

"What are you doing here in New York?" he asked.

"I live here now," she replied. He chuckled. "What's so funny?"

"Me too," he answered. "I live here now, too."

"Another BisCom?" she questioned.

"No. I sold BisCom, nearly six months ago. I'm an activist now, working on finance reform."

"Wow, that's great," Camille said.

She couldn't believe this. What are the chances that of all the places on earth, Steven would come into her favorite hangout, on a Tuesday, and at the exact time she was there?

In a hurry, he asked her to give him a call some time. He hugged her again and gave her his business card, then rushed out. Soon as he left, she took her seat on the patio, and called Maria.

"Hey, girl," Maria answered.

"You'll never believe who I just ran into."

"Here we go, again," Maria said.

"What's that mean?" Camille asked.

"You're always asking me to guess, and I never get it right. So just tell me already," Maria said.

"You get on my nerves," Camille said first. "Steven. Girrrrrlllllll, he lives in New York."

"No fucking way!" Maria exclaimed.

"Crazy, right?"

"That's so beyond crazy," Maria said. "What are you going to do?" Maria asked.

"I don't know," Camille replied.

"Seriously, Camille, you don't know?" Maria questioned. "You're not tired of drama yet?"

"What are you talking about?"

"Resist the temptation, girl. Life's just trying to see if you're going to make the same ole mistakes," Maria told her.

Camille and Maria talked a little while longer, Maria trying to convince her friend that this was just another test to see if she had learned from the last time. Camille thought about what Maria was saying and really took it to heart, wondering in silence if it was fate trying to bring them back together.

When Camille and Maria finally hung up, Camille was still unsure about if she'd call Steve. She thought about John, about how they hadn't committed to one another, only to Sammy.

That evening when she got home, John started talking to her about their relationship, about where it was headed, almost like he had been privy to her conversations with Steven and Maria. She wondered where his sudden relationship interest was coming from.

She had been back in New Jersey for a while now and he never mentioned anything about a relationship, not once, although they were doing all the things couples do, living together, raising a child together. John paid the bills, Camille was in charge of running the household, cooking and hiring a housekeeper on occasion. They even vacationed together. And sex with him was amazing, still.

If she allowed herself, she would know the best decision. But instead she flip-flopped back and forth between memories of Steven and thoughts of John and Sammy.

John left on yet another business trip that evening. Camille was restless. So, after she put Sammy to bed, she called her mother.

Lynn had been thinking about Camille too. She could feel her daughter's tension through the phone but didn't let on. She listened as her child talked, all the while praying silently. Camille told her mother what was going on, all the emotions she was feeling, her uncertainties.

After everything they had gone through with Mr. Young, the cancer, with Greyson, with Sammy, Lynn knew that there was only one right choice, although she refused to tell her daughter what she should do.

Camille longed for her mother's advice, but Lynn said nothing, allowing Camille to make her own choice. Camille wanted someone, anyone to decide for her, she didn't want to be wrong again.

Camille shook her head, she wanted concrete advice like...*stay with the man you love, stay with your child's father, if he's good to you*. But Lynn's only offering was, "Be still and know. The right answer will come."

When Lynn hung up the phone, she continued praying for her daughter, for her family. Then she went soundly to sleep, knowing that whatever happened, whatever Camille decided, they would get through it together.

Another piece of the puzzle in place, the healing had begun. Initiated by the wishes of a dying man, his last gift to his family was freedom.

It didn't feel that way at first when Lynn sat in the hospital room listening to the names of all the women her husband had betrayed her with. It didn't feel that way when Tania read the letter to Camille that morning in the rental house. But it was. And in time they would grow to appreciate his brave last act.

Lynn would eventually, years from now, look back on their relationship as she had before she knew about his affairs, sweet, and supportive, the first and only man she had ever loved at the time.

She would eventually forgive herself for knowingly and unknowingly betraying her daughters. She would forgive the seventeen-year-old child in her for loving Richard more than she loved herself, not knowing she was supposed to be her own first and greatest love. No woman had ever told her that or showed her. Nor had her father. He wasn't around.

Lynn would become the doting grandmother to Sammy and all of her grandkids. And eventually and unexpectantly she would fall in love again. A real, mature kind of love. Not needing anything just wanting companionship.

Tania would confess her abortion, the shame that accompanied it, her struggles to bond in relationships, her desire for other women. And despite all this, she felt loved and accepted.

Eventually she would find love, a man. They would marry, have a family, and move up north, relocating with his job, living the life she always wanted.

The sisters, over time would become best friends, again, resolving all the squabbles from the past. They would visit one another as often as their lives allowed. Their children would grow up to be as close as siblings, no residue of the dysfunction from the past.

And every year on their father's birthday, the sisters would go home again, visiting their father's grave, talking and praying, in appreciation for being released from the curse, from the family secret that had once contaminated their lives.

Once again Camille sat at her usual table in her favorite café, where a week earlier she had run into Steven. And although a lot had changed in their lives since they were together in Singapore, a lot had stayed the same. He really loved her, thinking back on it now. She cared about him, too.

Life is funny this way, never knowing how things will turn out, just doing the best with what you have, with what you know. And when you know better, hopes are that you will be better, that you will make better choices. The most you can strive for is to make better choices.

Camille fumbled through her purse for some change – she wanted a lemon bar. When she opened her wallet, she saw the number staring at her, almost like she was being summoned. *Why not*, she thought, *I'm a grown ass woman*. That's what she told herself, though really feeling like a child at times, still seeking acceptance and approval.

She pulled out her phone, slowly punching in the numbers one by one. With each ring, she considered hanging up, but didn't. There was no intuitive beckoning fighting against her this time, only fear.

This was an experience Camille had to navigate all on her own. No amount of preparation could soothe or make it any easier. Her chest pounded through her blouse like a fetus kicking its way around the womb when birth is the only next option.

Just rip the bandage off, she heard, something her father used to say whenever she felt intimidated by her circumstances. *Just rip the bandage off, baby girl*, she heard him say again. She was by herself, but she was not alone.

Camille smiled. She felt her father's love more now than she ever had while he was alive. And for the first time, when she thought about him, she didn't feel anger or hate or resentment or sadness.

Sitting there at her favorite café, she was surrounded by complete strangers. Outside, the salt and pepper clouds were threatening rain once again, and for the first time in her life, when she thought about her father, there wasn't an onslaught of bad memories. An unfamiliar existence, she didn't really know this Camille at all, but like a long-lost friend, she welcomed her with open arms.

"Hello," he answered.

Camille contemplating what to say next. Words that until only recently never had a reason to exist. She took a labored breath.

"Hello. This is Camille. Camille Young," she said. Not knowing what to expect, she was petrified. "Is this Greyson?" she stuttered. "…I mean, I mean Mr. Timmons?"

"Yes, this is," he said. "Greyson is fine," he told her. "It's so good to finally hear from you."

And for years to come, when Camille would run into to people who knew her family, in offering their sympathies they would say, "Your father was a good man."

Unwavering, Camille's response would be, "Thank you, he is. He is a good man."

the beginning...

Made in the USA
Monee, IL
15 May 2021

67480152R00189